potential absolute

timeline puddle

100000BCE - Prologue
6028BCE - 1st Manifestation, the seed. A Mesolithic Man
4500BCE - 3rd Manifestation. The Neolithic Man
4500BCE - 3rd Manifestation. Visions of the Neolithic Man
2200BCE - 2nd manifestation. 2nd Consolidation - Ptah
1000BCE - 2nd Manifestation. 1st Consolidation – Ilusha
546BCE - 2nd Manifestation. 3rd Consolidation – Thales
2060AD - 4th Manifestation. Meeting Fremd
2100AD - 5th Manifestation. Disillusioned on Erde
2122AD - 5th Manifestation. Christin returns to Earth
2124AD - 5th Manifestation. Escape from Erde
3200AD - 6th Manifestation. Inside the mind of Isten.
3200AD - 7th Manifestation. A new world, A new life
4300AD - 8th Manifestation. Meeting Ahatu.
4300AD - 8th Manifestation. Exploring Restu
4300AD - 8th Manifestation. Art of the Dream Maker
4305AD - 8th Manifestation. Creating a Life
4317AD - 8th Manifestation. Lost in the wilderness
4415AD - 9th Manifestation –Lélek's Transmutation
2127AD and **4415AD** – 9th Manifestation – Lélek's Legacy
4415AD - 10th Manifestation - The Tetrahedral site
Some when - The Rose Galaxy – Chamaeleontidae
Manifestations

prologue

100,000 BCE

Alone, Isten could no longer progress along his evolutionary path. It could remember Earth's naissance five billion years ago, and its own beginnings along that time line. Not so long ago, some seven thousand years BCE in Earth's time frame of reference, it had cast adrift a tiny portion of itself into the gene pool of the Homonids … a beacon of memory in a single cell to guide a new life back to itself.

Needing to review the progress of its seed it spared a thought in the seed's direction. It nursed the hope that one day the seed would evolve to enable it to merge with it. Together, as one, it could explore the eons yet to live and grow beyond its current limitations, and so progress to the next level of its desire on the path to attaining its absolute potential. A minuscule portion of itself was once called Lélek.

1st manifestation, the seed

a mesolithic man 6028 BC

Lélek wandered inside and sat on his favourite rock. The day's major hunt had not gone well. He'd woken in the morning with an uneasy feeling that grew as the day progressed. It had nothing to do with his mate Scritchen. She had snuggled up and kept him warm during the night and now she was tending the fire. It didn't bother him in the least that her rump obscured his view of the outside world from the cave. Lélek was thinking about much more important things. *I do not understand these dreams. They seem so real, yet I cannot catch them. Where is 'real'?*

He was a tall fellow, taller than most of the men in his tribe, and stronger. But that's not the reason he ended up as the chief. He was smarter than everyone else. Even as a child he was inventive, trying to figure out how things worked. One of Lélek's favourite past times was trying to understand why a rock placed on top of another rock kept falling off. Twenty-eight winters old and still the mystery of the falling eluded him.

The previous night he had a dream about being inside something round, like the moon, and not attached to the ground. He could look out of the round thing but there was not much to see, only a lot of blackness like at night, and many shiny things a long way away from him. There was also one very large round object that was mostly green and blue and white. But he could not look at it for long because of a very bright light beside it

which made his eyes hurt. *How can I have any hope of understanding such strange things when I can't even fathom the mystery of the two rocks.*

His art skills did help clarify some of his understandings. His father had trained him in the arts and he was very talented in depicting the animals and events of their daily lives. But what sense did circles on a cave wall make? There was really no point in trying to discuss anything with Scritchen. Not that she didn't have many sounds to use to discuss things, but it was all women folk talk about grubs and kids and whether last week's kill could still be eaten.

So Lélek sat there pondering for a little while. That in itself was very hard work and it gave him a brain ache. He had to constantly find new thought sounds to try and unravel the imagery of his dream to put them in some kind of context. In the end he gave up and started thinking about Scritchen's rump still jigging between himself and the fire. It would be his first watch that night so he would have plenty of time to think later.

As the sun sank slowly over the cold terrain, other members of the tribe arrived with small offerings for the larder; the women had a meagre supply of roots and berries, the men had little to offer in the way of protein. Prout sauntered in with a few rodents while Lélek's other son, Chut, eagerly showed off his stash of bats and a couple of owls. Still there was plenty left of the previous week's kill to last them a few more days. Life was a constant struggle. Lélek didn't dwell on that. It was routine, like the setting of the sun and the constant cold.

Dreams which began to feel like memories had become a more time consuming preoccupation. He knew what a normal dream was like. Each time one of his tribe had a near death experience, or he had his own brush with annihilation at the point of a sabre's fangs, nightmares re-living the experiences were a normal thing. But images of places he had never visited, or strange hairless people he had never met, were different. Initially they made him anxious, later becoming important things to analyse. Lélek had to decide whether these memories beginning to clutter up his mind were of any real importance. As a last resort he could always commit them to the wall of the cave for future reference.

While the women folk busied themselves with the children and the fire, the men discussed the next day's prospects for another big hunt. Lélek was forced to turn his mind to more important considerations to carry out his responsibilities as the head of the tribe.

"We must hunt again tomorrow," he said, "our meat will not last past a few days."

Ördog, his brother, volunteered, "I spotted a large herd of reindeer less than a day's run."

"Good. You can lead. There's enough of us to handle a reindeer or two." Given the tense relationship with his brother, Lélek took the opportunity to let him have his way for a change.

"Chut," Ördog said straight away, "you're at the back with Prout." Every male knew their job and their position during a standard hunt. Chut presented a conundrum. When it came to the final rush he was very fast and very accurate with the spear. During stalking he was a serious liability. As his name would suggest, he generally made the most noise. It was a habit Lélek could not get him to break. Every time Chut went out with Lélek to learn the skills as a child he would always be putting his foot wrong, or sneezing or making some other noise to disturb the prey. No amount of shushing by Lélek ever made any difference.

The last meal of the day, in this case the only meal of the day, was followed by the ritual of selecting sleeping partners and setting the watch changes. Wood on the fire was mandatory. It had to be organised with great care, as it was a precious commodity. It was the added responsibility of each watch to maintain it without wasting their timber. Lélek took up his position on an extra couple of skins on the ground to the left of the fire. He could keep an eye out for any movements out there without himself being seen. So settled, he returned to his ponderings.

The passage and use of time occupied as much of his thoughts as dreams. His father recorded changes, like the change from day to night, using a straight line drawn on the wall. Each morning he crossed that straight line with a short vertical line. Then each night he drew the longer horizontal line a bit further on. It all seemed pretty pointless until he introduced dotted lines. These he placed at equal intervals continuing the horizontal line, still using the long and short convention. He explained that these represented mornings and evenings which had not yet happened. Lélek was the first to understand the concept of planning for the future. He was just twelve winters old at the time. The tribe could henceforth plan precisely their next big hunt. Most importantly they could co-ordinate their activities with the neighbouring tribe when they needed to hunt together for the woolly mammoth.

By the time his father died, he had already introduced the idea of having a separate line for each new moon. Still maintaining the notation of days, they now had a way of recording the number of days to each   moon cycle. Somehow Lélek felt there could be an improvement made to the calendar. *These cycles keep repeating themselves. There must be a way to ... The Moon!* His most recent dream surfaced unbidden … the big round moon. He thought about the big round thing he was trapped inside in the dream. He thought about the huge blue, green white object he saw in the blackness. *Why are so many things round?*

It was getting near the end of his watch. He got up and walked outside of the cave to urinate. As the urine splashed into the dust it formed a rough circle in front of his feet. Lélek stretched, walked back inside to wake the next watch and settled down beside Scritchen. *I hope I don't have difficult dreams tonight.* With at least five hours before dawn there was time enough for a good sleep. With his children around him, Scritchen by his side and a very competent family to keep body and soul together Lélek was a contented man. Yet life had many challenges; the greatest of which was to resolve the mysteries of dream memories.

… Egek, his father, stood beside him at the edge of the lake. Together they watched the fish lazing near the edge. They were happy days. Lélek held his hand and peered deep into the still water. He knew he was dreaming again - dreaming and remembering. He wanted it to continue. Over the years Lélek had learnt somehow to stop some of his dreams from ending. So he kept holding onto Egek's hand and bent down closer to the water. Then he saw something he had never noticed before, not even as an adult when he went fishing with his sons. Sometimes the fish opened their mouths and shiny round bubbles escaped to float to the top of the water and disappear. They were beautiful.

It was a very still evening with a bright full moon. The flat smooth water reflected the moon creating two enormous orbs of light into which his father's words drifted magically. Egek tried to explain to his son that all things must die.

"The sun dies at the end of every day and the moon dies at the end of every night. But they get up again every morning and every night."

Lélek let go of his father's hand and threw a pebble in the water. It made ripples of silver run away from where the pebble sank. "Did the pebble just die?"

"No Lélek. It is at the bottom of the lake."

"Did the moon in the water die?" He could no longer see the reflection of the moon in the disturbed water.

"No Lélek. Wait a little and it will come back again." His father was a very wise man. As soon as the water stilled itself Lélek threw another pebble. More silver ripples ran towards him. So he picked up a handful and threw them all in the water, creating great chaos. His eyes could not follow all the circles of light chasing each other and crashing into each other.

He woke to Scritchen shaking his shoulder. "Wake up! They're getting ready."

The sun had just started to be born again. Lélek went directly to the fire, picked up a burnt stick and on the nearest wall drew a number of circles inside one another. He was very excited, but had to curb his enthusiasm because of the big day ahead. Apart from ensuring a successful hunt, he also had to cope with Ördog who always wanted to do everything his own way, which was not always the best way. He and Lélek constantly disagreed about many things, not just hunt strategy. For example, Ördog could not understand why Lélek wasted all that time painting on the walls. It did nothing to help them catch their food. It did not help them keep warm, and it certainly didn't deter some of the other tribes from attacking them from time to time. Very reluctantly he did agree the hunt calendar itself was not such a bad invention.

The men and some of the oldest boys set out on the hunt. They didn't expect it to be a hard kill. The wind blew steadily in one direction, clouds provided plenty of dappled shade and the ground was soft under foot. A big advantage, as it would help minimise the noise made by Chut. At the back of the single file Prout sauntered along sulking. He was a very capable tracker but the others could not stand the stench of his flatulence, so he was mostly banished to the back of the line. By the time the sun's position bisected the angle between the shoulder and the head they were in position at the edge of their valley.

A small herd of reindeer grazed upwind of them on the sparse vegetation. Several fawn, two groups of does and a big healthy buck. It had already been decided they would only take a doe. Under no circumstances would they harm the fawn. That was survival law. Any member of a tribe who broke Lélek's law was immediately banished. Squatting down, Lélek picked up a short stick and made two marks in the dirt opposite each other. One signifying their current position and the other the location of the herd. Then he drew a curved arc to the left between themselves and the reindeer. Pointing to individual members of the hunt he crossed the arc with short lines indicating where those individuals should go. Then he did the same thing to the right. Lastly he pointed to two youngsters and placed their marks on either side and in-line with the reindeer. Their job was to make a little noise to slowly encourage the herd to move towards the spaced out hunters.

Lélek stayed where he was. He had a little time to himself before the boys got into position. On this occasion Ördog, although always sceptical, had no objections to the strategy. It was a hunt by-the-book; tried, tested and highly successful. He moved twenty meters or so off to Lélek's right, still within view of each other. What Lélek could not see was the discontented leer with which he was being watched. Lélek kept an eye on his troops quietly making their way to their posts. For no particular reason he glanced down on the ground in front of him where he had drawn the diagram. The two ends of the arcs he'd drawn suddenly absorbed all his attention. Everything else went out of his head. It seemed like he stared at the diagram for a long time, before picking up the short stick again and joining the ends of those two arcs.

Eureka! Visions of his dream, the concentric circles he had drawn on the wall and his dad's calendar, all rushed into his mind at the same time. He knew what to do! Unfortunately, he almost did not live to see another day to do it in. Lélek had been so absorbed in his creative thinking he completely forgot the hunt. The two boys had done their job perfectly moving the reindeer in a straight line towards Lélek. The hunters on the flanks kept absolutely still quite confident that Lélek, an excellent hand with the spear, would make quick work of one of the does. It was Ördog who threw the first spear. It flew within centimetres of the top of Lélek's head to catch the doe in the flank. Ördog immediately leapt towards the doe, passing Lélek with a threatening grimace, and killed the doe with his second spear.

As was the custom of the hunt, priority was given to removing excess useless weight from the animal and preparing it for transport back to the cave. They should have been happy but the atmosphere in the group was electric. They had all seen what had happened. No one said a word, especially not Lélek. He knew he was in trouble, or more accurately his position as head of the tribe was in serious jeopardy. On the trek back he considered the various options available to him and made his decision in advance. He could think these things through because he was much smarter than anyone else in the tribe. He had learnt to plan ahead; he was a visionary.

Back at the cave they handed the animal over to the women and immediately went outside to talk. The women could read body language like the clouds. There was something very wrong going on. Scritchen became particularly alert. Lélek had not looked at her on his arrival. He had never omitted to do that before. She knew instinctively her mate had only three options available to him; demotion, banishment or death. He was still young enough to father children, so she hoped it would only be a demotion.

Ördog went straight to the heart of the matter. "You are our best tracker and you have the best nose." Everyone nodded, stamping their feet once.

"Today you have failed the tribe!" His voice rose rapidly. Everyone nodded and stamped their feet once, including the two youngsters. Lélek faced Ördog, spear point lowered to the ground, but said nothing as Ördog put the question to the hunters,

"Death?" No one moved, no one stomped.

"Exile?" No one reacted.

"Spear?" A unanimous nodding of heads and stomping followed.

Lélek still kept his peace. Slowly and deliberately he looked around the group. It was the privilege of a leader to choose his successor, unless the circumstances were extraordinary. His years at the helm had not failed to teach him some politic wisdom. Returning his gaze to Ördog he handed over his spear. Without ceremony Ördog broke the spear in half. Lélek was deposed and Ördog became the new leader. Lélek knew his brother was not mature enough for the role, but hoped he would grow into it quickly. The survival of the tribe depended on it.

With the matter settled they all returned to the cave. Lélek was well aware his value to the tribe had to be proven every day from then on. There were only two options left. He was in no doubt Ördog would look for the earliest opportunity to circumvent the necessity of his banishment. Ördog had political aspirations which could best be achieved by removing all possible opposition. Pretty paintings on the ceiling would not be enough to appease the new boss.

That very evening Lélek put his plan for personal survival into action by going back to the drawing of his concentric circles. He had a brilliant idea that he knew would please Ördog. Putting his excellent memory to good use he painted two animals on the wall, a woolly mammoth and a horse. Around each one he drew a complete circle, sectioning the circle into equal segments with short lines. He drew twenty-nine divisions, each representing one day in a cycle of the moon. Next to one of the lines he put a black spot.

Under the two circles he drew a new straight line to reproduce their existing calendar. Ördog didn't notice the new art work for several days, but said nothing even after he did. For an entire year he remained silent about it. As long as Lélek used his nose and tracking skills to find the game, Ördog could bide his time. He was in fact very content because Lélek seemed to be getting better and better at finding meat for the table. Ördog could not work out how he was doing it. He was aware however of the increasing number circles with different animals painted in them as the months passed.

After the end of the first year no more new circles appeared. By this stage not only Ördog but all the members of the tribe developed an intense interest in Lélek's work. They saw Lélek gradually add squiggly lines, dots, small irregular circles and small pointed dots to the interior of the circles. Each of the circles had different markings. Often his eldest son, Gloppel, contributed to the work. Ördog was not a complete idiot, in spite of his other character failings. He became intrigued one day after a hunt that was a long way from their cave, to see one of the previously unadorned circles with a meandering line and a very small animal in one part of the line.

He realized the drawing of the animal was the one they had hunted on that occasion. Gazing at the image his mind went back to the location of the hunt. His group had to approach the plain from the high cliffs which were several days walk from the cave. Before descending to the plain they observed a meandering river making its way across the valley floor, doing two sharp hairpin turns then continuing on its way. The prey was grazing in one of those hairpin bends. He could hardly believe his eyes. Lélek's squiggly line looked just like the river, and the small animal was painted exactly where they had found the herd of them.

"What is he doing?" Ördog asked Gloppel the next day.

"Maps." The boy answered.

"Explain."

Apart from his dad, this was the first time anyone had taken any interest in him, outside of the ordinary routines of existence. He was a clever lad with a good head for inventiveness like his father … and very keen to show off his knowledge. Gloppel had not yet fully realized the delicate situation between his father and Ördog.

"There are twelve circles, each circle is a moon. Twelve moons from hot to hot. Each moon, twenty-nine suns. Moon nine best for horse. Find horse in valley by the river."

For a very strange reason Ördog's murderous inclination towards Lélek bubbled to the surface. He immediately recognised the brilliant innovation of the ex-leader and could see the potential advantage it could represent to the survival of his tribe … if … no other tribe had learnt of this technology.

"Show me … which moon now!"

Lélek was out with the women carrying out one of the many menial tasks assigned to him since his deposition. Gloppel proudly took Ördog to the wall and pointed to one of the circles. Ördog looked at the next circle and immediately decided on a devious experiment. He would go out at one of the future moons on a hunt, without Lélek, guided only by the map. If his theory was correct he could get rid of Lélek. It would ensure the technology remained the property of his tribe only. He would rid himself of a potential rival, brother or no brother, and still retain the knowledge. *'The stupid kid knows all about it!'*

Nevertheless, Ördog felt it wise to learn some of the intricacies of map and calendar making. He may have been a ruthless, devious leader but he had patience. So from then on, every time Lélek settled to the task of painting, Ördog would just sit nearby and watch. He counted on the freeze between them to eventually thaw. By and by as the weeks passed Lélek became more comfortable with Ördog's presence and even started to explain the work to him. His dreams also took a turn for the better. Mysterious visions of the past began to replace the daily traumas of their difficult existence.

While Ördog plotted, Lélek dreamt. All things round became an obsession with him. In one dream he seemed to be suspended a very long way from everything. Although it was dark where he was, he could see small round objects going around larger round objects, and even the large objects looked like they were slowly moving around something else. His mind had no words for what he saw, but he still remembered the images. Lélek also remembered what triggered the particular dream; eyeballs. On one of their recent hunts they brought down a mammoth. It was shared between several tribes. He, as the chief tracker, had the privilege of eating the highly nutritious eyeballs. For the very first time the extraordinary smooth roundness of the organ impinged on his mind. After the dream, while out gathering berries, he asked himself highly obtuse scientific questions, like *why do round things roll*.

Ördog continued to plot. He had to be careful not to anger the rest of the tribe by depriving them of an able-bodied man. Every man … and woman … was valuable for their joint survival. The loss had to look inevitable. A hazy picture evolved in his mind of the possibility of an engineered accident during a multi-tribal hunt. There was always room for things to go wrong on those occasions. Many months had passed since Lélek started teaching him about the maps. He turned out to be a quick learner so Ördog took over the planning of hunts. All Lélek had to do was follow instructions. That suited Lélek very well. He and his son Gloppel spent most of their time talking science anyway during the initial stages of the hunts.

At last the day Ördog had been planning, arrived; a dangerous sabre-tooth tiger hunt.

"Lélek, are you ready?" It wasn't a question, but an order. Ördog couldn't help being tense.

Scritchen took a hold of Lélek's arm. While squeezing it tightly she directed his eyes towards Ördog, and whispered, "Watch out for him." Scritchen was always suspicious of Ördog, but there wasn't a lot she could do.

Lélek shook it off. "We've made peace," he whispered back. After all, hadn't he and Ördog been getting on so well lately. Scritchen had read their leader accurately. She knew she might not see her mate again.

Ördog continued with his instructions, "Bait, you know what to do, stay in front." Three tribes had come together for this special occasion. Normally they would leave the sabres alone. But this particular beast had developed a taste for human flesh. The other two tribes had already lost some of their number to him. Their leaders deferred to Ördog for this hunt, for he'd built up a good reputation in successful hunt strategy.

"Lélek will track him. You," indicating the north and south tribes, "form a wide circular cordon around it. I'll send in the bait when you're in place."

Expecting the Smilodon to follow its normal pattern of attacking from low overhanging branches to puncture its prey's jugular, they felt confident of spearing him before he leapt. All eyes would be searching above head height and with so many of them on the lookout Ördog felt sure of getting him.

"We will do the kill – you're backup, if it tries to escape."

Lélek was put in the lead to pick up the beast's trail, with Gloppel close behind, followed a little way back by Ördog. His mind on finding an opportunity to rid himself of his main rival. By the middle of the day there was still no sign of their prey. Even if it took two or three days they would not go home without a warm fur to help them through the coming winter. Meat had to be shared, but the fur went to the man who took the greatest risk. That happened to be one of Ördog's most trusted men. Despite that, even he was not taken into confidence about the true purpose of the hunt.

"There," Lélek pointed to the broken branch. It was late the following day he spotted the sabre. "He's going into the woods." Lélek followed it for an hour before alerting Ördog again.

Ördog gave the 'bait' a shove, "Go!" then dropped back to join the others. Unfortunately, Ördog couldn't see any immediate way to entrap Lélek. Within minutes a shriek rent the air. Before Lélek and Gloppel had even reached the perimeter to join the others the sabre attacked. The Beast was waiting for them. He had doubled back and perched on a perfect overhang directly in the path of the approaching scouting party. No doubt he knew he was taking a big chance with so many hunters after him, but he'd not eaten for many days and sometimes risks just had to be taken.

Lélek was taken completely by surprise. He was supposed to stay close to the bait, but not expecting the attack to come so soon, he had dropped his guard. That momentary lapse of concentration had given the sabre the perfect moment to strike. With the disadvantage of having weak jaws the tiger had to sink the sabres in quickly and let its prey bleed to death while it retired a safe distance to wait. It did just that, and fortunately so because the hunting party came on the scene within minutes. One of the other tribe's people had seen the events unfold.

"Lélek," he pointed the incriminating spear at Ördog's man, "did not kill!" He made the accusation to the master of the hunt.

The distraction and Ördog's main intent for the day ensured the tiger's survival. It was certainly the tiger's lucky day, for this was the opportunity Ördog was looking for. There was far more to be gained in making an example of an incompetent and unreliable hunter than in catching the old sabre. The 'bait' died shortly afterwards.

"Lélek, you must carry him." As custom dictated the dead man was tied to Lélek's back to take him back to the cave. He had no illusions about the outcome of his lapse of concentration. After three more days trekking they arrived back at the main camp, him carrying the dead man and the others carrying an odd assortment of smaller game to satisfy the immediate needs of all three tribes.

Lélek had ample time to reflect on his life, which was surely about to end. The children he sired attested to one of his many contributions to the tribe, one all could easily understand. The same could not be said of some of his other achievements. In retrospect he realised, from Ördog's reaction, that his brother harboured deep resentment. He finally understood that Ördog valued his 'enhanced' calendar for the power it gave him. Power which he could wield over the other tribes.

My time has come. Perhaps I'll be able to find the answers; my dream memories, why so many things are round, and why they roll. I want to know what makes the rock fall off another one. I want to know where my father is, for surely he is alive – in some way.

Lélek was well satisfied with his achievements, not just the enhanced calendar … a method for carrying fire on the end of a thick club dipped in fat … and especially the spear thrower which allowed them to stay further away from dangerous game during a hunt and still bag the kill. Above all he wanted to know for absolute certainty that there was something else after death. Then he thought of his mate, Scritchen. He thought about his neglect of her by not showing his affection more openly, for not supporting her in many little ways. But regrets never achieved anything. He regretted causing the death of the young man, yet it would not prevent his own.

Scritchen ran up to him as soon as they arrived. She saw the dead man on his back. "Lélek," she tried to find other words, but there were none that could change the inevitable. She let go of his hand. Tribal law now had to take its due course. His children wanted to run to him, but she stopped them. It was their first most serious lesson about survival in the tribe.

They arrived during the middle of an afternoon. First order of business was the case of the negligent hunter, a hunter who made repeated mistakes and had cost the life of one of their tribe. Ördog wasted no time in convening a full multi-tribe gathering. Everyone had to be there; all the men, the women and all the children. Lélek was stood in front of the wall of the cliff overhang, with the body of the dead man placed on the ground in front of him. After the initial shouting and accusations had died down, Ördog did not have to exert any great influence to achieve his ends. He simply asked two questions;

"Life?" To which there was not a single movement, not even a breath taken.

"Death?" All those who knew the law, and that was everybody, even every child over the age of eight winters, stomped their feet … just once. Hard, final and absolutely decisive. Before the dust had settled every spear but one found its home in Lélek's chest. Scritchen had refrained. For that, ordinarily she would have been punished. But she was held in great respect for the number of children she had birthed for the tribe.

2nd manifestation

in the void
6000 BC

Lélek didn't have to be forced to walk to the wall. He knew he was already a dead man. Eyes closed, hopes on the afterlife and mind on all things round, he made the transition. The biggest surprise was when he opened his eyes. Of all the things he had imagined, he had not thought to see what he was looking at immediately following his death. Temporarily confused he took a couple of steps backwards to get a better perspective on what was in front of him. He saw a man with head slumped forwards slowly falling to the ground, his chest pin-cushioned by spears. That man fell onto another, already lying on the ground. Turning his head away from that most intimate scene he noticed Scritchen with a hard set expression on her face.

"Scritchen!" He called out. His immediate impulse was to go over to her. But something held him back. There was a hand on his shoulder. He turned towards the hand, "Father? Is that you? He saw his father's face smiling at him. That was too much even for his highly evolved scientific mind, and he fainted. First thing he saw on recovering was Egek's face looming large in front of him. "How is this possible?" Lélek asked. He immediately remembered a recent dream he had with his father explaining about the dying of the moon. Then he remembered waiting in front of a wall to be executed. Was it all a dream? Was he still dreaming?

"Father, am I dreaming?"

"Come my boy", Egek said in a very peculiar accent, "I have to explain something very important to you."

"Father? Is it really you father?" The words escaped from Lélek more as plea than a question.

"Well … yes … and no. But I'll explain soon enough. Hold my hand and look over there."

Lélek's wide eyed gaze followed his father's pointing finger to see a large tribal gathering. Egek took his son to the edge of the crowd. "The man in the burial hole, the one on the left, is the man who died from the sabre's attack. You are the other man beside him."

Egek waited to let the idea take hold in his son's psyche. For a moment Lélek's mind could not grasp what he had just heard. Suddenly he let go of his father's hand and shouted with excitement, "I'm dead, but I'm alive. I knew it! I'm alive! I've always known it, like a memory from long ago. There *is* another life!"

"Yes, there are many secrets to life. You have just learnt one of them. I came to visit you recently, in a dream, and you asked me a question about the moon. Just like the moon we have many deaths and many births. Let me explain about myself and then we'll go on a little tour."

"Why are you speaking so strangely? Some of your words are hard to understand."

"I'm trying to speak the words I used to use, but my memory is a bit rusty. Actually, only a small part of me is your father. I am who I was before, but I am also the experiences of others who have become part of me, and I have become part of them."

"But you look like my father!"

"And I am your father, but in me there is also the mother of another, the son of someone else and the uncle of yet another. I am all of us now."

Lélek's eyes had started to glaze over. It is true he was an intelligent man and that he had solved many mysteries during his life, but what Egek was telling him made no sense. He could not get any of his thoughts to get a purchase on even the smallest part of what he was hearing. Egek saw the obvious struggle in his son's eyes.

"Think of it this way … into your water container put one drop of sabre blood and stir it. The blood and water are now one and you cannot tell them apart. Now put one drop of berry juice in the same water and stir it. Do you understand?"

"But how can you do that. You have hair and bones and flesh and blood. I can feel your hands and hear your voice."

"I am not what you see me to be. You are looking at an image I projected into your thoughts. It is convenient for you to see me like this while you make the adjustment. I am my spirit captured in my thoughts. I am the combined spirit of three others."

"So I'm not … that is … I'm not a body … I am just my thoughts?"

"You always were a smart boy, my son. I think you're ready for that little tour. Then I will have to leave you, but soon you will be joined by others."

While they talked Lélek was no longer aware of his surroundings because he was so intensely focused on his father. As he turned to look away he felt strangely unstable, and if he had not put out a hand to steady himself he felt sure he would have fallen. His hand did touch something and it did help to steady him. But it was not anyone from the burial crowd. Nor was it a rock or a tree trunk. It was definitely something he was inside of, but he could not see it. Casting a questioning look at his father he received the answer,

"You are inside the bubble of your being. There is no other way I can describe it for you. Perhaps when you have evolved a little more you will start to understand."

Lélek looked around at all the people gathered around the hole. The perfectly spherical bubble holding him captive was transparent giving him an uninterrupted view. His children were there helping to fill the grave, Ördog and the other men were there also, but Scritchen was nowhere to be seen. She was one of the emotionally strongest women in the tribe, but this loss overwhelmed her. Even when he was alive he was not a very demonstrative man emotionally. That and his death must both have been hard for Scritchen, he realised. Yet he was feeling completely divorced from everyone. It wasn't that he didn't care they were grieving for him. It simply had no emotional meaning to him anymore. He just wanted to explore his new life.

"Where's Arrgh, the man who died because of me? Shouldn't he be here watching?"

"You are a very clever boy indeed. He, like yourself is learning about his own thought bubble. But he has a different hunt to go on." Lélek felt that was a satisfactory explanation for the time being.

Then he tried to move forwards to get a closer look at himself in the hole, but his legs would not carry him. They were definitely there, he could plainly see them, but they just would not respond. He put his hand down to touch one of them - he could feel nothing. Egek was watching him with interest. He was considerably proud of his very clever son.

"Why can't I move, father?"

"When you were hunting and a problem had to be solved what did you have to do?"

Lélek thought this was a trick question, because the answer was obvious. "First I had to think of the solution, then I had to do it. Is that what you mean, father?"

"Exactly my boy. Now, all you have to do is think the solution. Just think of moving to the hole and see what happens."

So Lélek learnt his second lesson. He thought of himself standing next to the hole, and with the speed of the thought, while remaining inside his self-bubble, he found himself exactly where he wanted to be. Egek watched Lélek go through the slow process of awakening. But before Egek could explain one of the great mysteries of existence he had to take his son out into the solar system.

"Father, how did you know I wanted to get closer to the hole?" Egek smiled, but did not answer.

"I gave you a dream once – an image of yourself floating in darkness and looking at the bright white disk of the moon. Do you remember?"

"Yes. I saw another great very beautiful round thing, blue and green and white."

"I am going to show you that again. This time it will not be a dream. Nothing will harm you on this journey. You will always be safe. Watch and learn, my son."

Egek took his clever son slowly around their encampment. They floated high enough above the ground to accustom Lélek to the sensation. Then they rose a little higher following one of the well-trodden paths to the little river nearby, from which the tribe fetched their water. Egek could see his son was thoroughly enjoying himself. *Time to see what stuff he's really made of.* They rose high above the trees and still Lélek was not perturbed.

"There's a storm coming!" He called out pointing in the direction of the black clouds. The wind whipped the tops of the trees, yet his bubble remained perfectly calm. "Our cave, over there – and the river I drew on the wall! Lélek became very excited as he pointed out the many other landmarks to his father. Rather than taking him on an extended sightseeing trip around the countryside, Egek took his son straight up into the sky, all the while watching for his reaction. Birds flew past them, and through them. That made Lélek laugh so hard it brought tears to his eyes … at least he felt that was what was happening. He gazed in awe at the rainbow which stretched from one side of the land to the other until it fell into the sea. He had never seen the sea. Stories passed down through the generations told of a lake so big its sides could not be seen.

Lélek turned with ecstatic wonder to his father, pointed towards the ground from where they had come and said in a whisper, "Home."

"Yes that was your home, and may be again someday, perhaps. Are you ready to go on?"

"I want to see more. I want to know!"

Together, father and son ascended beyond the layer of atmosphere, where the curvature of the Earth dominated the scene in front of them. This time it was Egek who pointed at the bright white disc, "There is the Moon". Higher they went until up was no longer up. Lélek gazed at the Earth for a long time before turning his attention to the Moon … then to the stars … *So many lights!* Resting his attention on Mars just for a moment and the great ball of Jupiter, he raised his hands, turning around and around inside his thought-bubble, saying aloud, more to himself than Egek,

"Home! This is my home."

Egek was well pleased with his son, as was Isten watching the first awakening. Of all the previous new arrivals Lélek was the only one to begin to understand. It was time to tell him about one of the great mysteries of existence.

Egek spoke to his son for the last time. "You were alive down there on that beautiful great rock with all the water and the trees and the great lands. You had life, and that life was part of the universe. What you see around you is just a tiny, tiny part of the universe. You are alive still, and a part of the universe. But now you have life that is different. The words I am saying to you, you might not understand … yet … one day … I, you, all of your tribe and all men will be able to understand and transcend physical reality. We become the absolute pure energy of the sum of all our thoughts. That is what the universe is made of."

"Good bye my son."

That last business about the 'universe' and 'energy' and 'thoughts' made Lélek's non-existent head spin out of control. He didn't even realise his father had gone. The initial elation of discovering his true home had given way to apprehension, not fear. The unknown had never frightened Lélek. That is what made him one of the very few of his species who was truly unique. He did not panic. Instead he began to experiment. Not knowing what might happen next he began to indulge his greatest passion. The quest for knowledge.

Foremost in his mind was still the world of circles and spheres. He felt intuitively that perhaps great revelations were there to be discovered. *I want to have a closer look at the moon.* Without realising it, he had formed an image in his mind of being much closer to the orb. No sooner had the thought manifested itself, then he found himself exactly where he wanted to be.

It was at this time that Isten had cast its thoughts deep into the realm of its past. It perceived a great hoard of entities all at different stages in their evolution. One stood out immediately. It was the energy of the thoughts amalgam of one individual, not yet melded, engrossed in trying to fathom the spherical manifestation of a circle. For that was the only way his eyes could see it, conditioned by his many years of gazing at the bright disk far away in the sky.

This is truly a flower of my seed. Isten determined to contribute to Lélek's further evolution. Each 'thought bubble' containing the young embryo of an entity in its next phase of becoming had the potential to meld with at least three others. Just as three equal spheres could be joined so each sphere would touch every other sphere. At the joining, the point of contact would firstly transform into a common membrane, like the coming together of two soap bubbles. Gradually that membrane would dissolve as the entities shared each other's accumulated experience of life, so creating a new being; a unique entity, enriched by the essences of its contributors, yet with an entirely new potential.

Isten had seen many individuals suffering the outcome of inappropriate blending, for the process was truly random. The resultant aberrations became disruptive elements in the civilisations that they were eventually born into. Occasionally fortuitous conjoining produced greatness; minds that contributed to the welfare of their own kind, and the welfare of all other living things in the care of their kind. As with all things in the universe, these greater and lesser minds were evenly distributed among the planets of myriad stars. *I will help Lélek circumvent those random forces.* Then it could only watch and hope for greatness.

2nd manifestation

1st consolidation: Ilusha
1000 BC

It was one thing to pick a berry off a bush and watch it roll away because you dropped it, and an entirely other thing to comprehend its behaviour was largely due to its being spherical. The man whose survival in the past depended on keen observation of all he surveyed, turned his full attention to the rotating globe in front of him. He couldn't touch it with his hands for they no longer existed. But he could touch it with his mind. Slowly the rotating moon showed off its changing face to Lélek.

An idea crept into his consciousness. He was driven on by the compulsion of knowledge towards the outer edge of the solar system. Each planet he passed confirmed the notion. Yes, Mars was a sphere, and the great Jupiter. He could hardly contain himself on seeing the rings of Saturn. Such great wonders! They were all wondrous, magnificent spheres. *All heavenly bodies must be spheres. Perhaps even the 'universe' my father talked about, was a sphere.* But he could not yet quite fathom what that word 'universe' meant.

That train of thought brought him back to himself and his current predicament. He was in a transparent sphere, a sphere which now looked empty. But he knew he was still there. He could see himself in his mind's eye. *Father used the word 'energy'. Maybe I have become this word.*

The pure energy of thought. No amount of imagining could help him solve that mystery. He was so absorbed and so turned inwards into himself that Lélek didn't notice another bubble, just like his, approaching in the distance.

"I am Ilusha. Someone help me, please!"

*

Ilusha lived in the city of Ur on the banks of the Euphrates river, around 1000BC. She was happy in her husband's house, but not satisfied with teaching her children falsehoods. "Your father has been teaching you about our Gods. He is a good man, yet I believe he should allow you to make up your minds about such things."

"What do you mean?" asked the older one, not quite ten years old.

"Our priests teach us there are beings, very powerful people who lived in the sky, who make things happen. Like the sun climbing the sky each day, giving water from the clouds, making our animals healthy and so on."

"Daddy believes that. Don't you mummy?"

"No darling. Well, I'm not sure. But I think I should be able to make up my own mind about it. I have told your father. He's not happy about that."

"What do you think mummy?" asked the twelve-year old.

"I think the truth is that creation belongs to us alone and we belong to it."

*

"I am Ilusha, please, anyone, help me."

Lélek started to hear these words in his mind. It sounded like somebody calling from a distance. He looked around him, above him and below him. Nothing.

"Ilusha!" This time it seemed louder.

Suddenly there it was! To his left. The bubble was not quite like his. It was the same size as his and at first glance it also seemed empty. Its surface swirled with transparent colours, such as he had seen on the surface Jupiter. It seemed to be searching.

30

"Lélek!" he called with his mind. As soon as he finished uttering his name the other bubble was next to him, touching him. He felt her smiling, a welcoming relieved 'I have found you' smiling.

"I am Ilusha," she said again.

Spheres no longer occupied his mind. Questions and answers started flying backwards and forwards with the speed of thought. Time could not measure the length of their interaction. With each passing of Saturn's rotation they became more acquainted with each other, and the thickness of the membrane separating them diminished. Ilusha began her story, explaining why she was in the void, beginning with her beliefs about Gods.

"What are Gods," Lélek interrupted. This female was using some very challenging word pictures. Lélek had to work hard to understand her flow of thought. Ilusha told him what she had told her children.

"I have watched this great sphere with the rings, turning around itself. I saw no one pushing it. I think there is no God for this sphere." He stated.

"You are truly wise," Ilusha said, relieved. It made her feel elated to hear Lélek say such a thing.

"Did your mate believe as you did?"

"No. He became frightened, then angry. He truly loved me and feared for our lives. He bade me never to say such things for fear of death, for the priests would surely kill me if they heard my sacrilege. So I said nothing to my friends. But my children had to learn to make their own choices."

Lélek, could hear all of Ilusha's peripheral thoughts of course, about the years of struggle she endured by having to live the life of a hypocrite in her own eyes. She could hardly bare all the ceremonies and all the useless sacrifices made to the Gods that she also had to contribute to, all in order to safeguard her children and her husband. It was obvious she was not afraid for herself. It also became obvious that in the end it contributed greatly to her premature death. As Saturn continued to revolve, so Ilusha's story continue to unfold.

*

"Husband, I have tried to protect you and our children," she said one day after years of struggle, "but I do not think I can keep going."

"You have been a faithful wife and a good mother. What is such a burden to you?"

"Whether there are many Gods or one God makes no difference to our lives, so I have been able to come to terms with your beliefs."

"What is it then, woman?" He was beginning to sound impatient.

"Slavery," Ilusha responded simply.

"What have you been saying to our neighbours?" The husband became suddenly alarmed.

"Only the truth. It is an abomination to make slaves of women, to treat them as chattels, less than human." She said this quietly, with great conviction.

"If the priests hear of this it will mean your death! First you refuse to live by our faith, then you rebel against our laws. What do expect will happen!"

*

Again Lélek interrupted Ilusha's flow of thoughts. "What is this word, 'slavery'?"

"It is the way some human beings started to treat other human beings, as if their existence meant less than the dirt they were walking on, especially women."

"That is not possible!" He almost shouted.

"Believe me, it was a great abomination. But the greater abomination was that even free women were of less value than men."

"Impossible! They are the givers of life!"

"Nevertheless it was so. Our society created many rules to control us and to degrade us. I would not have it!

32

On market days, when we were allowed out of the house, I started telling other women this was not right. I was no longer afraid of what they would do to my husband and my children. The madness had to be stopped. Week after week I gathered more and more women around me, until one day the priests threatened my husband. I was not even worthy of being threatened to my face!"

"Is that how you came to be here?" There was compassion and understanding in Lélek's voice.

"My eventual execution was not pleasant, though thankfully quick. I refused to give in to the barbarism that had taken hold of our society."

Unnoticed by the bubble travellers, Jupiter had completed many revolutions around the sun. The shared membrane between their bubbles had completely disappeared. Lélek/Ilusha were no longer speaking to each other. He/she were simply reliving their joined life experiences and in the process learning and evolving. As one, they were greater than the sum of their joining. As one, they formed a new self-image.

Isten watched them, marvelling at their union. It was content to let the new Lélek wander in the garden of the solar system. Much had to be learnt about the nature of connectedness between life and after-life and as much about their separateness. The first tiny step was their realisation of the relative insignificance of the physical experience. Important as it was at the beginning, the true nature of sentient reality could not be limited by the constraints of physical perceptions.

Lélek reflected on the very recent events. Drifting out towards the Oort Cloud he found it extraordinary how his memory seemed to have two distinct elements. It seemed to him that he had been absorbing absolute freedom for eons. But at the same time his memory of caves and spears and deaths appeared to be so recent, though without sharp focus. He also had the sense of a great injustice having been perpetrated against him just because of some ideas he felt strongly about.

A wondrous excitement gripped his mind as he cast his attention towards the sun. The majesty of existence as he had never experienced it before energised every minute particle of his ephemeral essence. Before him, basking in the brilliance of the great light giver, orbited the larger and the lesser spheres with their attendant children around the orb of eternal warmth. Engrossed in the thought that soon he might fathom the mystery of the spheres, he did not see it till the very last moment. Speeding towards him out of the darkness Lélek recognised another little ball of translucence on a direct collision course with him, emanating panicked confusion.

2nd manifestation

2nd consolidation: Ptah
2200 BC

Egypt had not been known as Egypt for long. Before then it was known as Kmt; The Black Land because of the black fertile soil of the Nile delta before being called Hut-ka-Ptah, 'house of the soul of Ptah'. It was in this land at this time that a young boy called Ptah was born. The society had classified the variety of people there based on their origins. Ptah was the son of a farmer so he belonged to the Romut class. His childhood playmates were Blacks from Nubia, an Aamut from Asia and even several Temehu from Libya.

It felt completely natural for him to spend time with all these 'foreigners'. Besides, they were his friends, and more. In all their games of battles and sports they always elected him as undisputed leader. Their parents also liked him. He was always fair and never looked down at his friends as if they were in some way inferior. Ptah had a natural air of authority … and he was clever.

"But, father, I want to do more than just work the land." Ptah said, dismayed when his father tried to force him to be a farmer."

"I know you're clever, but who is going to look after your mother and me when we are too old to work the fields?"

"But …" Ptah tried to reason with him.

"No buts – you must learn all the skills of planting, harvesting and animal management."

"I want to learn all those things, and many other things as well." The only thing that could even remotely hold Ptah's interest was the management of their water resources. Irrigation was essential in that land. The soil was rich in nutrients and a great deal of water was needed to coax life from the seeds. Another year went by and Ptah continued his informal education.

His mother supported his ambition, seeking every opportunity to let him learn. Initially it was easy to get her husband to teach Ptah all he knew about the science of Hydrology. There came the time, fairly quickly, when Ptah knew as much as his father.

Out in the field at their main irrigation channel, Ptah asked his father, "What would happen if we tried a wheel with fewer blades, or more of the smaller blades?"

"It wouldn't work," the father replied without even considering the idea.

"Why not, father?"

"Because I know it won't. My father did it this way and his father before him. This is the only way to do it." He wasn't angry, just adamant.

Ptah didn't get angry either. He knew his father, and knew he would not budge on anything he wanted. So he spoke to his mother about his greater ambitions.

"There was a tax collector in the village today, mother. I watched him. He had a parchment with marks on it. Every time he collected the taxes from someone he put marks on the parchment. What does that mean?"

"The parchment is called papyrus and the marks are a way of remembering things without having to keep them in your mind all the time."

"Could I learn that, mother?"

She could see the great desire in his soul. On one of the God's feast days she took Ptah to the temple to see the priest. It was very expensive to get the priest to spend a few hours with the boy. Mother had to make a special sacrifice. It caused a huge argument with father because he said they could not afford such extravagance.

Ptah was such a quick student that the priest spent the next year and a half teaching the young boy the art. Of course this priest had motives of his own. He could see the potential in this young pup. A smart young man with ambition, charisma and a natural leader.

He even went to Ptah's father. "Farmer," it was beneath the priest to call the farmer by name, "I will take the boy and give him a career."

"No." The refusal was simple and final.

"He is a clever boy," the priest said, "he could become rich."

"NO!" The father reiterated. "I am already bent over double by the work in the fields. I need my son by my side to help look after the family." There was nothing the priest or Ptah's mother could say to change the father's mind.

"Father, please," Ptah pleaded.

"I said, No."

Ptah was furious. "What about all the time I spent studying and all the money it cost…" The father threw a murderous glance at the mother … "It's not as if I'd neglected the farm. I've always been there when you needed me."

The father held his stubborn ground, "No, and that is final."

"It's unfair, father!" Storming out of their hut Ptah shouted back, "I will not be a farmer all my life. There are great things I must do."

Several days later he went home early from the fields leaving his father to finish the tilling, to find his mother had already packed a few provisions for him. She knew her son well and the power in him for self-determination.

"I have to go mother." Ptah wanted to justify himself but his mother simply hugged him, saying,

"I will talk to your father. Be brave."

"I will return," he tried to tell her. Being a mother she sensed that would not be so. Perhaps he would not even live long. Mothers seem to know these things.

Ptah then went to see the village priest. He, seeing Ptah's clothes and his bundle guessed immediately that his protégé was about to embark on an adventure.

"You want to work with me?" Ankhfaret asked on the off chance it might be the boy's wish.

"I want to thank you for your teaching, Ankhfaret, but I cannot work with you. I have to see more of this world."

"Let it be so. Write this down and read it to my friend in Memphis. Tell him you wrote it. He will give you a job. Now, go." The priest betrayed no emotion although he had come to like this quite special young man.

*

Lélek reached out with his thoughts to embrace the panic stricken translucent sphere. He had the choice to evade it and let it fly past him. At least he would have had the choice if he was not a being with compassion. Ptah was only a young boy. He had no one to meet him as his transition was so sudden. Lélek felt immediately drawn to this youngster, for he had the energy of a creator and a leader about him. The new melding had already begun.

"Help me!" Ptah also felt a strong attraction to the force that stopped him tumbling out of control.

The experience of his death had left him bewildered and frightened. Images of the attack were still foremost in his mind. Lélek saw those images and started to absorb them into himself. Little by little Ptah settled, but he was still very confused in the enveloping darkness. He couldn't see anything except the sun and the planets. They had no meaning for him.

Gently Lélek spoke to the boy, "I am Lélek. I will help you. In a moment you will see me, but you have to close your eyes. Close your eyes and tell me your name."

"Ptah", came the immediate reply. Although apprehensive, the voice was that of a strong and confident individual. "Who are you? … Where am I? … What happened to me!"

Lélek had to be able to do what his father had done for him. He had to manifest himself in a form that could be recognised by those who had recently died. If he had still been his former self, without Ilusha, he could have projected his self-image into Ptah's mind. But now he was different. He still felt like a male but somehow more complete. It was as if he had gathered the experiences of at least two lifetimes. Thinking about who he truly was, opened the flood gates of myriad memories. Huge beasts fell to his hunter's spear after long days of trekking … feeding his children and teaching them about creating maps … teaching his other children about Gods, and women about justice. With every passing mental picture of Lélek's past lives an image quickly emerged in Ptah's mind about this stranger. With his unconditional acceptance of Lélek's image that same image was reflected back to Lélek … and Lélek saw himself through the eyes of another … and he also liked what he saw. The more the boy learnt of this man, the more he opened up himself and told his story. All the while that membrane separating them became thinner and thinner.

Lélek listened to Ptah's tale, impatient to ask questions. "Explain to me about this thing you call reading and writing"

Thrilled to be able to show off his knowledge Ptah thought for a moment before answering.

"Imagine a person can draw things, things which represent his thoughts. Then another person comes along and looks at those drawings and can understand what the first person was thinking, just by looking at the drawings!"

For a split second Lélek thought 'maps.'

"Yes," Ptah answered, "just like maps, but these are not drawings, they are little individual thoughts."

Without realising it, Ptah was communicating with Lélek with his thoughts … the membrane between them continued dissolving.

While Ptah told his story, Lélek's thoughts filtered into the boy about his own search for knowledge and his battle for equality for women among men. Ptah did not stop to dwell on those concepts, he was much too excited about the adventure into his own independence.

"I don't think I have ever been as happy in my entire life as on the day I left home," he told Lélek.

Although he'd never been far past his village, the adventure did not fill the young boy with fear, rather with anticipation and enormous excitement. The flood of emotion washed over Ptah and Lélek, and they both re-lived the joy of that moment. Very soon the dividing wall between them would disappear completely.

"It took me months on foot, always having to earn a little money with my scribing. And sometimes I had to make long detours. Wondrous things I saw. I never knew the world was so big and so full of things to learn. I wanted to see much more of this world. Living amongst flat fields of wheat, talking about planting and harvesting all the time made me feel empty. All I could ever see were the fields and the river. Then the time came when I had to escape …" As his mind travelled back to that important day it all came back to him.

"Ah! I remember exactly what happened! Am I dead, aren't I?"

"Yes Ptah, you are no longer amongst those who live along the Nile. You have another life now … with me … together."

Ptah thought about that for a moment. He didn't know why he was so attracted to this person. Already he was feeling the comforting reassurance his mother used to give him. He felt the strength of this man, as strong as his father but who had much more understanding. As his thoughts dwelt on the unique situation he found himself in, the last vestiges of the connecting membrane between their 'self' bubbles completely dissolved. Ptah still retained just enough of his individuality to realise he was communicating with Lélek, about to explain what had caused his death. He was no longer talking, simply remembering. Remembering in the way sometimes we all do, when we recall something in detail and tell the story of the event to ourselves. So it was with Ptah. He remembered and in remembering shared the memory with Lélek.

'On this one occasion I had run out of money and was very hungry. The old fruit merchant had so much fruit, I didn't think he would miss just a few pieces. Barely had I hidden the small melon and a couple of cucumbers, when the fruit merchant's two sons spotted me. I ran. They were not satisfied to just chase me. They followed me all through the town. That must have been very valuable fruit. They were big men and gaining on me, even though I was the fastest runner in my village. There was only one thing I could do … I dropped the fruit and ran towards the hills past the fields.

Can you believe it! … They didn't even stop to pick up their precious fruit. It seems I may have been more valuable to them to be sold as a slave perhaps. When I thought about it, I became very frightened and ran as fast as I could towards the higher hills. At last they stopped! I could barely breathe and dropped to the ground. After a while I wondered why they had stopped so suddenly. I didn't really care. That was too close and I was happy to have escaped. When I stood up and looked around I could see the hills rising in front of me, and the whole town laid out in a chaos of streets and buildings behind me towards the river.

I had never been on anything higher than the roof of our hut and one of the palms in the corner of our field. It was wonderful to be able to see so far. I was still very hungry, but I wanted to see more of the world, so I climbed higher. The higher I climbed the lower the sun fell. The world was beautiful! I wanted to stay the night there and see it all in the morning. There might be snakes, but I was used to those and crocodiles would not bother me. So I started looking for a shelter.

For a second I thought I saw a shadow on the ground pass over mine. Just as I turned to look behind me, it attacked. All I remember is the lion in the air coming straight at my head.'

Taking a moment to collect his feelings Ptah was no longer just Ptah. In his mind's eye he was watching another hunt and remembering. The predator was not a lion, but something that looked a lot like a lion with very long fangs flashing out from below its gums.

Lélek felt a new youthful vigour in his mind. He recalled his childhood only indistinctly. However, the awakening he had experienced when he had first learnt to read and write still left him with a great sense of unlimited possibilities. The sun continued to shine brightly in his eyes and once again he was drawn to that speck of blue/green sparkling planet not far from it. So the three entities that had become one moved a little closer to their previous home. He stopped somewhere near the largest planet of the solar system. There were so many spheres going around in circles around this enormous coloured sphere that he simply had to have another look.

Mesmerised by the spectacle of the four large Galilean moons he began to wonder why they did not roll away. Why did they keep going around in circles? He recalled the round berries he had dropped on the ground as a boy and how they rolled away from him. Even the combined experiences of all three entities were not able to comprehend the phenomenon. Although knowing the answer did not seem as important as before. There were other, newer, more important things to think about and understand.

2nd manifestation

3rd consolidation: Thales
546 BC

"**Y**ou may be the shining light at Plato's Academy," commented Aristarchus, "but you must keep in mind you have made an enemy at the Lyceum."

"I don't understand it, my friend," Thales shook his head slowly, "you are the mathematician, you have the proofs. I'm only supporting your theories. It is not possible for the Earth to be the centre of the Universe. Surely Aristotle cannot dispute this."

"Nevertheless, you will have to take care my friend. Aristotle is powerful. He has great influence and can have you removed as the head of the Academy."

The two men often discussed this conundrum. Yet Thales, in spite of his being a mathematician, astronomer and philosopher in his own right with a brilliant mind, could not comprehend the fierceness with which his rival would oppose him.

At first Aristotle was patient. "Be reasonable, man. Don't you trust your observations? Have you not seen the sun revolve around the Earth while we stand perfectly still? Have you not seen the moon and the planets pay homage to us in their nightly rotations, while the Earth remains solid, stable and unmoving?"

After years of arguments on the subject Thales had become exasperated with the great man. "I have demonstrated the mathematics to you time and again, as has Aristarchus and yet you will not concede the truth."

Then Thales make the fatal mistake of questioning Aristotle's integrity. "You are afraid of losing your reputation. You know the truth but your ego will not let you admit it. You would rather live a lie for the rest of your life!"

Aristotle held his anger under control, which did not dissipate until he had undermined Thales' reputation with his peers at the Academy and amongst his students. Thales should have known better than to fly in the face of the establishment. He lost his respected position and the time of the great plague found himself almost destitute. Of the three previous new arrivals to the cosmos, his death was the least comfortable.

Still enthralled by the spectacle of the heavenly bodies, though trying to contemplate his new existence, Lélek heard the voice of an obviously educated man.

"There was a man once in a country surrounded by a great sea, not far from where you came from. His name was Aristarchus of Samos. He knew the secrets of the spheres you are observing."

Another transparent bubble appeared beside Lélek. He was not in the least surprised. After having spent a long time exploring his new world, he didn't realise thousands of Earth years had elapsed, and he was still looking forward to more new experiences. Lélek felt this was not going to be a fleeting occurrence.

He asked, conversationally, not showing any surprise at the unexpected presence of another sphere, "Who was this man, Aristarchus?

"He was my friend; a man with very great knowledge. Not many people wanted to believe in his knowledge, but I did. I was not only his friend but his student. My name is Thales."

Projecting an image of himself, Lélek introduced himself and asked, "Why do you mention him to me?"

"My teacher understood a little something concerning what you have been wandering about."

The two spheres were now touching, and the final melding for this cycle had begun.

"Do you not want to know where you are?" Lélek asked.

"No. I have a vague recollection and all this is not so strange to me. I was expecting to meet someone."

Lélek was keen to learn from this man who had previously been through the metamorphosis.

*

Isten beheld the latest coming together. It had chosen wisely it seems. Already there was a bond forming between the two men, even though Thales was quite an old man in comparison, over seventy revolutions of the Earth around its sun. The melding of the four would result in a wide range of life experiences, gathered over a good span of ages and from a broad spectrum of sentient life on Earth. Their combined attributes of a thirst for knowledge, a strong sense of justice, an adventurous spirit and the wisdom of learning with an open mind, created a formidable foundation for their continued evolution.　Isten looked far into the future with a renewed hope.

*

Lélek listened as Thales told his story, both of them keenly aware of the thinning of their separating membrane. Soon, very soon, Thales would become an integral part of Lélek's memories.

"Tell me what happened after you became destitute and how you died." Lélek had already absorbed much of Thales' previous memories.

Before being immersed in the personality of Lélek, Thales wanted to ease the memory of his suffering by the recollection of it. "Aristarchus could not protect me from the ridicule of my peers. Eventually I had to find another means of existence outside the benevolence of my teacher. A great disease found me begging in the streets of the city. Unfortunately, winter had passed, which would have made my death mercifully quicker. As it was the plague wracked my body and my mind. I can see that you, collectively, have not experienced true prolonged pain. I tell of it in the hope future memory of it might engender some small compassion for others."

Lélek had experienced his fair share of suffering; hunger when prey was scarce, beatings from his father when his father felt that the loss of crops was his fault, maltreatment by a supposedly 'good man' when that good man felt his partner had dishonoured him according to the dictates of his culture by refusing to believe in the Gods, or refusing to accept slavery. Nevertheless, Lélek listened as Thales continued his tale. The patience he had learnt very early in life while hunting with his father always had its reward.

"Headaches at the beginning were bearable, until the third day when my body became covered in a rash. Reeling from a fever, coughing up blood and doubled up by stomach cramps I could neither sleep nor eat. By the fifth day I was wishing for a quick death. Thirst, agonising, absolute thirst even drove out the pains of vomiting and dry-retching. By the eighth-day uncontrolled diarrhoea almost drove me to insanity. As quickly as the torture began it had pity on me by the tenth day. Weakened by the ordeal, I slept under the stars without waking for two days. It was a miracle I awoke at all. For the first time in my life I was truly grateful to be alive - but I was blind. What else could I do but laugh at the joke perpetrated by the great cosmos! But that was not the real joke. In my delirium of mirth and darkness I walked off the side of a tall bridge, breaking my neck instantly. Immediate recall of previous transitions allowed me to continue enjoying the ironic spectacle of the blind man who thought he had been saved from death. So now, you see me content and ready to contribute to your adventure."

With those parting thoughts the last vestiges of the membrane dissolved. Lélek, the augmented Lélek, could continue his journey.

3rd manifestation

a neolithic man
4500 BC

Proud as only new parents could be, Yon and his mate Ide celebrated the birth of their son with a feast. It was a special day for their longhouse. He was the first born to their house after a harsh winter and the first born in the village after many mysterious stillbirths for months. Events of this magnitude required feasting. Each longhouse contributed from their saved larder, and for an entire week the strongest hunters had been stockpiling the meat. The village elders confidently foretold the future of the baby, certain of their prognostications for a great future leader amongst them. In previous days of consultations with both the parents, and with the spirits of nature, the child's name was selected for him.

"He shall be called Lelke; Soul of the tribe," Elliou announced to all who had gathered.

Feasting lasted for days, from early morning to the setting of the sun. Emboldened by a variety of herbs of a spiritual nature, Elliou, the chief elder and shaman, took it upon herself to create the myth of Lelke. She was by no means the oldest of the leaders, but she was considered to be the closest in spirit to the land that gave them life. Why should they not listen to her about their future, carried by the baby Lelke. After all, Elliou could tell if it was going to rain the next day just by looking at the moon. Wild birds would sit on her hand and flowers sometimes bloomed the following day just from the touch of her hand.

"Give him to me," Elliou asked. She wrapped baby Lelke in a warm blanket, placing him comfortably on her knee, facing her. She waited till all heads of each longhouse seated themselves in a circle by the main fire in Yon's longhouse.

Elliou looked into the baby's eyes, her breath becoming shallow and her head bending to her chest.

She spoke her quiet words to little Lelke. "You have come from yesterday and from tomorrow and you will leave us, never to return. Four winds blow into your spirit and you will be carried very far from your home. Before you go, you will lead this tribe with your heart and with your mind." Looking at the child she felt his intense scrutiny piercing through her mind to her inner being. This child of Yon and Ide was of their body, but he was also of her soul.

Each of the seven heads of the houses stood and in turn touched the child's forehead giving thanks to his parents. At the end of the ceremony they all returned to their respective houses to spread the good news. Members of Yon's longhouse were proud of their child. Each individual, young and old, felt it their duty and their privilege to be Lelke's guardians.

The time had come for sleep. All but the main fire was put out. Members of the household settled in their private places scattered around the central part of the longhouse. Baby Lelke's eyes would not close just yet. Mother's milk made it very difficult to stay awake, but he had important things to think about. He was not yet old enough to be overwhelmed by the new reality he found himself in. As a child his senses reacted to the new environment, but as his former self he could still remember all that he was before his birth. In that vortex between manifestations Lelke remembered.

Still encapsulated in his sphere Lélek approached Earth cautiously, slowly. Perhaps it was chance, or perhaps it was destiny that the first land mass he should see was southern Europe. Or perhaps in his previous manifestation in that land he had left some things unfinished. Without any warning he suddenly found his sphere undergoing a spectacular metamorphosis. Moments ago all his thoughts, the total of all he had become, was traveling in a perfect, transparent sphere. Next moment his being was sleeping soundly in the warm womb of his mother, encased in the body of a foetus waiting for the right moment to be born. Part of him could remember the past, and part of him marvelled at the future.

Why all the fuss? He asked himself. *She's nice, Elliou, she has a good smell like mother. I like what she said. Perhaps this is a land where we can explore our potential. We?* He checked himself, *"yes – we."* Gradually his eyes closed, falling into a deep sleep.

Almost two weeks had passed since he was born. Lelke's memory of Lélek was dimming with each passing day. So much sensory information was pouring into him that sometimes Lélek felt he barely existed as a human being. The machinery of his early survival allowed him very little choice to direct his own future. Before coming to Ide he had a definite sense of purpose, without having to be too specific about it. Being back in the restrictive physical life manifestation, that purpose was being overwhelmed by his body's primary imperatives. *Why can't I remember any more?* - 'Don't be afraid,' he heard a young encouraging inner voice, *'Elliou will help us.'* Content in that belief Lélek allowed himself to be overcome by his babyhood. Tomorrow he must concentrate on surviving. In the greater scheme of things there was no real hurry with the evolution of his being. Time was only a temporary condition, but still, he must not waste it.

Infancy was boring in many respects. Lelke simply had to absorb and learn. Language was the greatest challenge. The awakening of his spirit and his mind out of the fog of infancy began when a sound Elliou and his parents often used in his presence suddenly meant something to him. "Lelke!" They were referring to him – *I am that sound!* From that moment his brain went into a frenzy of analysis. Storing every sound and correlating it meaningfully with three dimensional reality. It wasn't until around his second birthday Lelke began to dig into that stored databank of sounds and make meaningful sounds of his own.

"Neh!" *I'm hungry.* "Neh!" He kept at it until at last …

"What do you think he wants?" Yon asked Ide, as he was being disturbed by the infant's noisy chatter.

"I'll feed him. That should keep him quiet for a while." Ide didn't know what he wanted either. She just acted through past experience.

"Neh – Neh – Neh!" *They understand!* It was his first great thrill. It made him giggle. He knew they thought his name was Lelke and he knew that now he could command peoples' attention.

Though his parents hadn't fully realized the significance of Lelke's achievement, Elliou was fully aware. She spent more and more time with him, offering Ide relief from her constant nursing of the child. Elliou had motives other than just neighbourliness. As a community of two hundred odd people they all looked after each other. It was only natural. But Elliou felt the power of this child's soul. She was irresistibly drawn to it. She spent hours and hours over many months conversing with Lelke as she would with an adult. Sometimes she asked questions, and always stopped to give him the opportunity to respond. Before Lelke was three years old he had started to reply to Elliou's questions.

Whenever he was not with Elliou he was content to just listen and absorb. Of course he had affection for his parents, and showed it lavishly. But his relationship with the Shaman had already become a major driving force in his life. By his fourth birthday he'd begun to ask Elliou questions of his own.

Among his peers Lelke's outstanding nature was clearly visible. When he asked for something it was with such an air of confident expectation that he was always obeyed. He never commanded, always asked. Lelke had already started to become the leader of the mini tribe.

When he was just past four years old he asked his mother a question which confounded her. "Where did I come from?"

"You are my son, Lelke. I gave birth to you. You came from my belly."

"No. Where did I really come from?"

"Don't you understand, dear. Babies come from their mothers."

"I know where *babies* come from, but where did *I* come from?"

Ide couldn't understand her son's insistence about such a simple thing. All children asked where they came from, and all children were satisfied with the normal answer. A frightening thought suddenly flashed into her mind. Perhaps there was something wrong with Lelke. She immediately asked for Elliou's help. "Lelke doesn't seem to understand when I explain to him about where he came from. I hope he's not a little ... strange."

"He has an exceptional mind that wants to see deeper into things," Elliou said soothingly, smiling inwardly at Lelke's precociousness. She already knew about his strange obsession with his origins. She did not want to worry Ide unnecessarily. "I'll take him for a walk and have a serious talk with him." It was late in the day and soon it would be dark. Ide felt secure in letting her son go out with the Shaman even though they would not be home before dark. Their compound of seven longhouses was well secured, and the fields were not prone to predators frequenting the area.

Elliou, hand in hand with Lelke, walked out of the compound just as the sun was setting. Lelke had been outside in the dark before, but never before had he ventured out of the compound; not even with his father or mother.

"We are going out into the field to look at the night sky. What do you think about that?" Elliou told him. She detected absolutely no apprehension or fear in the little boy. She was elated, not just by his comfort in a new and potentially dangerous environment, but especially because he had asked that big, big question.

Far enough away so the lights of their compound would not disturb their view, Elliou stopped. "Come sit beside me on this large rock." The field had not yet been planted, so there was no chance of being surprised by a wild animal. "You asked your mother a question today. Do you remember what that was?"

"Yes."

"You can ask me that question and I will try and answer it for you. But before you do, would you do something for me?"

"Yes."

"Put your arm around me, and look into the sky. Look around very carefully, take your time … and find a star you really like."

Lelke's smile stretched from ear to ear. He could not remember ever being so happy. Why? Because Elliou understood him, because she knew there were important things he had to know. At almost five years old he already needed more information than the average child in order to grow into his self-hood. Imagination was the realm of children, but he did not need that as he scanned the night sky. With a new moon and a cloudless sky, the river of the Milky Way stretched before his seeking gaze. He looked in front of him and to either side and behind him. Twice he searched the entire dark dome before slowly raising his hand to point at a sparkling dot almost directly above his head. "I like that one – mother Elliou."

Elliou was a very wise Shaman indeed. She knew there was great hidden knowledge in this child. "Is that your favourite star?"

"Yes."

"Why is it your favourite?"

"Sometimes, when I sit outside our house at night, I look up there … I see all the stars … that one is watching me."

"You can ask me your question now."

Lelke responded without hesitation, "Where did I come from?"

"You know where babies come from. You have a little sister now, and you saw her being born," she said, not to annoy or test him, but to try and understand the context of his question.

"I know where *babies* come from … but I want to know where *I* came from!"

"Have you thought about it? Do you have any ideas?"

"Yes. But I'm confused. Sometimes I think I came from a place where there are not many trees and a lot of dust. Then sometimes I think about a place with so much water."

"Are you telling me about your dreams?"

"No … I see pictures in my head."

"They must be very good pictures. When you are just a little older I will help you see those pictures better."

Lelke listened and thought and then he asked, "can we stay a little longer … to watch my star."

So the two of them sat side by side, watching the cosmos breathing in and breathing out, she the younger and he the elder.

They were not gone for long. Ide was pleased to see her son return, smiling broadly. He gave her big hugs and kisses before going to bed. "Thank you mother, for letting me go with Elliou."

"There is nothing wrong with Lelke. He's just got a big imagination and a very smart mind." Elliou's words reassured Ida, for everyone in the tribe trusted their very wise Shaman.

As the years melted into one another, Lelke didn't ask his mother any more of the hard questions, though they never left his mind. Ide and Yon always encouraged him to spend time with all the people in the community who had knowledge in every facet of their existence. They particularly encouraged him to learn from Elliou. Lelke had a strong sense of responsibility, never shirking his duties around the compound, in the fields or on the frequent hunts. He was very capable in all those areas. People trusted him. By the time his head reached his mother's shoulder many members of the community had already started to rely on his advice and his knowledge.

Yon, took Lelke aside to prepare him for the next phase of his life. "Next year you will become a man. Perhaps you will sit at the right hand of our chief.

The people trust you. But this year you are still a boy, with the freedom to explore our world."

"Thank you father." He felt particularly grateful to this man without really knowing why he should be appreciating such freedom. "Tomorrow I should like to go further than I've ever gone before. There must be more to this world beyond the boundaries of our fields and our hunting grounds."

"Of course, Lelke. But first consult Elliou."
"Yes father."

After almost an entire day of trekking he reached the hills which could just be seen from his home. They were more than hills; they were great rocky mountains. It was already late, so he would have to spend the night. His mother and father might worry, but he knew Elliou would allay their fears. Finding a substantial rocky overhang that would suffice as shelter for the night he settled to watch his favourite star before bedding down on previously gathered leafy branches. Sleep came quickly after an exhausting day, as did the awakening at first light.

Early morning light flooded under the overhang creating sharp shadows over the surface of the rock. His attention was drawn to a particularly dark area not far from where was sleeping. As he approached he saw it was the opening of a cave. Lelke had never seen such a thing. Fear had never entered his soul, not even when he was a child. Without the least hesitation he decided to explore, making as much noise as possible in case there was an animal there that needed to be frightened away. He did have his spear, but he didn't want to kill any creature.

He advanced slowly and with him came the light of the sun. He'd taken no more than two dozen steps when the light revealed the most amazing thing he had ever seen.

"Ah! – What is this!" He couldn't help exclaiming.

The entire wall and ceiling of the cave was covered in myriad images of animals and people. The colours were fantastic! Nothing like the drab decorations on their pottery at home. He became absorbed in the minute examination of every image, every line, every colour before him. Animals in exquisite detail from every angle being hunted by people. Strangely the people were not very well done. The stick like representations did not do justice to the skill of the artists. He particularly like the abstract drawings of circles within circles, and the images inside them as if a story was being told.

Then in one corner of an outcropping he noticed the most wondrous image of them all … it was a hand; a large left hand with the fingers spread wide. Not a painting and not a drawing. "How did they do this?" at first he could not understand. Raising his left hand and spreading his fingers he brought it close to the image, slowly adjusting it to lie within the image boundaries. A picture immediately flashed into his mind, and flashed out just as quickly, so fast it didn't give him chance to think about it. He saw his hand, just like that with the fingers spread, touching something he could feel but not see … and strangely it felt like that touch had stopped him from falling.

However, his mind was far too involved with the image on the cave wall to think more about the fleeting insight. As he examined his hand against the wall he saw there was colour all around it. Around the palm of his hand and around every one of his fingers. "That's a very small hand. Maybe it was a boy like me." Difficult as it was to tear himself away from the magic cave, he had to find some food. The next few hours searching satisfied both his hunger and thirst. So he hurried back to the cave, with not a single thought of going home that day.

Lelke was about to experience another great awakening. The third and most important of his short life. He went directly to the hand, but the light was now very poor and he found it difficult to see. Again he spread his fingers and put his palm on top of the image … moved it a little to the left, then a little to the right … then all of a sudden an unbearable excitement took hold of him. "I have an idea!" He shouted, forgetting there could be prey animals about.

Lelke rushed outside into full daylight and let his eyes adjust. He put his hand, fingers spread, against the wall and spat at his hand, over and over again. A wave of electric energy surged through his body making all his hairs stand on end. Ever so slowly he lifted his hand away from the wall … and there it was … a hand … *his hand!*

"That is *my* hand!" He had created an image of his hand! Lelke stared at it till the moisture all dried up. Then he did it again until his mouth ran completely dry. He had done it again! Lelke whooped and jumped around and shouted for sheer joy. He wished Elliou was there so he could show her the magic. Running down to the river he made some mud, put one hand on the ground and with the other threw mud at it. Again and again an outline of his hand kept appearing when he lifted it away from the mud splatter.

It was a cruel night that night with a darkness that could not seduce him to sleep. He had not been so excited since the day he discovered his name. Lying there on the bed of leaves all he could think about was millions of ways of creating his hand. Around and around it went in his head, until eventually it all spiralled back to another image. Lelke remembered the flash when he first put his hand on the wall. Since his visions of dry dusty lands and enormous lakes of water where he could not see the other shore, he had had few other visions.

What are all these pictures I see in my head? I don't remember those things happening before. When did they happen? Did it happen to me? The endless questions just kept coming and coming until he eventually did fall asleep.

An unusually cold night woke him well before morning. Bundling himself tightly with his animal hides, he decided to wait out the morning, looking at the stars. Winking at him between the clouds was his favourite. He knew exactly where it was by now, at any stage of the night. Then as dawn began to break, with a much more settled mind after all the excitement of the previous day, he went to sit in front of the hand and await the light of the sun.

In the rays of a new day Lelke watched the hand reveal itself, slowly, majestically. In its fully exposed splendour he experienced his awakening. He went to the wall and made his own hand, slowly and calmly. That was not just a hand. It was not just his *hand*. That hand represented himself! ... and he said aloud to the sun ... "I am."

It took far too long to get home. He'd been away for almost three whole days. His mind had aged three decades. Of course everyone came rushing out to greet him.

Ide was furious with him. "You should have told us you were staying away for so long! It is not safe out there by yourself!" Then she almost squeezed him to death.

"We thought you had been killed," said Yon, relieved. "It's not the kind of world to be out by yourself for any extended period and hope to live too long." They were all so preoccupied with his return no one noticed the change in Lelke, no one except Elliou.

She took him aside, also hugging him while whispering in his ear, "You left us as a boy, and returned home as a man; a man with a wisdom beyond your years." Lelke held Elliou at arm's length and again looked deep into her eyes, as he did when still an infant.

"What happened to you?" she asked.

"I ..." He tried, but the words did not come. Elliou just hugged him again, joyful at his discovery without knowing what it was. But the boy understood. That's all she wanted to know.

As a credit to his humility Lelke did not behave any differently. His mind certainly worked differently, and he had become patient, more thoughtful. Lelke had also learnt to trust himself and accept his visions.

3rd manifestation

visions of the neolithic man
4500 BC

"**T**ell us the story of your hand again," asked Tilit, his friend. It was one of his favourites. He and Johee, also his close friend, and Lelke spent many hours together, never tiring of Lelke's fascinating mind. If it wasn't Tilit asking the questions, it was Johee. "Why are you so fixated on round things?" He would often ask, never quite satisfied with Lelke's explanations.

The experience in the cave had a profound effect on Lelke. He no longer played with the other adolescents, instead doing normal chores, learning life crafts and attending elder's meetings. There remained very little time for himself. The two boys, his closest friends, still managed to keep him company. Tilit and Johee seemed to make a special effort to be Lelke's companions. They were the other two smart boys of the community. The three of them made quite a formidable trio. Since Lelke's return they were rarely seen out of each other's company.

Tilit, the most practical of the three could turn his hand to almost anything. Not brilliant with ideas, but fantastic with execution. His even temper had become legendary even among neighbouring communities. Lelke of course was the ideas man. A bit absent minded, not always focused on what he was doing and much too trusting. To balance out the two of them Johee seemed to be the most 'sensible'. Partly keeping Lelke's feet on the ground, finding the practicalities in his various outlandish ideas and partly making sure Tilit didn't over engineer everything. The most valuable characteristic of the two young men was that they always listened to Lelke's ramblings.

Tilit said to Johee confidentially, "Sometimes I think he's a little crazy, but don't you just love his stories?"

"I don't think they are just stories. I think he's a shaman like Elliou. I think the things he says are important. I want to be with him. I want to hear more."

"Me too," confided Tilit. "Come on. Let's see what he's up to today."

They were particularly enthralled when Lelke spoke to them about his visions. Lelke trusted them. It helped him to understand his own thoughts to be able to share those thoughts with them. Not that Elliou wasn't there for him. But she was now much older and more set in her ways. Lelke loved her with an affection he thought he was not capable of. He loved her as his teacher … he loved her for her womanly wisdom and her compassion … he loved her as if she were his true mother. They still found time to sit together under the stars.

Several years passed without any major events. When not busy with trying to create pots that were perfectly spherical, and generally quite impractical, or finding new and interesting colours to paint with, he was consulted at every death and birth in the compound. It was soon realised Lelke had an inner vision. He did not need to dance around a fire at night, breathe the smoke of pungent weeds or hold special ceremonies. He just spoke in a normal, quiet, authoritative voice. Sometimes the people almost felt as if there were different people speaking through him at different times.

On more than one occasion he was invited to be both the head of his house and the head of the whole community. Not that it would have made much difference, since he was already carrying out most of the important roles of a leader. He always refused as he was jealous of his independence, knowing the time would soon come when he would have to leave the community if he was to satisfy those inner insistent urgings.

Lelke was asked to officiate at the birth of a girl child at one of the neighbouring communities. As always the three men set off together. Camped in the open at dusk, for it was always safer not to travel at night, Lelke was in one his moods. Tilit and Johee sat close, ready and eager to listen. Their lives changed as a result of Lelke's revelations.

"Johee, Tilit, what I am about to say I would not even tell Elliou. She is too … spiritual … and would misunderstand. You are my best friends. You know I trust you both." The two companions glanced at one another – they felt the same about Lelke. Sitting comfortably between his two friends Lelke raised his arm, stretched it to its limit and pointed into the sky.

"Look. Can you see that star, the middle one in that row of three?"

It took a moment for the others to locate it and confirm. "You mean the one that seems to be blinking all the time?"

"Yes. I have stood beside that star. I have looked at the sun and I have seen the Earth."

The sounds of the words came out of Lelke as if he was speaking from inside a cave, quiet, deep and distant. Johee was the first one to look directly at him. Lelke was not inside his eyes at that moment. Tilit also noticed the strange otherworldliness on Lelke's face.

"Lelke?"

No answer.

"Lelke," called Tilit a second time, putting his hand on Lelke's shoulder. Lelke turned to him slowly.

"What?"

"What did you just say?"

"What do you mean?"

"About standing beside that star."

"Oh, that star … that's my star. It watches over me." There was still a dreaminess about him, although he seemed to have returned.

"You said the word Earth. What is Earth?"

Lelke returned his gaze skyward. After a little while new words made their leisurely journey from his inner selves to his companions. "This is the Earth. It is a jewel in the sky kept warm by the sun as it travels around it endlessly. The stars are my home. They will be your home too."

They turned their eyes back to the stars. At that moment a substantial meteor shower illuminated the landscape. A spectacle never before seen by any of them. They sat there, together, transported to another reality … just for an infinitesimally short moment the three of them became an intimate part of the cosmos. In that millisecond the light of the celestial display burnt Lelke's words into their minds. Lelke himself let out a long breath … *One day I must go back.*

A distant sound of life brought them all back to their campsite. No one spoke for quite a while. Then Tilit was the first to break the silence, "I want to go with you." He looked at Johee and repeated, "*We* want to go with you."

"I will take you as far as I can … in this life."

Nobody spoke again. Not that night, not in the morning, not until they arrived at the other community compound. Then they were forced to become their normal composed selves for the hour of the ceremony.

Johee and Tilit had no forewarning Lelke was about to upset their traditions. Girls were not valued as highly as boys. Boy babies were lavished with every possible care and comfort to ensure their survival. The community needed their strength to hunt, to work the fields, to drive off warring communities. In short they were essential to survival.

Girls … girls were important as well; to have the babies, and for other small contributions they made. They were not seen as essential in the long term. Lelke felt differently. It was not because of his mother and not because of Elliou. He just felt deep inside himself that men and women should be treated equally and valued equally. When the moment came for naming the child, he addressed all his comments to the baby. He had another of his visionary flashbacks, still retaining awareness of all things around him, but establishing contact with the mind of the unborn soul. He knew the child would come to understand.

The sounds of chanting and dancing diminished. Smoke cleared from the central hearth to reveal Lelke sitting with baby wrapped, lying in his lap.

He looked into the infant's eyes, as Elliou had looked into his. "Your name is Rain. As you bless the earth with nourishment, without favour of one over another, so you should be treated in your life. No more, no less than any other because you are a girl child."

Total silence thundered through the longhouse. The crackling fire ceased its crackling feeling self-conscious. Tilit and Johee scanned the faces of the crowd. Everyone showed the tension of being overwhelmed by such momentous statements.

Tilit nudged Johee, whispering, "These people are outraged. They're scandalised by Lelke so blatantly disregarding their age old traditions. I think we'd better get ready in case they decide to put the blasphemer to death because he'd offended the gods.

"No, wait," Johee was a little more astute at reading people.

The silence seemed to stretch to eternity. Rain's mother slowly, deliberately raised herself from the ground to stand in front of Lelke, her face a mask of stone. She touched his forehead with her right hand, a sign of great respect … bowed her head three times, a sign of acceptance and picked up her baby, Rain. The father of the child followed his mate, and likewise showed great respect and acceptance, without the slightest hesitation. All the elders and all the members of the longhouse followed in procession. Lelke's reputation had preceded him. If it had not been for that, they may very well have ended their lives prematurely and in ignominy.

Tilit and Johee had a close friend called Lelke. Certainly they were friends, more so than ever before. The boys now felt this man was more than ordinary, more than just clever or strange. This man was the future, if only the future would accept him.

Tilit and Johee exchanged a quiet vow. "For the rest of my life I will go where Lélek goes," He said to Johee.

"And I will look after him, support him and defend him with my life." Johee joined his friend in making the life-long commitment.

As was customary the trio left without much ado, given provisions for the return journey and accompanied by the blessings of all. The last faces Lelke saw was of Rain's mother and father. Her stony face was replaced by the most ecstatic beaming smile he thought he would ever lay eyes on, and the father stood erect, grave and gave another three quick bows of the head.

Lelke never knew what happened to Rain, or how she was treated throughout her life.

Journeying home took as long as a wet week. But if one believes in the wisdom of the cosmos, there is a reason for all things. The three were granted the time to consider their future. They were delayed by torrential rain. Unusual for that time of the year, it caused flooding of a river forcing them to take a detour. One night after the abatement of the rains, with the moon almost full, they let the fire die down in their rocky shelter, to better see the moon. So Lelke spoke about the moon, for he was again very strongly drawn to the silver globe.

Knowing the signs by now the two boys eagerly anticipated … something … anything Lelke could share with them. For a while all three sat there gazing at the brightness, wondering what all those darker markings were on its surface. Without warning Lelke spoke, more to himself than the others.

"It's like a ball and it is always dark around the other side, where the sun cannot look upon it. It is like a dry desert of dust and rocks. I saw a very large rock fall onto it and make a big hole. The moon is a ball that rolls around the Earth on an invisible path in the sky."

He was almost in a trance, remembering the time when he became … more … more complete. During the day, when he was busy with the affairs of men he could not remember such things. Even his dreams did not help. They were mostly confusing. At times it felt like they were not his dreams at all but other peoples', people he had never met in his present life. The other most confusing thing was that he knew things he had never learnt, certainly not from Elliou or his parents.

"What makes the moon move through the sky?" Johee asked quietly so he would not disturb Lelke's trance.

"It is the Earth that controls the moon, and the sun controls the Earth. I have seen the moon go around the Earth, and the Earth going around the sun."

"We don't understand."

Without really concentrating, Lelke picked up a stick and by the light of the moon he drew random circles on the ground, corrected himself and drew one large circle. He put a largish stone in the middle, and a smaller one on the circle. Then he put a little pebble next to the stone on the circle.

Coming out of the trance he said, "We have to find a crossing tomorrow. It will take us many days to get home."

A crossing was difficult to find. They had to travel a long way out of their intended route, then double back. During some of their rests they talked about their future.

As usual, Johee was the first to speak his mind. "I cannot imagine spending the rest of our lives doing all the boring things everyone else is doing, not after being with you, Lelke, listening to your wisdom and your visions."

"I like being at home," Lelke said, "but there's these voices inside my head urging me to see the world. And I *want* to see the world."

Tilit was curious, "Just how much of the world do we have to see? We know what it's like; mountains and trees, rivers and snow, rain and wind. And everywhere we go there is the sky."

"I would like to see more of the sky." Whenever Lelke asked himself why he felt the need to explore, the answer always alluded him.

"There are many people who could benefit from your wisdom, Lelke. And think of all the things you could learn in your travels." Johee tried to sound as convincing as he could, for he truly believed Lelke could not advance much further in their own compound.

Tilit observed, "Besides, your visions seem to come most often when we are roaming the land. We will go with you, look after you, help you in everything."

"You are both truly good friends, but I need to thing about this. Let's take a little detour."

The boys never objected to detours as they always ended with interesting experiences. Some of the mountain ridges and valleys started to have a more familiar look about them as they neared their compound. So Lelke decided to take his friends to his secret cave. Very excited the boys were eager for the new adventure, because Lelke had told them about the fabulous paintings, though he hadn't told them about the magic of the hand print. Arriving late the following day, he decided to postpone the revelation until the next morning. The magic was so much more exciting in the rays of the rising sun.

Indeed, the effect on the two was as he had anticipated. They were overwhelmed. Rushing from wall to wall, touching every image, they were shouting and jumping and hugging each other. Lelke just let them absorb as much as they could. Eventually their enthusiasm relaxed enough to bombard him with myriad questions.

"No, I did not draw them. No, I did not do the painting. No, I don't know who did make them," and so on. They were not satisfied with the short answers.

"You have been with the stars, you should know!"

"Come with me, I have something special for you to see." Keeping the best till last, Lelke took them over to the corner where he had discovered the handprint. The boys, very disappointingly, were underwhelmed. After seeing the magnificence of the hunted animals in their glorious colours, drawn from almost every angle, the bland silhouette of a single hand did not seem to excite them.

Lelke kept urging them, "Look, Look!" Obediently they examined the image.

"What do you see?"

"A hand," Tilit replied, "just a hand."

"Look closer. Don't you understand?"

They did not understand. They did not understand how it was done, they did not understand the significance of what they were looking at. A thought flashed into Lelke's mind. He said to them, "Perhaps when you come back next time, as more than one, it will mean something to you."

Tilit could see his friend was clearly disappointed. "Show us how it was done." He didn't fully catch onto what Lelek had just said, so the three of them went down to the river to fetch some water.

Back at his old campsite Lelke prepared for the exercise. "Go find some rocks of different colours." Eager to obey and eager to discover they were soon back with a good selection.

"Now – crush one of the smaller rocks to powder and mix it with water till it's almost runny." Lelke had learnt a great deal over the last few years. They took all the prepared paint of different colours to the wall. Lelke put his hand on a clear section of the wall, took some of one of the pigments in his mouth and blew it at his hand. It took just one second for Tilit, then Johee to go completely silly! They dashed about putting their hand prints on any clear space they could find, mixing different colours indiscriminately to achieve magical effects.

For a while Lelke let them enjoy themselves. Before all the pigment ran out, he thought of a little experiment. He called them over to a clean section of the cave wall. They came running like faithful dogs, faces looking like designer mud, with grinning mouths and gleaming white teeth. "Watch," he said with a sly grin. Lélek made his hand print with the blowing technique. "Now you Tilit, put your hand on my hand print and make your own."

They stood back in amazement at the beautiful artwork. "Johee, your turn." Johee was already at it before Lélek finished speaking.

They stood back, gazing in wonder at the three superimposed images. Each could see the outline of his own hand and the outlines of their friends' hands. Johee turned to Tilit and Lelke saying most seriously, "We are truly brothers now!"

The boy's admiration of Lélek continued to grow with each passing day, almost with each passing hour. Knowledge and mystery … an irresistible attraction to any intelligent man.

Tilit whooped and Lelke smiled warmly at his friends. It gave him a strange sense of satisfaction, even fulfilment, to see the blending of the different images into one. The next few words he uttered even he could not comprehend. They burst out of him like wild water freed from a dam, rushing over the cliff,

"I am not one … I am four!"

The boys became a little worried as they had never heard Lelke burst out like that before. He just stood there staring at the superimposed handprints.

If they thought that was strange, the next few words were even stranger. "I *must* take my selves to meet the world!"

Well, that at least made the two friends very happy. But whatever did he mean by 'selves'? Exchanging a knowing glance, independently and together they came to the conclusion they would never understand their teacher, but they would always support him.

From the cave it only took another day to reach home. Unknown to them, the community they visited sent out runners with news for all the neighbouring communities. So even before the trio arrived home the new 'law' given them by Lelke was known to everyone within many days running. His mother was extremely proud of her son. His father had been elevated to a much higher level of respect within the compound as a result of his son's wisdom.

Tilit and Johee's parents, from two different longhouses, also shared in the fame of the returning sons. They also benefited from their sons' wisdom. For inevitably some of it had rubbed off from Lelke. Now, with the diplomacy of the two boys, some long standing differences between their two longhouses were settled, bringing greater peace to their community of many hundreds of souls.

Elliou herself had gained a considerable boost to her reputation. For indeed Lelke was a leader. She had foretold he would lead with his heart and his mind. At the very first opportunity after the welcoming feast, and Lelke's inauguration into the position of their Chief's official assistant (for he would not accept the chieftainship), he sought out Elliou.

"Mother," - Lelke had decided to call her by that title as a show of great respect, - 'when I was still a baby you said some words over me. I don't remember exactly what they were, but I heard you say them."

"How could you possibly remember that, you were only days old?"

"I have been having many strange experiences and I need to understand them. When I was still that very young baby I had a mind I brought with me. That mind was me, but more than me. I could remember things from before I was born, and I could glimpse the future. Do you remember what you said to me?"

"Four winds blow into your spirit and you will be carried very far from your home." Elliou responded, wondering what all this was leading up to.

"We had an experience on the way home. I couldn't understand it. For a moment I felt I was not just one person, but there were several of us."

"Be happy. You are on your right path. You are now my teacher, young pup. Don't let it go to your head!" She embraced him then slapped him gently on the cheek. As always Elliou knew exactly what to do and what to say, and how to keep things down to earth.

For a year or two the normal rhythm of life claimed dominion over the enthusiasms of the famous trio. Considered to be not only a wise and knowledgeable man, but also eccentric, Lelke was granted the luxury of private accommodation for himself and his two companions. The community didn't expect them to participate in the general monotonous labours of the others. However, each of them had specific responsibilities to ensure the safety and the wellbeing of the tribe. Least of which was ensuring their new status as being the most advanced in the region was maintained and enhanced wherever possible.

Lelke mastered the potter's craft, some of his work meeting the every-day needs of scullery demands, storage necessities and so on. The rest of his output became an irresistible conundrum to be solved by any who could think past the acquisition of their next meal. He had set himself a challenge. To make a perfect sphere. His potter's studio-come-dwelling was situated some way from the longhouses. He had plenty of room to experiment in. He laid out a number of concentric circles using small pebbles closely set, with his hut at the centre. The hut he decorated with orange and yellow splotches of colour. In itself a curiosity, because it seemed to have no symbolic meaning.

Progressively the circles of pebbles acquired pots of various sizes and varying degrees of roundness, but he only used the very best ones. Many were thrown out, and many given away, and then thrown out. As much as the people respected his wisdom, they could not work out why he made such round pots that could not stand. Some actually had two holes, completely useless as far as they were concerned. Tilit asked Lelke about that.

"They have two holes because I need one to look through, and the other one to let the light in so I can see the inside of the pot."

"But it will not even hold water. Why do you need to see inside it?"

"So I can see my hand print! I have finally worked out how to do it! Come, have a look." Sure enough, right there, opposite to the viewing hole was a handprint.

"Lelke … why is there a handprint inside the pot? Shouldn't the decoration be on the outside?"

"It is not decoration. That's me … inside the pot."

"I don't understand at all."

"Tilit, my friend, it's time I spoke to you and Johee about something very important. Please fetch him home."

For some time Lelke had been troubled by a re-occurring dream. No amount of meditation had helped. He thought that perhaps if he could talk to his friends about it they might be able to help make sense of it. When Johee arrived Lelke took his friends outside the compound, away from the hustle and bustle of everyday life. He also took his very special pot with him. There was a particularly serene area, only an hours walk away, where he always felt very comfortable. It was a like a smallish amphitheatre with a small creek running through it, with good sitting rocks, and almost completely surrounded by a ring of low hills.

"We will have to go on a journey soon. Do you still want to come with me?" Lelke asked when they were all settled.

"Of course!" They responded together.

"Perhaps we will never return." Lelke warned.

"Tell us about this pot," Tilit asked. "I mentioned to Johee what you said about being inside it and he became rather concerned."

Lelke closed his eyes to gather his thoughts about his peculiar obsession with spheres and circles; particularly about this idea that he was inside a sphere. Many minutes passed before he spoke, very quietly, more to himself than to his friends.

"When I first discovered the cave with the handprint and realised my existence, it made me feel very ... er ... re-assured. Later, when we went back together, I had a realisation there were others as parts of me, whom I did not know ... they were all me and I felt I was all of them. Still there was something missing. Then I started to have these flashes of memory again, about being trapped ... no, not trapped ... embraced, by something large and round I could see through. I could put my hand on it, but I could not see it." Lelke lifted his head and smiled, re-assuring his friends he had not become unhinged in some way. "Thank you Tilit, Johee. I wasn't able to understand some of these things before. Even now it is very misty, but I'm no longer worried. I want to finish the circles first and then we can go. We have to go to where the sun sets in the evenings."

*

Life went on as normal. Nothing seemed to have changed, except all three of them seemed much happier. Lelke eventually finished his circles and spheres design. He kept two of the most perfect spheres, one larger and one much smaller one for a special circle. He didn't know why, but he felt those two had to be placed on the third circle of pebbles. He put the bigger one right on the circle, and the smaller one fairly close next to it, but not on the ring of pebbles, slightly off to one side. He spent days looking at his circles and spheres and then decided to make one more very large one, with lots of very small ones. These he arranged on one of the furthest circles from their hut. Again he placed the big one on the ring, and the little ones around it, just on circles of their own on the ground.

Elliou was sensitive to Lelke's moods, feeling something imminent was going to happen, something she had foreseen a long time ago. As always, showing interest in all his work she first asked him about all the circles and all the spheres. "Tell me about your work of art. I am sure it has great significance.

Without the least hesitation he answered with just four words, "That is my home," as was often the case, without knowing himself what it meant.

Accepting that without comment, having a fair idea what he was alluding to, she asked, "What are your plans for the future, dear boy?"

"I have to go. We all have to go," meaning also his two friends, "I cannot find the answers here."

*

Three young men with long beards and worn animal hide clothes stood on the plains looking up at the Bükk mountains. For three long years they followed valleys and rivers across Europe. Stopping in many places and meeting many people their knowledge of the world and civilisations grew to be greater than that of any other men alive. Tilit and Johee often urged Lelke to stop and settle down. Sometimes they stayed in one place for months at a time. Eventually Lelke always decided to move on. It was only when they came to this place in the mountains of Hungary, and met a large community whose potters were even better than Lelke, that he decided to stop their journeying. It was not just the outstanding quality of the pottery, but also their shape that had decided his mind. The Pots were almost perfectly round. Globular bowls were an everyday item.

. . .

Lélek, Ilusha and Ptah had travelled forward in time taking their strength of purpose, raw energy and strong survival instincts all fused into Lelke. Above all their thirst for knowledge knitted them together and drove them on. For the first time since their coming together they found themselves excited about the future. Thales had travelled with them into the past taking with him civilization, science and philosophy. These people of the mountains seemed to have fertile minds. An irresistible attraction for someone like Thales, who, like Lélek, Ilusha and Ptah no longer existed as an individual. They lived in the fullness of Lelke's anima.

...

Not inherently suspicious by nature, more by necessity of survival, the Bükk people did not immediately warm to the strangers. However, they were young and strong; perhaps they could be an asset. The trio also realised that the first mandatory matter to be resolved was a demonstration of their skills and trustworthiness. No better way to do that than a successful hunt.

"Johee come with me, we'll bring them something substantial for the table. Tilit, they're building something by the stream. Why don't you go and show them what you can do." By the end of the first week of their arrival it became apparent to the Bükk tribe these three wanderers were no ordinary men.

Over the subsequent months, language barriers eased and little by little they were accepted into the new community. Johee turned out to be the most proficient linguist, initially acting as an interpreter between Lelke and the leaders of the community, who in turn quickly discerned Lelke had a wisdom beyond his years.

"My father has passed," the chief told Lelke, "come to the festival." The invitation, though simple in in its delivery, was nevertheless significant in the respect it demonstrated for Lelke. It was their most important funeral of recent times, giving Lelke comprehensive exposure to their belief system. "We will gather at his house at sunrise. You will speak." This part of the invitation was less of a request.

On his arrival Lelke was pushed to the front of the gathering, almost falling into the hole dug just under the edge of the house. He focused on the body, laid in the foetal position, covered with a variety of obsidian tools placed on its side and temple. The image of a body at the bottom of the hole brought back a flash of memory. He saw himself, or at least someone he thought he should remember vividly … standing in front of his own grave … watching his tribe covering the hole, with himself at the bottom.

He became too preoccupied with his own thoughts to listen to the ceremony until he was asked to contribute a few words. It took him several minutes to speak. Even then Lelke was not fully conscious of what he was saying. "Apa is standing beside me, watching as you say good bye. He is pleased for his body to have a resting place by his home, but he will leave you soon."

After the hole was filled and before the festival began the chief consulted Lelke. "We are reassured yet we are confused. We believe our dead go on living, with us. But why do you say he must go elsewhere? Where else is there to go?"

Now, fully in the present, Lelke had difficulty gathering his thoughts about this obscure subject. It was the stuff of his dreams, which he did not fully understand himself. "I have visions and memories that have not been part of my life here." That's all he could truthfully say. It was enough. More, would have obscured his credibility.

Another year passed with many more burials and many births. Lelke officiated at most of these, always taking particular care to emphasize the respect due to both sexes. Even within such a short time he was held in considerable esteem, partly because of his sense of justice and partly because of his creativity.

He continued his work with the spheres and the chemistry of colours.

"I have found new rocks we could grind, some we've never seen before." Tilit excitedly told him one fine summer morning.

"Get some of the apprentices, we'll gather some for experiments," Lelke was always quick to take advantage of opportunities to learn.

Within the hour Johee, Tilit, Lelke and several others had come together, with bags ready. Tilit showed one of the boys a sample, "Where can we find more of these?"

"Best we hurry while the light of the sun is still flat. Easier to see the sparkles," the boy replied. A good place to find what you are looking for is up on the hills, over there," he pointed directly ahead.

The ridge was close by. From a good vantage point, when they spotted some likely specimens, some went to the right and some to the left. Johee stayed with Lelke. Most peculiarly Lelke started to behave like a frightened child. He was quite overcome with anxiety. Just as well Johee was with him.

Shaking and taking hold of Johee's arm, Lelke made his confession. "You know I fear no man or beast," Johee couldn't believe what he was hearing, "but being on rocky hills fills me with an irrational dread. I cannot explain it. I haven't had any visions or flashes of memory to give me any clues." He was at the point of whimpering.

"Look around you, there is nothing here, except rocks. Stay here. Don't move. I'll look around, see if there is anything to be concerned about."

For a few minutes Lelke jigged about on the spot, constantly turning and fidgeting until he could stand it no longer. Before Johee had a chance to return Lelke had run over the edge, tripped and tumbled down the pebble strewn hill side into the morning shadows.

As the ground levelled out slightly he raised himself to catch his breath. It was the last breath of his life. A bull auroch, hidden by some bushes and spooked by Lelke's noisy descent, charged the first moving object he saw. Fully mature, with well-honed horns he dispatched Lelke at the first stab. Lelke didn't see him coming and he didn't utter a single sound as life shook off its corporeal mantle to stand beside the man known as Lelke. Wasting no time on a lifeless body the auroch turned and fled further down the hill.

The Lelke energy stood there looking down at the ground, transfixed. Then memory flooded back into him … a long, long time ago he was released by a lion on a rocky hillside.

4th manifestation

meeting Fremd
2060 AD

Isten watched and waited and hoped. *I was not wrong to entrust my future to this seed. The potential has revealed itself. This manifestation will evolve.* Isten touched Lelke for the briefest moment.

Lelke must have stood there alone, lost in deep thought for some time before Johee and the others came running down the hill to the prostrate body. They could all see the puncture wound, the brutal reality silent, absolute. Johee became so distraught by the loss of his friend he could not compose himself enough to help carry the body back.

The whole village gathered around to hear how Lelke had died. One of the other men saw the tracks left by the auroch and worked out the scenario. Although Lelke had only been in the village for a relatively short time, he was much respected and admired. As an indication of the high esteem in which he was held, the elders decided to bury him near the place where all the most important matters of life, death and faith were dealt with - the ceremonial house.

Up to that point Lelke felt no desire to abandon his body. Still in shock, he followed the group home from the mountain, then followed the procession to where the grave was dug. As part of the burial ceremony the very words *he* once used, were said over him by Johee, his dearest lifelong friend.

"Lelke is watching as you say good bye. He is pleased to have a resting place with you where he made his new home, but he will leave you soon."

The message of continuity after death was not only reassuring, but by hearing those specific words it was enough to help him realize what had happened. Deep emotions stirred in him as Johee and Tilit placed one of his most perfect spherical bowls in the grave with him. Lelke did not stay to watch the grave being filled. Remembering his first father, then Isten – previously an unknown name - helped him to decide what he had to do.

The new sphere in which he travelled to the moon was larger than the first one he had. Life as Lelke, had taught him many lessons. He had not wasted his life, or the lives of those who had melded with him. Although there were still aspects of his condition of pure thought energy he did not know about, his general philosophy of existence had been polished by his selfless contributions to all the people he had met. The richness of his inner being could only be accommodated by a larger vessel. For his current level of comprehension, that was the only explanation he could think of.

Moonlight was as beautiful as it had been before. The rings of Saturn even more majestic. He slowed to admire Neptune and the rings which gave it a grace and elegance he had not noticed the first time he was there...

When was the first time? Just a thought ago? But I have so many new memories. Was I on Earth? ... Yes ... I don't need to live there again. So many thoughts and questions and realisations claimed his attention that he drifted far from the solar system through the puddle of time. His thoughts had no limitations in the fabric of space or the conundrum of time.

For a moment his introspection abated. Lélek looked around into the depths of the cosmos. Overwhelming darkness and chaos threatened panic until he saw below him something that looked like a spider's spiral web. He could not comprehend the spectacle. There was no reference anywhere in his entire existence that could give him the slightest insight. *Surely no spider could create such a thing.* He could clearly see the pattern of spiral strands starting from the centre, gradually diminishing in brightness the further those strands extended from the middle. Everything around him was dark, except for that enormous bright spiralling web below him. Far, far in the distance there were bright spots of light shining like the torches of hunters returning from a night hunt.

Still engrossed in his wonderment Lélek didn't immediately hear the soft voice near his sphere.

"I heard you were coming, so I thought I'd meet you here."

Lelke turned in the direction of the sound, "You 'heard' me?"

"Not exactly. It was more like tuned into your thoughts. I see you still use your sphere. New at this I presume?"

"Second time. How did you get here?"

"Just a thought, that's all it took."

"I'm still having trouble understanding a lot of things, like what we are looking at down there."

"I'll explain that shortly. My name is …"

"Fremd. I see. My name is …"

"Lélek. I see also," replied Fremd.

"Why did you come to meet me?"

As the conversation rolled along, Fremd seemed to grow louder and more distinct in Lélek's mind. He didn't have a sphere, but he still managed to keep an image of himself 'concentrated', without dissipating in space.

"I know someone called Isten, who knows you. I believe you know the name."

"No, I've never met this person, though the name is – I've heard it before. Who is he?"

"He said we are to evolve together. I believe you have decided not to return to Earth. Obviously you have a higher purpose, even though you may not know it yet. Since I've been melded several times, with individuals whose experiences can help in our joint evolution, we are also to be joined. Any objections?"

"I don't know you, but I didn't know my others either. Tell me about yourself."

"If I explain what we are looking at, that will also tell part of my story."

"Can we go closer?"

"Soon. I see you have examined your home planets. Earth, Moon, Saturn and the others moving around your sun. Do you understand what they are?"

"Yes. They are the spheres that live in my world."

"There are many more suns and planets. They are all down there, but a long way away from each other. Your sun and your Earth are there as well, about a third away from the edge of those spiral legs ... look, there," Fremd pointed his thought for Lelke to follow. "My world is very close to yours. Follow me."

The two of them approached that part of the galaxy slowly so Lelke could get a sense of perspective and size. The closer they got the more the light of comprehension glowed in Lélek. All those circles he'd been drawing ... and all those spheres he'd been putting on them! He understood! If he had been seeing the spectacle with only his eyes, of course the immensity would have been overwhelming. But his enhanced mind could grasp this little revelation that the universe had granted him. It gave Thales in him great satisfaction.

Fremd pointed out Lélek's sun to him, then he indicated the location of his own red dwarf. "My world revolves around that red sun. It is much older than your sun. We call my planet, Erde."

"How do you know so much about my world?"

"Because we originally came from there."

More challenging concepts for Lélek. "How is that possible? It is so far away. It took me three years just to walk to the Bükk tribe. How could your people move so fast? Did they all die and 'think' themselves there? But then how did they have life again? … How …?

The questions flooded his thoughts to such an extent Fremd found it difficult to interrupt him. "I can answer all your questions, but not at once. We were brought to Erde a very long time ago by … friends … who had … who could travel very long distances without using their legs. But let me finish telling you about Erde first, so when we go there it will not feel strange to you."

"Have you visited Earth since you left?"

"Yes, I have … a few times. But most of the people on Erde have not. I was a scientist … kind of like your friend Tilit the architect … I built ideas instead of buildings, about everything you see out here."

"I have ideas. Many ideas!"

"That is one of the reasons we will be together. Now, to get back to my world. It is the fourth planet from our sun, not like your Earth which is the third from its sun. It is a very beautiful planet with many plants and animals and water. A great deal of water. You will not find the plants or the animals strange either, because most of them evolved from those on Earth."

During the monologue they drifted closer to Erde, close enough so Lélek could see the continents and the clouds and the seas and the mountains. "This is very beautiful indeed, like Earth." Fremd then explained about the temperatures on Erde.

"Did you notice, we have no moon, and the sun is very big in the sky. That means that living life is a little different than on Earth. One side of Erde is always facing towards the sun and the other side always facing away from it."

"Just like my Moon, but how do people live where it is always dark?" Lélek had not realised he'd referred to the Moon as being 'his'.

It will be a pleasure to be part of this man, who, in spite of his primitive origins has such an agile mind. "Most of us live where there is sunshine. Only a few live on the dark side when they have to work there … like hunting … for important things to help us live.

While they were 'thought' discussing a variety of essentials about life on Erde, Fremd manoeuvred themselves to drift into an area of space outside of the Milky Way that had a very low density of cosmic matter with very little activity. He chose that environment in order to start introducing some concepts to Lélek concerning the realm to which bundles of thought energy gravitated. At this stage of his evolution it was only important for him to realise there was more to 'life' than corporeal existence. More even than the various transitional stages of the mind, manifesting as thought bundles wandering about in the universe as unique forms of energy waiting to become physical again.

"The universe, a small part of which we are experiencing at the moment, is a complicated fabric of energies manifesting in many forms. You already know about some of these. From reading your thoughts I can tell that once you were fascinated by the reason rocks fell off one another. The thing that makes it happen is one form of energy. When you burnt wood at night to keep warm, the burning wood gave you heat energy."

"Is that like the sun giving heat energy during the summer?" Asked Lelke excited. He liked this kind of talk!

He never heard anybody at home or among the Bükk people talk like that. Just another reason he didn't want to go back there. Everything was evolving much too slowly on Earth.

"Exactly. Now, when you start thinking about things, or anything really, there's a kind of energy that is generated in your head to make those thoughts. When you have finished thinking those things, you can remember them later. Even a long time later."

"I liked that! Being able to remember and then to keep thinking about them and adding more thoughts to them."

"You never lose the energy that makes all those thoughts. You actually become all the thoughts you've ever had. That is what you are now. Your thoughts, and the thoughts of the others who have joined with you. After a time, or I should say, after many changes and additions to yourself, all that energy will go to a special place. I have not been there, so I can't tell you what it's like. Our legends tell us we all go there eventually. That it is like a universe between the universes we already know. A place where the essences of all living things come together."

Lélek listened with rapt attention. It all seemed so – comfortable – to think such things. During the earlier phases of his being there did not seem to be much sense to anything. Just living from day to day, struggling to survive without much joy or meaning to it all; then one day to be suddenly dead! Even when he was able to create and have adventures with his friends there was fleeting little satisfaction in solving the most basic mysteries of his life. The more he listened to Fremd the more enthusiastic he became about the future. He was actually able to cast his mind forward and contemplate possibilities. Yet for the moment, talking about universes was just a little too overwhelming. He felt much more drawn to the place where Fremd came from than exploring universes.

Of particular consequence, which Lélek had already asked about, was the origins of the people of Erde. The melding process was well advanced, so much of their individual memories had become common property. But it wasn't enough to get the concept of planet colonisation across to Lélek as clearly as it was needed.

"Tell me how we - you - came from Earth."

"Do you remember," Fremd asked, "that sometimes your tribe raided a neighbouring tribe to capture some of the people?"

"Yes, we had to do that if we had too many deaths and didn't have enough men for hunting or women to breed children. Sometimes we got raided for the same purpose. That's just how life was."

"Down there, among the spiral arms of our Galaxy, live many different kinds of life. On some planets they are a little bit like us from Earth. For a long time, a very, very long time one of those civilisations regularly visited Earth. They wanted to learn about us, because they wanted to take some of us to their planet. But they couldn't take us there straight away, because their water and their air and their food was so different. So they had to do it in stages. The first stage was to get us used to living somewhere where the environment was compatible to both species."

Lélek was understanding the general drift of the story. "Sometimes we found tribes that were so strange we didn't think we could breed with them."

"So over a few years, they came in their space spheres, and took many humans to Erde. They helped the humans build their houses and grow their food. They also bred with some of the humans."

"Are you one of those – new – humans?"

"Yes. My parents, their parents and their parents before that, were all, new humans."

"But you look normal."

"That's because I'm showing you the image of my human father. Not that the strangers were so different, they just looked a bit strange."

"Did the strangers have strange thoughts?"

"Their thinking is very much like ours. But they have lived for a much longer time and know a lot more than Earth people. Are you not comfortable with me?"

"Completely. I wouldn't have known you were 'strange' if you hadn't told me. You know much more than I do. But I like that."

Fremd unfolded the history of his civilization in words Lélek would understand. Some concepts simply could not be simplified and Lélek had to do the best he could to fill in the gaps. Gradually the two entities, Lélek, a composite of four, and Fremd a composite of twelve came together in harmony ... Lélek a descendant of Cro-Magnon man, and Fremd a product of an abductee from Earth and a human-like alien.

*

Lélek watched the galaxy parade its enchantment as he listened to Fremd filling his mind with great mysteries.

"Between the years 1920 and 1990 on Earth there was a concerted harvesting of humans by my alien ancestors for re-colonisation and breeding. Their civilisation had evolved to plague proportions on their own planet. Their genome had become degraded and contaminated by over engineering."

"I don't understand some of your words," Lélek commented, though keen to hear Fremd's story.

"The Opians needed to raid a neighbouring tribe to get fresh blood to make them healthy again, except that tribe was on another planet. They faced a daunting task in trying to save their species from extinction, needing not just fresh blood but also a fresh planet where both species could survive. That's why we are on Erde now. Though the Opians and Humans had evolved in similar ways, and in spite of their highly advanced culture the niceties of 'civilized behaviour' assume secondary importance when a species is fighting extinction."

"So the – Opians – did survive. But why are you here with me now?"

"Don't be so impatient. It's important for you to know our history so your – our – journey will fulfil its potential. The legends of the Earopians, the resultant species from the mix of Earth people and Opians, tell tales of behaviour that would be considered brutal by either species. However, the circumstances were extraordinary, leaving little room for inter-species etiquette. Yes, the legends say humans were abducted, examined and experimented upon. Their robustness in general, and their breeding potential had to be known."

*

"So these are the kind of people we are going to meet?"

"Yes, you are beginning to understand why I have to tell you these things. Some humans were rejected. Many, particularly the homeless and those without families, were transported direct to Erde. None were ever returned. The legends also say none ever wanted to return."

Of course Lélek would remember none of this information directly after re-entry, even if he had understood it all, but it did predispose his essence towards an openness to the new world he was about to enter.

"Most of the things you've said to me are very strange but also very exciting. But I want to know more about where we all go – in the end."

"You are right that our coming together is only a small stepping stone in our journey. Our time on Erde will be short. "I am surprised you are not full of questions about details. That is a good thing. If you are capable of understanding the big ideas, the details will explain themselves. What I'm about to tell you is partly what I know, and partly what Isten has told me. So some of it is a mystery to me as well."

At this stage in their relationship the distinctness between their unique entities had been considerably blurred as they drifted closer to Erde. Their thoughts transfer was interrupted very gently by the image of a youthful looking person. It introduced itself as Isten. They couldn't tell whether the image was that of a man or a woman. Nevertheless, it was most sympatico and its voice felt reassuringly soothing to listen to.

"I will tell you a little of what you want to know. Your father has already explained some of it to you. Do you remember your first name?"

Lélek needed no more than the gentle prompt. "My father was Egek! He called me Lélek. And then my new father was Yon, but he did not name me. It was Elliou. She called me Lelke. I liked that name as well."

"Egek told you that one day, with all your thoughts joined with many others' thoughts, you would become part of the universe. That is going to take a very long time. But before it happens you get a chance to become aware of a great many mysteries. You will go to a place that is in-between universes. Yes, there is more than one universe. Look at your sphere. You can't see it, you can't see where it's edges are but you can feel it is a sphere."

In his mind's eye, Lélek reached out his hands to feel the limits of his enclosure.

"A universe is just like that sphere. It holds in itself all the energy it needs in order to exist in its many manifestations, some like Earth and Erde, some like the

Earth people and some like the Opians. It is not eternal. This one had a beginning and it will have an end. It will end when it joins with another spherical universe. Just like you and Ilusha once joined."

"People like yourself, when they are ready, will go into a space between universes. There you will all learn and grow and join with many others, and when you are mature you will … that's enough for now. I will tell you more next time."

Isten's words were mesmeric. It was saying wonderful, exciting things. They made Lélek/Fremd want to do great things. He wanted to become part of the new universe. His mind began searching for a way to achieve that, a purpose for his future. That desire became the impetus of his manifestation onto the planet Erde to a civilization of Earopians.

5th manifestation

disillusioned on Erde
2100 AD

Twelve months after he was born he met his potential parents for the first time. Immediately after birth, all babies were isolated from their biological parents. After all, it was not efficient to indulge a 'product' prematurely, especially if it developed faults early in its existence.

Kra, his biological father was mostly Opian. Dyl-An, his biological mother was newly arrived from Earth about twelve Earth years ago. He was greeted with little ceremony and little emotion.

"Stand there," his potential father pointed to a spot on the ground directly in front of him. The child obeyed, emotionally neutral. Kra looked him in the eyes, "Hmm," uttering a non-committal 'he-might-do' grunt. That was normal behaviour.

The child held his ground, his eyes not moving off Kra. If the child had shown the slightest sign of timidity, he would have been assigned to another colony. Dyl-An was a little more personal. She picked him up, holding him close to her breasts, and monitored herself for signs of bonding. If that was weak or missing the child would have been assigned to another colony. He remained limp, yet focused, in Dyl-An's arms.

Since Dyl-An arrived from Earth, a voluntary emigrant in her case, she had been put through a complex series of re-socialisation procedures. It was necessary all emigrants left their culture behind as much as possible. Their greatest value to Earopian society was their pure genetic heritage, uncontaminated by diseases and failed or inappropriate engineering, and free of extraneous loyalties.

Kra and Dyl-An were members of an elite group of Earopians specially dedicated to the genetic development of the combination of the two races, without resorting to invasive genetic engineering. With the initial stage of the introduction to the child completed it was time for the naming. Within this elite group the custom was strict on naming procedures.

"Put him down," the Director ordered. He put a notation on record, "He will be called Kradyl-On," 'On' denoting the fact that he was the first born to the parents. Neither biological parent registered objection at this initial stage to a possible commitment.

Kradyl-On was not required to say anything during the naming procedure. By that age the children had a good grasp of the language and had been disciplined, from a very early stage, to do as they were told. So Kradyl-On said nothing. But his mind was not silent. All the preliminary tests had been completed on the child.

"Kradyl-On's tests show all aspects to be normal. Any objects to final assignment?" The Director carried out the procedures with clinical disinterest.

With the final approval given by the parents the child was permanently assigned to them. Permanently meant exactly that. There were no circumstances under which that assignation could be changed. The parents had strict responsibilities with the raising, and preliminary education of their assigned children ... and they, the parents, were just as strictly monitored. The long term future of the Opians depended on it. The survival of their species depended on it.

"Come here, child," Dyl-An held out a hand to him.

Kradyl-on did not move. The father raised his eyebrows, more surprised than anything else. "Come," she said again.

At one point during the recording of all relevancies regarding the birth and parental acceptance, Kradyl-On had reached a decision. As the adults waited for his compliance he announced in a clear, perfectly pronounced Earopian accent,

"My name is Lélek!"

Dyl-An's hand remained hanging in mid-air, Kra's eyebrows raised themselves to their limits. Everyone was stunned! No child had ever had the ill manners, let alone the courage, to choose his own name. He wasn't just choosing his own name – he was defying his parents and the regulations! He was speaking when he should have been silent! No one knew what to do. Dyl-An, being most attuned to the child, perhaps because of her Terrestrial origins, responded first.

"Kradyl-on, I am your mother and you must …"

"My name is Lélek," insisted the child in a matter of fact tone.

That left no option but for the adults to call a conference. The parents, a leading child psychologist, a prominent educator, Mani-Tre, and of course the conventions enforcement hierarchy, discussed in serious and controlled tones this most unusual child. The decision was not unanimous to allow the child to be known as Lélek.

"I suggest terminating him," the Director just wanted to be rid of the problem.

For some reason both parents wanted to persevere with the child. "No," Kra said, with the authority of the official father. "The child is healthy and has a good mind." He looked at Dyl-On for support, which was given with a firm nod. "However, we want him to remain here for another year."

"You may proceed," said the Director reluctantly, astute enough to recognise a potential asset to the breeding program. "There are conditions."

The psychologist made those quite clear. "Such a child, one who shows such a high degree of self-awareness and such confident self-assurance, has to be treated as a special case. He has to be monitored closely for any emerging aptitudes, and those aptitudes have to be nurtured to the fullest extent. Am I understood?" It was an order, not a question.

While the conference was in full swing, Lélek quietly contemplated his circumstances. It seemed to him that once before, prior to immersion in the consequences of being given corporeal existence, he could remember things after he was born that had happened to him previously. Although a year had elapsed he still recalled wondrous things said to him by someone special, perhaps it was because he had asserted his actuality. The things he remembered made him feel there was purpose to his existence. He recalled Fremd who had taught him so much about the life he was about to live. Most of all his mind replayed the visions of magnificence surrounding him – the galaxy and the planets and the suns and the vastness of space. Most of all, he knew his name was Lélek. Once before it had been changed, but never again. It wasn't just his name – that is who he was!

As if waiting for acceptance of his pronouncement, his mind went over and over the name, until he could think of nothing else. When at last his mother acquiesced and called him by his real name, Lélek had already lost the insight into his past. He was just a child on the planet Erde, with parents who were as fully dedicated to his future – as he had been. He smiled, but found it difficult. Nobody on the planet had needed those muscles for countless generations, and so they atrophied, except for new Earth arrivals. In spite of the rigours of their new life, they found much to smile about. Dyl-An noticed her son trying to smile and she smiled also. *There is more human in him than Opian.* There was more human left in her than she knew. *Such a strange child; already trying to smile at this early age.* "We will return for you after you've had further education." That was the last Lélek heard from or of his intended family, until a full year hence.

*

Lélek took his mother's hand. His life on Erde had at last begun after waiting for two whole years.

It was dark outside the Inculcation Institute. With his very large eyes and pupils wide open he could see into the darkness quite easily. His parents lived mostly on the periphery of the dark side of the planet, as did most of the population. The light side was almost always too hot and too bright for survival without dedicated structures and protective clothing. The eyes were particularly vulnerable in the bright light, as they had evolved for very low illumination.

Every now and then he looked at his parents sitting in the transport vehicle as it glided through the clear tube. He felt he would come to like his mother. She had, what seemed to him, nice proportions. He was not sure about his father. The man was rather tall and skinny with very large hands, or at least very long fingers. Kra looked back at him with an expressionless face, tilted his head slightly and nodded. Lélek held his eyes fixed on his father's. Somehow he felt Kra was not entirely displeased with him. That was a pleasant feeling. Perhaps he would get to like Kra as well, in time.

It was a long journey from the Inculcation Institute to their home, through some extremely rocky terrain making Lélek feel strangely uneasy. He was just getting used to it, so it came as a shock when suddenly it all changed, causing him to jump in his seat. This time it was his father who spoke.

A quiet, slow and measured voice said, "You are looking at grass and trees and a lake."

The landscape made him as uneasy as the barren, rocky terrain did. It made no sense at all. For the first twelve months of his life he had lived in an artificial environment undergoing intensive targeted conditioning. Nutrition and exercises were paramount. This planet had a gravity 1.3 times that of Earth. Not impossible for Terrestrials to manage, but difficult. Genetically he was only partly Earopian, leaning more towards the Earthly spectrum. So he needed the exercise and the special diet to help him compensate for life on the outside. Neither was Lélek's mental development neglected. By no means kept in isolation he had considerable interaction with other infants, and many adults. He was taught about his planet through holographic images, but it was still a shock when he saw the real world.

Before long Lélek's attention came back into the vehicle. It was only then he became fully conscious of the other individuals with them. He knew the theory, but it was strange to see them there filling up the tube car's empty seats.

"Father Kra," he asked, as convention dictated, "who are these? Why do they all look the same?"

The caretaker androids did indeed all look exactly the same, except for an identifier on their front and back. That identifier denoted the identity of their charges. Slowly Kra turned to his son, considering the two questions for a moment before answering.

"They are our carers. We each have one. Everyone on the planet has one. They are with us during our entire lives. It is their responsibility to help us during the day and when we are asleep. You will very rarely have to ask them to do anything for you, and they will always obey you. Now listen very carefully to what I say – do not ever break this law. You cannot ask your carer to harm itself, you or anyone else. You cannot ask it to put itself in danger for any reason, other than to protect you. It will do that without being asked."

Kra waited a little while for his young son to absorb that law, all the while watching him. Then he turned his mind to the other question. It was the first time in his entire experience a child his age had asked about the uniformity of the androids. Why? What possible reason could he have? What answer can he give a two-year old child.

"Because we decided to make them that way. Why do you ask me this?"

"Father Kra – because I want to know." Lélek said this completely naturally, quietly, even seemingly pensively. Genetically he was certainly the product of the two species. The motive force, the spark of life, that essence of 'being' which inspired his genome into sentience was something else. He looked away from his father, examined his android with dispassionate curiosity, glanced at his mother then turned his attention to the outside world again.

Kra determined he and Dyl-An would have to be especially vigilant about answering Lélek's probing questions as he grew into manhood. He was certain this child would test their resourcefulness.

Lélek could not yet understand the importance of the comprehensive bio-diversity of life he witnessed on the way home. Holograms could not give even the slightest sense of reality in contrast to seeing life in the wild; bewildering in their size and some in their ferocity. Eat and propagate or be eaten and die, seemed to be a universal law of ensuring the cycles of eternity. Distracted by the manifestation of life in general, Lélek didn't notice the tube car turn onto an exit tube and after a little while slow to a stop.

They had arrived at the complex which housed the people of their specialised colony. There were many of these complexes around the planet, each housing about a thousand families. Every 'hive' had the same structure. Tubular elevators, extending eight hundred meters, some below ground level and most above, serviced ninety homes per building. Each hive consisted of ten such buildings.

"Father Kra, what is this place?"

"This is where we live, child," Dyl-An answered. Kra watched the boy as Lélek scanned the environment. "We are on level sixteen, building eight. Remember that - level sixteen, building eight."

For Lélek the spectre of the rising columns, parks and forested areas were incomprehensible in comparison with the restricted environment of the Inculcation Institute. Standing in the open, while waiting for their personal pod, that environment burnt itself indelibly into his mind. People were coming and going about their business, greeting each other, and them, without paying any particular attention to him. That would change soon enough.

"Why are all the buildings the same, Father Kra?"

Dyl-An turned to Kra, "Are you prepared to educate our son? He seems extraordinarily curious." Again the raised eyebrows from Kra, this time confirming his mate's instruction to do just that.

"They are all exactly the same," he said to Lélek, "outside and inside. All the dwellings are furnished the same and decorated in the same colours." He should have anticipated the next question.

"Why do they have to be the same, Father Kra?"

The pod arrived, all of them disembarking including the androids. Kra took a moment to formulate an appropriate answer. "We distinguish ourselves and express our individuality by our actions, thoughts and our contribution to society, both at home and in the world at large, not by inconsequential external ornamentation."

"Do you understand, Lélek? You can ask as many questions as you like," said Dyl-An warming to this seemingly exceptional little person.

Arriving at building eight, the design of the structure came into clear focus. Lélek immediately noticed the slow rotational motion of each of the irregular circular platforms making up each level, noting those movements were not synchronised. "Why don't the platforms move together, Father Kra?"

Dyl-An smiled, already reconciled to a lifetime of enquiry. "If the child is that curious, he might as well have detail. One day he will understand," Kra said to Dyl-An, then to Lélek, "each floor has a single self-contained environment, set on a slowly rotating platform of one hundred and twenty metres diameter. This allows for the main dwelling and an external space dedicated to leisure, gardening, and food. The height between 'disks' is twelve meters, which is enough for light and rain for each level. Do you want to know more?"

"Yes Father Kra."

"The underground levels are dedicated to storage and maintenance."

"Come on Lélek it's time to go up to our level." Dyl-An was eager to settle the newcomer into her home.

Lélek couldn't immediately take in the scale of the building as they stepped into the large tubular elevator and travelled up through layers of vertical gardens, each layer resplendent with birds and other creatures. On level sixteen the door opened directly onto their main living space, facing the large panoramic window to their gardens.

Lélek ran outside, right to the edge of their platform, his eyes wide in amazement at everything around their building. Each building was set back from a central community environment, which was directly below him. In general, each colony occupied a circular patch of land at least three kilometres in diameter. Engrossed in the moment, Lélek had no burning questions.

On their platform, both Kra and Dyl-An let themselves relax, encouraging Lélek to do the same, and gave themselves over to the ministrations of their android carers. Priority item for the day had been concluded with the successful transfer of their son.

"You had better have a little rest as your first play session is due to begin in an hour. You will meet some of the other children down in the community area." Kra was grateful not to have to deal with any more questions.

Until Kra had actually accepted responsibility for his son, having satisfied himself the child was a suitable progeny, he could not proceed with arrangements for the child's higher education. That started immediately after the end of the second twelve months of his life. The Earopians were a long lifespan species. Those who chose to do so could live for up to the equivalent of two hundred earth years. Few elected to do that, particularly in the past as the specie's genetic structure had been so badly re-engineered that the quality of their lives was seriously compromised. But that was gradually improving with the purity of the human genome beginning to have a noticeable effect.

The hour's downtime passed quickly. Kra ushered his son down to the ground floor giving him a word of advice about his foreseeable future.

"Time now for you to play and make friends. There will be regular play periods for you, but for the next ten years your schooling will be intense in the basics here at our colony's education centre."

"Will my teachers be able to answer my questions?" Coming from his son it was no surprise at all to Kra.

"I would expect they will – by the end of that time we will know the correct career path for you."

"What if I should want to do something different, Father Kra?"

That, the father did not expect. "Go and play now. We will discuss such important matters later."

The following day Lélek was introduced to his first class. Mani-Tre wasted no time on pleasantries or introductions. The children could do that themselves in their own time. "You are here for one reason only. If you fail in that endeavour you are of no use to society and will be treated accordingly."

Lélek stood between two other boys, they looked at one another feeling somewhat apprehensive at the announcement, except Lélek. "Master Mani-Tree, what is that treatment?"

Mani-Tre glared at Lélek and continued, "Understand this – the acquisition of knowledge is the driving force of your life for the next ten years. Your self-esteem depends on it, your acceptance into our colony revolves around it. The purposefulness of your life is defined by it. Do you have another question, boy?" The Master kept one eye on Lélek. He was the only one fidgeting.

"Master Mani-Tre, why have knowledge?" Lélek could hardly contain himself for this is exactly the need he felt deep inside himself.

"Your social and professional position in this world will depend on the use to which you put your acquired knowledge." The Master waited for a reaction, but received none. Lélek withdrew into himself to ponder the proposition, while the other children stood frozen to the spot in fear of reprisals for Lélek's disrespectful behaviour. That first day set the pattern to Lélek's interactions with his teachers and his fellow students, not without some attended unpleasantness from time to time.

This philosophy of usefulness to society was introduced to the children on the first day of formal education, to be reinforced constantly throughout their lives. There was no higher goal than the attainment of understanding. From this point of view Lélek should have been the most contented child in his group. Not so. Perhaps it was his humanness, perhaps it was his predisposition based on the constituent parts of his melded beings, that continually pushed him to question everything. From the end of his fourth year, those questions became more specific. Other children asked their parents … Why? … about such and such.

Lélek asked … Why … following it up with How, When and Why not do it differently.

He had stored in his memory Kra's response to his very first question as to why the androids all looked the same. One day, without forewarning he said to his father, "Father Kra, you said the androids were the same because they were made that way. How are they made the same?"

Since Kra had dedicated his life to Lélek's education, on the following free day he took Lélek to one of the local android manufacturing facilities. The workers were assailed by myriad questions from a six year old boy, probing every conceivable aspect of production Lélek could think of. His insatiable thirst for knowledge had become a source of pride for Kra. It didn't do his standing back at their colony much harm either. For Lélek the factory visit proved to be both enlightening and disappointing. He learnt about the vulnerability of the android programing. Clearly, intentional high level controls built into their logic systems made them open to external covert interference.

*

In the second ten-year period of higher education the emphasis was placed on the practical applications of knowledge acquired. This aspect pleased Lélek, though he was again disappointed by the restrictions placed on parental visits. The students were required to live-in at their educational institution, parental contact being discouraged. It was considered to be too distracting to the students.

"Lélek, what you and your little band of followers are doing have attracted a great deal of criticism," Master Mani-Tre told Lélek after having put up with years of his insubordination. "No good will come from your methodology," he tried to warn the boy he'd come to admire over the years.

"Is it not our duty to test the theories you teach, Master? Is not the best approach to disprove them in any way possible?"

"Well, yes – but do you have to apply that to everything? It is one thing to play with the sciences, but if you attack our ethics …"

Lélek considered the word 'attack'. "My friends and I are not attacking anything. We are trying to show the balance has been lost, especially in the realm of this great re-engineering enterprise we all seem to be a victim of!"

Perhaps he'd gone a little too far in proclaiming themselves 'victims'. The Master's anger did not manifest in the usual emotional manner one could expect of a human being. He was third generation, like Lélek's father, yet the colour did rise to his face. This boy he admired often pushed him to his limits.

In a constrained measured voice he tried to make the situation clear, "Your tutors are fed up with you and your gang – your parents are concerned and have been warned by a higher authority – the other students do not wish to be associated with you. Do I make myself clear?"

Initially this young fellow's antics only drew questioning looks from tutors, parents and neighbours. But as the years progressed and Lélek became more adventurous, the academic elite became involved, then the local ruling establishment. Lélek simply refused to adhere to the accepted rhythms of academic life. He adamantly proclaimed, "Our research and experimentation require our absolute dedication to the exclusion of all else. Sometimes our methods have to be ruthless and uncompromising to your laws, your ethics, even your attempts to rejuvenate your genetics." It pained the Master to hear this brilliant mind divorcing himself from his own society, let alone rebelling against it.

Kra saw the extraordinary potential of his son, and was prepared to endure all the angst it caused him. Dyl-An became outspokenly supportive of her son. It was through her intervention the entire school programme routine was altered to make room for her son's unorthodox methods of self-education. Perhaps it was this last matter which threatened the establishment. Perhaps it was Lélek's dangerously subversive attitudes that eventually caught the attention of those in Government.

By the time Lélek was twenty years old he and his band of followers were assigned a wholly new role in the inter-species programme of the Earopians. Lélek's extraordinary academic progress, including some scientific innovations which had been implemented for the overall benefit of the species and his outstanding dedication to work, had earned him full qualification as a research scientist. At that juncture his formal education officially ended prematurely, by one year.

Master Mani-Tre enjoyed telling Lélek, "Not only have you earned yourself an early graduation, gaining your freedom from this place," he stopped for a moment sure Lélek would understand the pleasure the release afforded both of them, "you have also been given a prestigious assignment."

The director of the Inculcation Institute was there to give Lélek the good news. "We are sending you into space. Once again we have to deal with a problem, that is *you*." As officious as always the Director could not resist putting Lélek in his place.

Completely unfazed Lélek shot back, "And you want me to do what, exactly?" He could barely contain his excitement … Space … where he'd always wanted to be since he could remember.

"Do what you do best. Look around and ask questions." The Director, the leading scientific authority of the day and also the individual who sanctioned most of the 'exploratory' surgery on prospective abductees from Earth, wanted to find out the young man's true potential; any way possible. If all else failed, neural electro-incursion was still an option … probably without inflicting too much damage. He didn't mention this possibility.

The Director had a major problem, partly exemplified by Lélek. The Earopian species was having problems with the assimilation of Terrestrials. It appeared the human genome was quite persistent in propagating itself with minimal changes, in spite of the dilution by the Opian gene pool. Kra was also an unfortunate example. A true Opian would not indulge their offspring's unconventional behaviour, let alone take pride in it. There was simply no room for emotional attachments. Finding a solution to these and other anomalies may lead to using another species more successfully, either in conjunction with Terrestrials, or instead of them. That's where Lélek might become an asset. The Director was prepared to give the young man some rope – he might yet prove to be of some value.

Ignoring the unpleasant nature of the man Lélek asked, "Is there anything in particular you want me to research?"

"That is all," The Director said to Mani-Tre, turned and left without bothering further with Lélek.

As a young man of not quite twenty-one years, substantially immature in the ways of life on Erde, whichever perspective one chose, he was extremely excited by the prospect of going into space to be with his stars. On many occasions, unknown to his parents, he'd taken their pod deep into the dark side of the planet just so he could look into the black sky. Those excursions presented little danger, as he always had his android with him. Lélek would stare into the sky awestruck by the spectacle of the Milky Way. He felt such a strong craving to be out there. On those occasions he did not feel like a Terrestrial nor an Earopian. What he felt most strongly was that there was something or someone out there waiting for him.

Even the many thousands of years of advanced sciences, well beyond that of Earth's knowledge, could not explain the phenomenon of cellular memory. The depth of neurological understanding had not unravelled the mystery of the repository of thoughts within the brain. They understood how memory worked and how it could be enhanced and suppressed, a technology often used on human abductees. Still the mechanisms of how memories could be handed down from generation to generation eluded them. They could neither locate the source of the process nor download any of the accumulated data.

Lélek experienced many memory recall events when he went on his nocturnal outings. He remembered things he didn't even know he had experienced. An outstanding example, baffling him every time, was that he could remember his name. Not that it was a name he wanted to give himself, or a name he liked – simply that it was actually his name. No question. Absolute certainty. He wanted to know why! So when he found out he was being sent out there ... well ... he was simply elated. One thing he did know for certain ... the answers he was looking for were not to be found on Erde.

There is a star out there for me, watching over me. Perhaps I can ... he let the though go for fear of more disappointment.

Preparations for the space flight became prolonged as protocols had to be established. Some concerning the crew, some about experiments and data collection in space, and some about monitoring Lélek. Because of the nature of Earopian society, Lélek had a considerable amount of power which issued from his extraordinary accumulation of knowledge, his scientific innovations and his highly successful though unorthodox methods. He was not fully aware of this until Kra alerted him to it.

"There is no more I can teach you, son," *This is the first time Kra Father has ever called me 'son,'* "and I have done little enough over the years, given your degree of self-sufficiency. You know without my telling you that you have a brilliant mind. That is well recognised – and greatly valued. Your knowledge, though you be young, and your potential gives you considerable power. I know you are not aware of this, and that is to your credit. Once, a long time ago, I explained the law to you about the treatment of your android. You understood that. Now understand this ... you can ask ... no ... demand ... certain things, which cannot be refused you. What you are also not aware of is that your mission is not a frivolous acquiescence to the precocious talent you have shown. It is the first step in a new program aimed at accelerating the adaptation of our species to this planet, and the rejuvenation and repair of our genetic structure."

"Why me?" came the predictable question.

"Because there is more human left in you than any of us. You are an unpredictable anomaly. You must be solved and used – or - terminated."

"What kind of people are these, Kra Father? I believed that knowledge was their greatest goal. Why are you telling me these things?"

"You must not mention your knowledge of the true nature of the mission to anyone. Not your friends, especially not your android. By the way, I know about your escapades to the dark side, and your pre-occupation with the cosmos."

Lélek smiled. He had become used to using his smile muscles. He did it many times with his mother, and often enough with his father. He smiled at the emotion his father was showing him, the trust he was putting in his son. He smiled because he was now a preeminent research scientist about to embark on his first mission … on his terms. The Opians had their idea of what the mission was about, and Lélek had his own.

At the Inculcation Institute the Director reluctantly acquiesced to an interview with Lélek. Knowing what was at stake Lélek needed to be – circumspect. "I want to select my own crew." He was brief and to the point. He knew now his position of strength. "Each crew member must have a companion of their choice." The Director tightened his lips, slowly lowering his eyes so he would not have to look upon this – this – extreme annoyance. "Each crew member is to be no more than one generation Earopian."

"Anything else?" The Director squeezed out between thinly slitted lips.

"If I feel it necessary I will extend the duration of the project beyond the twelve months."

The Director did not respond apart from raising his eyes enough to see Lélek's back as he left the office. Lélek took his silence as acquiescence to every demand.

He can have whatever he wants. He will be in my absolute control! The Director could barely control his frustration, which made him even angrier. All the androids' loyalty had been re-programmed from the control of individuals they were looking after on the spacecraft, to the Director's, without compromising the well-being of their charges. He also insured the on-board computer systems had a remote override function installed. In neither case did he take into account Lélek's curiosity about even the simplest, least significant deviations from normality. And finally, every crew member was put through an additional conditioning process to ensure their psychological profiles retained minimal human disposition. Christin, Lélek's choice as an assistant science officer, was the only exception. But she was implanted with a homing device, having only arrived from Earth relatively recently.

5th manifestation

Christin returns to Earth
2122 AD

No ceremony accompanied the departure. Given the critical importance of the mission that was surprising. The hierarchy did not want to make the mission look more important than being the final stages in the education of a brilliant mind.

The crew was made up of the pilot/navigator, Mlad - a medical officer, Apoli - Lélek and his three companions. All of them under thirty years old. Christin, Lélek's personal assistant was a new Terrestrial arrival, strong both physically and mentally. A prodigy, who had become a research fellow at the Max Planck Institute of Astrophysics, before suffering the trauma of alien abduction. Lélek could find no logical explanation for selecting her from hundreds of possibilities. Other Earopian astrophysicists of far greater capability were available. When he scanned the list of names, hers just jumped out at him. He liked the name. Then when he met her, he liked her, and he liked her field of knowledge.

His other two companions, brothers Adrik and Edik, were those two kids, back at school, who had the courage to hop into his zero-friction contraption that had no brakes. Their own career paths had taken them into the sciences and qualified them for the mission. Adrik was the life support systems man and Edik, communications.

Lélek confided in his two friends before asking them to join him. "You know what they say this mission is about. What if I told you I have other plans as well?"

Grinning broadly the young men immediately agreed, "We're with you all the way – as long as whatever plans you have are fitted with brakes!" They all laughed.

"We could be gone longer than expected. Would that worry you?"

Adrik and Edik looked at each other as if that possibility couldn't concern them less. "All the way," they reiterated together.

Lélek was the Commander and the spacecraft's engineer, having a comprehensive understanding of the two drive systems of the vessel. He chose Christin as his assistant, officially; but unknowingly more as a companion, perhaps he felt the chemistry.

Christin had been on Erde for several months and well advanced in her re-socialisation process, but proving to be a tough nut to crack. Not that she let on. Her self-discipline, coupled with a highly organised mind gave her an extra edge in resisting the brainwashing. Christin did not like being coerced and was going to make damn sure the aliens were not going to get her mind easily. She didn't know of the possibility of going on this mission. Her first inkling was during a personal interview with Lélek at his instigation. There was an immediate reciprocal compatibility. She had already made up her mind to go after Lélek explained the mission. The icing on the cake was that tiny bit of information about Lélek, which he volunteered, that his mother was from Earth. Being a survivor she did not make long term plans ... however ... in the deep recesses of her mind, Earth started to look a little closer.

The crew of six, and five androids (Christin did not yet have one) wasted no time. They were all keen to get away. The pilot and doctor, blissfully ignorant of the real adventure ahead of them were – simply, excited. The others dreamt of impossibilities becoming possibilities.

They were expected back on the planet twelve months hence. The roar of the engines seemed to know better.

The thrust emanating from the cosmic dust fission chambers, gave the ship slow speed manoeuvring. Lélek had no input into the development of that form of propulsion, but he did improve on its efficiency; specifically, in the area of cosmic dust collection and storage, pre-fission. Seated beside Mlad he watched the slow progress through the planet's atmosphere. G-forces distorted all their faces as the acceleration pushed them through the ionosphere into black space.

Having achieved primary cruise velocity, Christin, seated next to Lélek turned to him, smiled, and touched his hand. "Do you know where we are going?"

Taking a moment to enjoy the touch, "No particular destination," then facing her he asked, "Is there anywhere in particular you would like to go?"

"Perhaps." She could not yet trust Lélek, nevertheless, she felt just that little bit nearer to Earth and just a tiny bit happier.

They had to maintain slow speed for some days before engaging the Gravon drive that would take them from star system to star system very quickly.

"What do you say Lélek, a short jump to start with?"

"Good idea. Let's try for Kepler 22b. It will give us a chance to test all our systems." It was the most logical choice for several reasons; it gave the impression they were following the mission plan. The planet was classified as a warm superterran mesoplanet according to the Earth Similarity Index. Most importantly it gave Lélek time to check things out on board and make a couple of changes.

Mlad plotted the course, initiated the Gravitube and within five hours was able to engage the Gravon drive system. The crew did not have to make any special provisions for the jump, other than to be aware it was happening. The process was instantaneous. Christin, although aware they were shortly to travel at an extraordinary speed, nevertheless was taken by surprise at seeing what appeared to be the universe suddenly contract, then expand just as quickly. She felt nothing physically, and could no longer see Erde.

"Where are we now?" She asked Lélek.

"Near a planet called Kepler 22b, about 536 light years from Earth apparently," replied Lélek using all Earth references to ensure Christin understood. He also wanted to set the precedent for the others, to use Earth as reference instead of Erde.

"Explain the drive system to me! When I was taken I was drugged, so I had no idea how long it took to get from Earth to Erde".

"You were drugged? Were you – hurt?"

He seemed genuine in his concern so she answered, "Not enough to cause permanent injury."

His eyes lingered in hers for a moment before responding to her question. "There are two systems, neither of which requires us to carry fuel, so in theory we have unlimited range. The first system allows us to use slow and relatively fast speeds while retaining steering capability. The second is not constrained by speed considerations, so nothing is too far away for us, but it has some other drawbacks. You know about cosmic dust and I know you personally have been involved in some experimentation to exploit its potential. We," he corrected himself, "the Earopians have perfected a propulsion system by capturing, storing and condensing that dust and finally using it in a fission chamber to extract its nuclear energy."

"Don't you need a considerable amount?" Not letting on she noticed his rephrasing.

"Yes. As long as the tanks are fully charged there's no problem. To fill an empty tank can take weeks. The other system, about which Earth scientists have only an unverified theory, is the use of temporary worm holes to move through the fabric of space almost instantaneously from one point to another. It's not practical from two aspects: the time it takes to generate and stabilise the funnel and the second issue is that there must be a specific target destination of a cosmic entity sufficiently large to generate a substantial amount of gravity." Lélek enjoyed the conversation, or more accurately, enjoyed interacting with Christin.

"But how does it work? Can't you be a bit more specific … you said you were aware of my field of expertise, so I'll probably have a smattering of understanding if you would be so kind as to not talk down to me." She touched him again on the arm, involuntarily, but did not remove her hand.

He was careful not to move his arm as he answered. "Well, here's the rudiments of the thing. You understand how light behaves and how you can concentrate light into a beam. Gravitons, which are like a particle aspect of gravity, conduct gravity like photons conduct light. We concentrate the gravitational radiation, which has a negative energy signature, thereby generating an anomaly in space-time, vis-à-vis a worm hole. That hole will have a life span of no more and no less than your journey through it. In fact, it closes behind you as you move through it. The entrance and exit are closed, forming a sphere at either end like a membrane, which our ship has to pierce. Happy?" As much as he liked being near Christin, other matters were pressing on his mind.

"No! It must need an incredible amount of energy to create such a tunnel. Where does that come from?"

"I can explain, if you must know – but later. I want to ask you about something else also, but later. I'd love to talk more worm holes with you, but there's a few critical things I must take care of … Edik! He called through to the other chamber. We have work to do."

During the entire conversation Lélek's android hovered around finding bits and pieces of unnecessary things to do. That was unusual. The androids were programmed to be completely unobtrusive, to appear only when necessary or when called upon. Lélek made a mental note. Something was different. Why? And how? "Wait here," he commanded it.

"Edik, ask your thing over there to wait where he is while we go and do a full system diagnosis in comms. I've already instructed mine."

The two androids simply stopped everything they were doing and stood there, in the corner, out of the way. Whereas androids back on Erde would be completely inactive at this point, these two were not. Their surveillance systems, fully functional, scanned and transmitted everything back to Erde.

The comms, a rather small restrictive area, barely large enough to hold two people, was a perfect place to have a private conversation. "Before we start, I need to know if you are with me. You've probably worked out there's things I want to do other than find civilizations for those Earopians to mess about with."

That last phrase jarred a little on Edik. "What exactly do you mean by 'those Earopians'?"

"I think you know exactly what I mean." Lélek left it at that to gauge Edik's reaction. Edik was an astute fellow. He'd been Lélek's friend all his life, from that first day at school. They knew each other well, and Edik knew how Lélek felt about what the Earopians were doing. In particular, how they were treating people from Earth. He felt the same about that, perhaps even more strongly – he was only first generation.

"Sure – I'm with you all the way. What are you going to do?

"I'm certain we're being monitored. We need to find how, and stop it. We also need to get the others with us. Christin will be no problem. What do you think about Adrik?"

Edik being the older of the two knew his brother looked up to him, and trusted him − in all things. More of a gentle soul than Edik, Adrik also looked to his brother for guidance, perhaps protection or even just plain brotherly support. "He'll go where I go, do what I do − without question. You can count on him."

"That only leaves Mlad and Apoli. They are only first generation and lean heavily towards their human natures. But still, do you think they can be trusted to join us?"

"Well − they appeared to toe the line back on Erde. But I've overheard them speaking amongst themselves. They are not impressed with the way their human parents are treated, and how they have been brainwashed. Mlad especially has been feeling powerless to do anything about it. It's worth the risk. Just come straight out with it and tell them where you stand. By the way − what's the plan?"

"First we do a full system check and see if we are being bugged. We have to scan ourselves for devices that may have been implanted, and lastly we need to power down the androids. I noticed they were paying us too much attention when it was not necessary. That can only mean they have been tampered with."

Lélek found opportunities to assess the 'loyalty' factor of the other members of his crew in private. They all seemed to go along with the idea of being out in space for a much longer time than planned. Hence they understood Lélek's insistence on the 'companions'. But they were not taken into his full confidence just yet. He also explained to them about the homing device and the remote override in their computer systems, which would soon be switched off. They concurred with the de-activation of the androids, which was scheduled to happen to each of them at exactly the same time.

Christin was livid when she found out about her implant. "The bastards! It wasn't enough for them to go poking around inside me, then try to bend my mind – now this! Bastards!" Her fury was tempered only by the hope that perhaps Lélek would try to take her back to Earth. "Can you rip the dammed thing out?"

"Yes, but not just yet. We have to make them feel sure they've got control over us."

"Them? Meaning …?" This time she pushed a little.

"I think you know what I mean." Lélek touched her arm lightly.

Over the next few months they made a number of excursions to remote parts of the galaxy, to planets unexplored before, not expecting to find sentient life. Full reports were sent back to Erde to ensure they felt 'secure' in their deception down there and that their subterfuge was firmly embedded. Lélek took great care to make the destinations completely random so no pattern could be discerned from their journeys. Mlad particularly enjoyed the navigational challenges.

They did not discuss their plans, waiting for the appointed time to put it into action.

The timing had to be perfect. With only several minutes of communications time delay it meant everything had to be achieved almost concurrently. At the pre-determined hour, while all the companions were asleep, every android was simultaneously powered down. Within seconds Edik had pulled the homing device out of the comms system, and switched off the remote override function. At the same time Apoli cut out Christin's homing bug, giving no indication he might have had any qualms about it. As far as Erde was concerned the spacecraft had suddenly disappeared.

Previously Mlad had plotted their next jump, and the tunnel was ready. All he had to do was engage the Gravon drive. Not only had they disappeared from view, they had disappeared from their previously recorded location.

The small band of space rebels were now free. Their companions were still unaware of the machinations going on behind their backs.

"Remember I mentioned a while ago that I wanted to ask you a question?" Lélek prompted Christin during a meal in the craft's dining area. "Would you come to my cabin later?"

Christin certainly did remember, but why the secrecy? "Discussing a spacecraft propulsion system doesn't need secrecy – unless …"

"It's a private matter, specifically private to you."

"Oh. When?" A little flush on her cheeks betrayed her suspicion. Lélek noticed its swift passing, choosing not to correct her. It made him smile.

Later that evening the two of them met in Lélek's private quarters. He'd a strong feeling about this girl, and strong feelings towards her. It was time to put the proposition to her. "It's always been my intention to find Earth." Christin caught her breath, her heartbeat suddenly increasing. "Do you want to go home?" Before he'd finished asking the question she was in his arms.

As could be expected, the location of Earth was not made common knowledge by the Earopians – especially not to Lélek or his crew. They had now been in space four months. The search for Earth began in earnest. They had no starting reference point other than the location of Erde. Drifting for several weeks, ostensibly to replenish their cosmic dust tanks, Lélek and Christin found themselves growing closer together after that first night of intimacy. Those initial moments of compatibility that each experienced at the interview blossomed into something quite personal. Neither of them wanted to get too close to the other. Christin knew that if they found Earth, she would leave him − without hesitation. Lélek knew he would insist she went. His future had no place in it for a companion.

Still they spent more and more time together as the weeks flowed into more months. They even started sharing the same accommodation. Some evenings, while Lélek was busy looking at possible directions for the Earth search, she would sit in their cabin and cry. It was inevitable they could not stay together. Yet Lélek started discussing the future in the plural 'we', forgetting that the loyalty of the 'companions' was still an unknown factor. One night, one particularly emotional night, when Christin's monthly cycle prevented certain intimacies, they were discussing what they would do when the moment arrived for them to part. As usual, Lélek being a mere male, droned on about impossibilities. Christin's mind wandered back to the time of her abduction. Extremely painful memories flooded her mind. Painful because of the loss of her family, because of the loss of her home and painful because of the trauma of the 'probing' with which they tortured her.

"Stop!" She shouted suddenly in the middle of her painful memories and his inarticulate drivel. Lélek was cut off in mid-sentence.

"I've got it!"

"What have you got?"

"A way to find Earth!"

As soon as she finished explaining, Lélek rushed off to wake Mlad. It just might work. "Her period started on the day she was captured", he blurted out. "The cramps had just started and they always lasted exactly five days. When she had arrived on Erde, the cramps continued for one more day."

"That means we have at least the possibility of a search perimeter with Erde at the centre. Our on-board star map is quite sufficiently comprehensive. Given some parameters the navigational computer could narrow down the search pattern!" Mlad had become just as excited as Lélek. The great adventure had truly begun.

After a further seven months, with hope running very thin, the latest jump landed them near a giant gas with at least sixty-two satellites in orbit. Christin could barely fit into her skin. "That's Saturn! I'm positive. Look at all the moons – and there's, Titan. We are in the Solar system!" again she flew into Lélek's arms, not surprising anyone.

"I can't take us any closer, Christin. They'll see us. We'll just sit here in your Saturn's shadow and send you down in a landing craft."

"I've called this meeting to let you all know where we are, and why we're here." Lélek could not put it off any longer. Although the reasons for deactivating the androids had been settled, there was still some discontent amongst the companions.

"I know where we are – we're in the Sol system to visit Earth. If we've come here to pick up more alien volunteers why the problem with our androids?" Asked Apoli, apparently the spokesperson for the others.

"We are here to do the opposite, to return Christin to her home." It was only at this critical point Lélek realised the full extent of his love for the girl, and his compassion for her circumstances. He could not explain to himself why he should have felt so strongly about her, even from that first meeting at the interview for the mission. Quietly he told the gathering, "None of them were volunteers. They were all forcibly abducted and tortured."

Lélek had not foreseen the degree of opposition to his revelations. The companions were outraged. They refused to believe his story about the abductions and torture. Amid the drama of imminent revolt and the emotional departure of Lélek and Christin to Earth, the atmosphere had become highly charged aboard the ship.

...

Isten watched the drama unfold. At last Lélek had arrived at a critical juncture in his evolution. *He has to make his own decisions. I cannot interfere.* As difficult as it was for Isten not to help in the situation, it would have been pointless if it truly wanted this manifestation to proceed along its own unique path. It could not even give the slightest hint to Lélek as to why Christin was so important. Once before he had no choice in abandoning his mate, now it was time to make the decision of his own free will.

...

Leaving Apoli, the medical officer, in charge Mlad, Christin and Lélek made the slow five day trip to drop off Christin at her home in Garching, Germany, near to the Institute. Separating from Lélek was nothing compared with the problems she was about to have after being absent for almost two years. Despite the ensuing drama, she was at least back on Earth.

In spite of the short time they had been together their bond to each other had become unreasonably strong. Neither had realised they had a previous connection, thousands of years ago. Christin too had experienced a melding, when Scritchen died not long after her mate's execution. Back then Lélek did not have the emotional makeup to enable him to reciprocate Scritchen's devotion to him. His opportunity was now. But he was torn apart by his devotion to her and the absolutely firm conviction that his future could not accommodate such private luxuries as personal love.

The emotional upheaval of the parting had a dramatic effect on Lélek. "I will not return to Erde. They are barbarians!" He confided to Mlad on the way back to Saturn, unable to control his emotions.

"Lélek, I have tried to keep an open mind, but I cannot forget what the Earopians did to my mother when she arrived." Mlad broke down under the barrage of memories. "I too renounce all things associated with the Earopians. I want to go with you, wherever you chose to go, whatever you chose to do."

Lélek should have foreseen the possibility of a mutiny. He was too caught up in his passion for Christin to take heed of the earlier warning signs.

Edik tried to warn, "We've got problems, Lélek. Apoli couldn't hold his ground," he said over the comms.

"What exactly do you mean, my friend?"

"They've …" and the link went dead.

"What do you think Mlad?"

"Whatever it is, we have to go back to the ship. We can't stay on Earth."

Some major changes had taken place on board the ship. Only himself, Adrik and Edik were left of the original rebel group. The 'companions', of whom there were four plus the five newly re-activated androids made a formidable opposing group. Apoli had to make a decision and he vacillated. His convictions were not as strong as that of Mlad, and he gave in under pressure.

In fear of the consequences of what they had done, the mutineers decided to try and salvage the situation. Mlad was to pilot the craft, Lélek would be taken into custody and they would all return to Erde. Apoli decided that on the way they would return to one of the planets they found during the Earth search, which had some sentient species, to take a few specimens back with them.

It all went according to plan. Lélek's android did nothing to stop him from being manhandled. He was not surprised. Communication was re-established with Erde. Within two months they had their fresh cargo and had arrived home. News of the entire mutinous enterprise was suppressed. Action by the leadership was quick and decisive. The new 'specimens' were treated with negligent contempt. Even though their level of evolution had not met the Earopian criteria for inclusion in their rejuvenation programme, still they were subjected to a wide gamut of experimental procedures. Lélek later learnt all had died after much suffering, offered up presumably to the advancement of Earopian scientific knowledge. Mlad, Edik and Adrik were all immediately subjected to a more vigorous re-socialisation regimen, then assigned to menial tasks on the other side of the planet, never to be allowed to return to their respective families.

The situation regarding Lélek required intervention by the Erden government. The Director of the Inculcation Institute put the case succinctly, "He is still young and has demonstrated further outstanding attributes."

"He has also done a great deal of damage. Are you able to keep the matter confidential?" It was not so much a question as an order.

"Though his escapade was unsuccessful thanks to the loyalty of our people, Lélek has revealed some additional admirable qualities."

"Be brief."

"A high degree of initiative, ability to attract loyalty and substantial leadership traits. All of which could still be used in the rejuvenation plan. The question is how to go about turning him without damaging him."

"Do a standard de-briefing, let his parents visit. But keep him in custody for the time being."

At the de-briefing facility, which looked more like a detention centre for unsuccessful products, Kra was only told that his son's performance was under review. As a result, his attitude towards his son became somewhat clouded. He was expecting laudits and recognition for Lélek, not what amounted to incarceration.

"Something is very wrong here," he whispered to Dyl-An.

As they entered the visiting room Dyl-An could only glance at her son before bursting into tears. Emotional outbursts like that from new Terrestrials always meant painful readjustment for them.

"Mother, control. You know the consequences." Lélek became extremely concerned, particularly because of the way he was being treated. What would they do to his parents. There was still a great deal of human emotion in him.

Kra was brief, "Your two best friends have been sent on a permanent assignment, to the dark side. Did they tell you that?"

"No, Kra Father. Why?"

"Mutiny – and loyalty to you. Was it necessary to do whatever it was you were doing out there?"

"Did you know they tortured Christin? That they abducted her forcibly from her home? Mother says she was a volunteer – do you believe her?" Lélck glanced at his mother, who was still sobbing and appeared not to hear his comment.

As the situation began to clarify in Kra's mind he decided to tell his son about the passengers they brought back. "Those new aliens you brought back turned out to be of inferior quality, and were consequently disposed of after the examinations."

Lélek found it hard to listen to all this. A couple of those 'aliens' had actually shown him some understanding and compassion when they found out the story of how he came to be locked up with them. The meeting was short and altogether unsatisfactory from Lélek's point of view. The opinions he had gradually formed of the Earopians during his higher education, then during the year he spent in space were further exacerbated by what he had just heard from his father. He decided to bide his time and see what these people were up to.

Lélek had no other visitors, though he was hoping to see some of his other friends. They, both from his early schooling and higher education days who had taken part in the 'special' curriculum with Lélek, had all gone their separate ways into various influential positions in Earopian society. But they had all kept in touch with him in the past. Lélek was sure he could count on a few of them for help when he needed it.

Two days after the parental visit, the Director went to see him again. This man, who had very little human left in him, matter-of-factly explained what had happened to the alien specimens, and to his co-conspirators. It was quite clear there was an implied threat woven into the conversation. When Lélek showed no sign of taking the hint, the man brought up the subject of his parents.

"We hope your parents' lives will continue untroubled in spite of your serious misadventures."

At that Lélek did react. He responded in a quiet controlled voice, "Surely, any re-adjustments to Dyl-An would not be necessary. Kra had amply demonstrated his loyalty to your society, which could in no way be influenced by the 'wayward' son. I am quite confident nothing *I do* will harm them in any way".

He said directly into the eyes of the man, holding his gaze for an uncomfortably long time. The director's swift departure left Lélek in no doubt he would have to act quickly. This Earopian civilization was so morally bankrupt as to even try to blackmail him with the welfare of his parents. He would not be able to change society, but he did not have to continue being a part of it. As he matured into full adulthood, and his personal heritage from the time he was first known as Lélek to the present day, brought into focus more clearly that he had some greater purpose driving him forward.

If he could escape off the planet there would be no point in threatening his parents or further maltreating his friends. Although he had some Opian blood in his veins it did not make him vengeful, in spite of his overactive sense of justice, but it did make his anger come to the boiling point. These beings were not chattels to be treated as slaves. He really could not fathom where that came from, but if there was some way he could prevent the way Opians and their Earopian descendants treated other sentient species, then he would surely try.

5th manifestation

escape from Erde
2124 AD

Whilst still in the final year of his formal studies a small group of his closest friends, all of whom were first generation Earopian, formed an alliance. Being of one mind about the unacceptable ethics of how their very selves came into existence, they vowed to help each other if any of them found themselves in serious need. To that end, and as a precautionary measure, they engaged in a bit of biological manipulation themselves. They developed and implanted into each other a small transmitter and receiver, with neurological signatures connected into their sympathetic nervous system. It was engineered in such a way that no form of technology of the day could detect their presence. It could be activated simply by the individual experiencing an involuntary or voluntary emotional overload. The signal would immediately go out to each member of the group, who would take all possible measures to render assistance.

Within a few days Lélek was free from detention. The order for his release came from the highest level of the governing authority. Lélek never found out which of his friends in the alliance, or how they had managed to engineer his freedom. The Director had no option but to release his prize possession. Nevertheless, he had Lélek followed. Lélek was not so naïve, in spite of his youth, as to not realise he had to be cautious. He first went to see his parents. That in itself was innocuous enough and bought him a little time.

"They let me go, for the moment anyway," he said before Kra could get angry. Of course at the first sight of him Dyl-An burst into tears, which made it even more difficult for Lélek to tell his parents his plan. "I must leave Erde - for good." His mother couldn't cope with this and left the room. Before his father could respond Lélek continued, "Kra Father, you told me yourself what had been done to my two friends, and to the aliens we brought back. Is that just? What had the aliens done to deserve being tortured! What you don't know is that the Director threatened me with your welfare, and mother's, if I did not co-operate with them. How is that reasonable in our advanced civilisation? It is primitive, cruel and completely unacceptable to me. There is only one way for me to keep you, my friends and myself safe. I have to leave Erde."

Kra was a reasonable man. He listened to his son, finding it difficult not to show his emotions. "Don't tell me your plans. Though I would like to know where you will go, what you intended to do – don't tell me. If I don't know they cannot get it out of me. I will not help you either. It would put your mother in grave danger … they could use her against me."

Lélek absorbed all he was hearing, understanding his father's difficult position; the position he put him in. "Kra Father, I am sorry to have done this."

"I will not choose between you and your mother."

For several hours the two men tried to reassure Dyl-An no harm would come to her son. "He has many friends," Kra said to her, "they will help him." When eventually both his mother and father had resigned themselves to his decision, Lélek left his home. Deep inside himself he had the firm conviction he would never see them again.

The next few days were a blur. He kept moving from one friend to another within his circle of conspirators.

Eventually they managed to help him shake all attempts at surveillance. That itself made things more urgent. By some devious means and influential intervention, the group gained access to Lélek's spacecraft. It was still in quarantine.

"We've fully re-stocked it with provisions and fuel – and – we've set up a nice little surprise. All you need to know is that when you're far enough in space for a jump, activate this protocol." Lélek only had to commit to memory a simple password – 'Christin'.

"You can't take a companion either, though you can have your android."

Lélek responded quickly and harshly, "Don't be an idiot! I'm not taking that *thing* with me."

"Take it easy. It's been reprogrammed. I did it myself. It now has absolute loyalty to you."

"You sure about that?" He was more than sceptical.

"Sure I'm sure. It's too risky for you to take anyone else. Anyone missing from their normal designated duties would immediately draw suspicion." It was inevitable the subterfuge resulting in his release would be discovered.

"You have to leave this very hour. No time for any more good-byes, my friend," Ansi-On urged. "We know and appreciate your concern for the aliens who continue being harvested. We will do all we can to help them, regardless of their origins. Sentient life deserves more than to be treated with contempt." Lélek may not have been able stay with them, but he did leave them with his sense of compassion and justice.

The craft left without incident, first heading to the dark side of Erde, making immediate detection more difficult. He was lucky to have several hours start before the theft of the ship was discovered. His friends had even provided him with his re-programmed android. Absolute loyalty to Lélek was not the main attribute. Its ability to pilot the craft and to navigate was beyond the current state of the art available on Erde. After all, his friends needed a little technological challenge for themselves.

Erde security had several ships in pursuit within hours. They could go no faster than Lélek, so until he reached the critical distance he was safe. It gave him a few days to contemplate everything that had happened over the last year. His relationship with Christin kept coming back to haunt him. But it was more than just the relationship. He kept going back to the moment he saw her name on the list. *Why did that name jump out at me? It seemed so familiar, like a long distant memory I should never have forgotten.* Often his mind drifted to visions of magnificent spheres he had seen in space. Even Erde was a beautiful planet. Earth was extraordinary. It drew him like a powerful magnet. He had never before experienced that overwhelming feeling of belonging as he did when he took Christin home, standing there on the soil of Earth. He had stared at the moon unable to tear his eyes away. Mlad and Christin almost had to manhandle him back into the landing craft.

And so the days passed; remembering, dreaming, wandering – and planning. He had no idea what he should do. If Earth had made him feel so – comfortable – it was incomparable to the feeling he had in space – the freedom, the silence – the sense of unlimited possibilities.

This is my home!

It was not a new feeling, the very awakening to the realisation gave Lélek comfort. *Where should I go? Does it matter? Perhaps I'll seek out another sentient species. Where do I look? How would I know if they are intelligent?* These kinds of thoughts led him back to his better self, to the normal, inquisitive, brilliant minded Lélek. There was another reason he had to be in the arms of the cosmos. He was absolutely certain that was where he would find the answer to why he knew his name was Lélek.

"Lélek," the android advised, "we are ready for the first jump." Since leaving Erde, the computer had been setting up the Gravitube and the worm tunnel was ready. Lélek entered the password, 'Christin' to activate the escape protocol, putting into effect a chain reaction of events. It was a password he would never forget.

The Director aboard the leading pursuit craft watched as the image of Lelke's ship exploded into a chaotic ball of luminescent energy. "Keep after him!" The Director screamed at the Captain.

"There is nothing there to follow Sir," the Captain replied, "only debris. They have been obliterated. It must have been an overload on their reactor."

"Not with Lélek on board. Go closer!" The Director only saw copious amounts of debris, all consistent with the materials and components of his prey's vessel."

One second after the contrived explosion and the jettisoning of old spacecraft parts, Lélek disappeared into the worm tunnel heading for another galaxy. Like all worm tunnels, Lélek's was closing behind him as he advanced through it. So there was no discernible evidence of it ever having existed. He was free to seek the answers to his personal mysteries. As far as the Earopians knew, Lélek was dead - no longer their concern. They had to carry on with their rejuvenation programme without the brilliant mind of that part Earthling.

The Director swore under his breath, "I don't believe it! He is out there somewhere!" They never saw the man with the brilliant mind again.

Lélek was on the way to the Andromeda Galaxy. An unlikely place they would search for him because of the size of it, even if there was a good enough reason to initiate a search, especially after the explosion and the ships flotsam. He arrived in the vicinity of Mayal II, a globular cluster. While the android set about the search for earth like planets in the vicinity, Lélek contemplated the parameters that would help him to recognise sentient life forms. He had no doubt they were out there. After all this universe was made of the same substances as the universe where Earth was, with an extremely high probability of similar conditions that could give rise to life. The trick was to recognise it. The universe was undeniably composed of the stuff of life.

"Set up a spherical search pattern, with us at the centre," he told AL – he'd decided to give the *thing* a name seeing he was going to be stuck with it for who knew how long, "unless you can think of anything better. Besides, I really like spheres."

"No, Lélek, that is appropriate." AL replied in an unmodulated tone.

Sometimes Lélek entertained himself by trying to work out why the majority of cosmic bodies were spherical. *If, like the universe, planets and stars and moons are spherical then why are galaxies flat structures. They should be more like bubbles in a pond, not the ripples on the surface, unless space was a woven fabric. If gravity works equally in all directions from a central core, then it makes no sense for galaxies to be flat.*

Finding planets capable of supporting recognisable life seemed less of a challenge than finding a way of recognising the existence of sentient life he could interact with. There was no point in trying to communicate with a 'blob' of life-like matter if it could not talk back to him. Out of the dark, a peculiar thought occurred to Lélek. *If I was able to create life, what form would I give it – what criteria would I use to define it? Would I let it do whatever it wanted?*

The very idea entertained him, let alone the wonder of having the idea itself. *Imagine that – being able to create life.*

...

It was only an instant ago Isten entertained a though of Lélek and yet he impinged on his consciousness again. *My seed wants to create. Shall I be patient?* He asked himself. *He is not yet ready.*

...

While AL went about the routine explorations, Lélek immersed himself in a little fanciful daydreaming. *What I don't want to end up with is a clever android. So apart from being adaptable, mobile, dextrous and capable of reproducing itself it has to be – to be – a bit human. Ha! That's a disturbing thought.*

AL interrupted his reverie. "We may have found something." It seemed the universe was so fecund that even after just a few months there was promise.

"Go for it, AL." Lélek was obviously in a good mood after his ruminations, and keen to get back on that track of thinking.

Right, human, - so it would need to be self-aware, think creatively, absorb and integrate all forms of information. Yes! And I would give it empathy. That should do it – and – I would give it pain. He seemed very pleased with himself, never giving a single thought as to how he would go about achieving all this.

The weeks and months rippled in the puddle of time as Lélek lost himself in thought and wonder – and space.

But he was not lost. AL, never one for unnecessary conversation, piped up, "We have arrived."

"You have found life?"

"Yes."

"Will we be able to communicate with it?"

"You will have to determine that, Lélek. It has community, so perhaps."

But how to initiate contact without danger to himself? Lélek had not considered this. In spite of his better judgment he could not think of any way other than the tried and tested methods of the Opians. Under cover of darkness, find a secluded area of sparse population, 'invite' a native aboard the craft, forcefully if necessary and attempt communication. Their computer's linguistic systems would make that simple enough, if the species was prepared to co-operate.

It was ugly, even by Earopean standards. *This is not what I would make my creation look like!* That was Lélek's initial reaction on seeing the creature. For one thing, the stodgy roundish lump didn't seem capable of efficient mobility. Lélek was determined not to harm it in any way. So rather than force it to be a 'guest' aboard his shuttle, AL took the translator outside to meet the individual.

The alien waited, seemingly quite relaxed as Lélek considered what to do next after achieving a rudimentary greeting. Suffice it to say that when it settled into a resting position on the ground it was not attractive to Lélek's eyes. Most off putting was the smell of broken eggs left in the sun for a day, wafting in a sickly yellow haze around it. No doubt the alien found little pleasing in the form of a rather tall, heavily built individual towering in front of it. No doubt Lélek's only four thin extremities, much too thin in proportion to his body, with elongated wiggly bits on the ends seemed less than functional from its perspective. Most of all, it must have been hard for this tall creature to protect its elongated head set on a thin stalk, emblazoned with huge eyes.

Mutually incomprehensible noises were exchanged for a few hours, until eventually the computer worked out the language and they were able to communicate through its intervention. This particular specimen was not in the least aggressive and even seemed eager to involve members of its own family in the 'cultural' exchange. It was not even put off by the very odd looking metallic creature who continually hovered around Lélek.

"What is that?" It asked.

"My companion."

"Is it alive?"

"No – Yes."

"Do you not know?"

"It is an intelligent machine. Do you not have …"

"No," the creature replied, "we are all alive. We do not have machines that pretend life."

It turns out they were not particularly advanced technologically. No space flight capability, no computerisation and it seemed nothing in the way of weaponry. All this was rather odd. Lélek subsequently found out from this particular head of the family that the species had been evolving longer than Opians, but in quite a different direction. Initially Lélek had no idea why he felt the need to search the cosmos for more sentient species. Perhaps the reason was to learn what this elder had to teach him. The 'cultural' exchange continued without further digressions.

They had no religious structure, and they had no faith structure. "We believe in what we know. For example, we believe there were other intelligent species among the stars, because we have met others before. Some not as 'nice' as you. We believe life is temporary only from one particular point of view."

This immediately sparked Lélek's interest. "What exactly do you mean?"

"We know there are other energy manifestations for life because we have evolved to perceive those energies in their myriad forms. I can 'see' heat as well as feel it and I can see our planets magnetic field. I can even see gravitational energy reaching out its radiating tentacles into space. That is how I knew you were coming."

Lélek was about to ask a question about the sphericity of heavenly bodies, but thought better of it. It was too trivial in the context of the conversation.

"Now I will tell you something you need to know. I can see the strength of your life force. You are not one, but many, combined with many. But you are incomplete. You will have to use several more hosts in order to grow. Your current host may not be suitable for much longer."

For a moment Lélek thought it may have been a veiled threat, but just as quickly dismissed it as an unfortunate aspect of his experiences on Erde.

"Thank you for those insights, please continue." He was eager to hear everything this strange smelly globular creature had to tell him. Somewhere in the back of his mind he was even beginning to think that if the smell wasn't so bad, the rotund nature of the alien could even be considered attractive in a squiggy sort of way.

"It comes naturally to us, as no doubt it will for you in the future. The life force of your host body, which you animate with your own life force, is a different entity to you. You both exist in the cosmos as energies which manifest in different ways when you are together and when you are apart. You interact with the universe in different ways. Host bodies are always temporary, but serve a very useful purpose. You, on the other hand are always permanent, but subject to great transformations. The host body does not change. It simply re-cycles to do the same thing over and over again, like water. It has limited potential."

Lélek was a little taken aback by the surety with which these things were explained to him. His thoughts rushed off into impossible tangents about fleeting visions which had recently started coming to him again. It took him a moment to respond when the alien asked,

"What can *you* teach us?"

That was a completely expected question. He felt decidedly inferior to this unattractive thing after that dissertation. What could he possibly say that could be of any value to it. For no explicable reason Lélek found himself saying the strangest thing, "We are all going in the same direction, to the centre of the four universes."

"How do you come to know this?"

"I have been touched by the mind of one who knows."

This was no surprise to a species whose evolutionary path had steered them towards the true nature of reality and away from focus on the corporeal impermanence and its attendant delusions. It was certainly a big surprise to Lélek. He had no idea such thoughts lurked in his mind. Eventually both species found themselves satisfied with the encounter and each went their separate way.

It seemed to Lélek there was definitely some guiding force involved in his life. He had a vague idea some important things to be done lay ahead of him, but what they were or where to do them … well that would come upon him when he was least ready. This he knew well enough from the past.

It was no little thing to find himself in another galaxy. The experience with the globular life form was most illuminating. Perhaps not the most encouraging thing to be told that "Your current host may not be suitable for much longer." In another way it was comforting to have one's suspicions confirmed that there was more to existence than the apparently insignificant petty things he'd had to endure on Erde. Not that at the time those experiences had no value. Certainly one gets out of life what one puts into it. That was obviously a universal truth. *But where do I go from here?*

'Go to cruise mode, please AL. Re-charge the cosmic particle tanks and continue the search for other habitable planets. I'll look for anything else that could be worth exploring."

The Why and How of things never stopped being a major driving force in his short life. The more time he spent in space the more that short life took on a less temporal perspective. Spheres of all types continued to attract his attention. So when he saw what looked like a sparkling translucent bubble, some light years in diameter, he headed straight for it in spite of the Androids warning.

"It is photon sphere, around a black hole. I caution against going any closer to it." AL's suggestion, delivered in his usual flat tone, lacked all sense of urgency. Not that Lélek would have taken too much notice.

It took weeks to get close to it so Lélek had a chance to analyse it. He'd never seen a photon sphere before. The computer of course had a good deal of relevant data about it. This phenomenon was most exciting. He had learnt that light did not always travel in a straight line. He knew light could be bent, but not that it could be restrained to such an extent as to form a sphere. *Fantastic! How could this structure even exist: zero thickness, photons moving along tangents to the sphere and trapped in circular orbits?*

What was not so fantastic was the thing making it possible; a rotating black hole. AL had expressed several more warnings in the course of last week, with the latest, most urgent only hours ago. "We are being drawn towards the centre of the sphere, into the hole. I recommend reverse thrust immediately." Its even tone did not inspire urgency due to the matter.

"Continue on our present course. The event horizon is still far enough away. I want to get as close as possible to the sphere, even inside it if possible." The thought was particularly attractive. Why that was so, he did not get the chance to ask himself. "Prepare for a jump. I'm sure our Gravon drive can handle it."

Because a photon sphere is intrinsically a delicately unstable phenomenon, any disturbance to the photon curtain has major consequences. As soon as the ship touched that curtain an immediate fluctuation of space-time engulfed the travellers. That in itself was not fatal to an organic life form. The disturbance of the photonic energised particles caused two things to happen. AL and ship's systems were completely disabled causing them to become helplessly adrift inside the photon sphere. So much for the jump.

Then Lélek experienced a sudden and painless reality warp. He turned to see what the noise was behind him. AL had collapsed into an inert mass, but what caught his attention was a shimmering, mirror-like apparition in front of him. For a moment he thought he saw a grossly distorted image of himself.

It was indeed Lélek – not the Lélek he'd become familiar with, rather a history of his journey embodied in the images of a motley group of individuals. These multiple projections into real space in front of him represented the constituent parts of his current essence. They were as stunned as Lélek staring at them. The small group, who had become immersed in Lélek's being, recognised him of course. Their surprise was that they could still appear as unique individuals with their own personal identities and thoughts intact. They scanned each other, recognising each as having been a part of each other in the melded form with Lélek.

Lélek's consciousness needed a little longer to decode this experience. He looked at each in turn, intensely, questioningly. No one spoke. It took many minutes for the light of recognition to ignite his memory ... the most recent memory ... Fremd. He remembered Fremd, the scientist who had met him just before he was infused into the Earopian species. That opened the floodgates to a swarm of memories all wanting attention at the same time. He acknowledged Thales as his teacher with a nod of respect. His arms opened up for Ptah. Though it was not possible to touch him, it still put a huge smile on the young boy's face. Lélek wanted so much to hug Ilusha, his first. The feeling was obviously reciprocated from the look in her eyes. With somewhat of a shock he stared at Lelke, his first intermediate self, and Lelke stared back. The eyes seemed to say that each felt ennobled in the presence of the other. Lélek had to concentrate hard on the next and last apparition. It seemed to be out of focus and substantially unrecognisable, until his mind was pierced by the sound of a voice, "Lélek!" It said in a strange guttural accent.

That immediately brought the image into very sharp focus indeed.

It was himself!

Dressed in animal skins, dishevelled long hair and beard, carrying a stone axe, Lélek looked out at himself standing there with that strange elongated body and large round eyes staring back at himself. It was difficult to tell who was more proud of the other. Their eyes told each other everything. The Cro-Magnon man eventually moved his two arms, as did the Earopian, simultaneously - after all, they were of the one mind - each of them describing a sphere as the fingertips navigated north-south and east-west. At the conclusion of the voyage each had the same concept in his mind,

We are home.

Each apparition now content, resumed their previous condition.

Time behind the photon sphere curtain slowed. The closer the vessel drifted towards the Event Horizon, the longer it seemed to take. It did not feel like it to Lélek from inside his ship. He could not readily account for the elapsed time shown on the computer. He tried to retrace his actions backwards to tease out his memory of the events of the last few days. There were flashes of something vague – but pleasant; extremely pleasant. In fact, he felt more complete than at any other time in his life … and he was content. Not happy – just content; completely, unconditionally contented. All that in spite of the rather disturbing fact of his disabled vehicle being sucked into the black hole, without AL to help him. Still, he was content.

The Event Horizon was not something he could see or his instruments detect like the photon sphere outside it. Lélek in his ship with the defunct Android, had just passed it. Being in the grip of the gravity of a rotating black hole made his life simple. He knew death was the only option and that it was imminent. A small consolation was that the spacecraft may end up in another universe if it was lucky enough to hitch a ride in the worm tunnel generated by the black hole. Academic really if one's context was the state of being dead.

6th manifestation

inside the mind of Isten
3200 AD

This was the first time Lélek knew an absolute; an absolute certainty he was going to die, and how he was going to die.

The little globular man was right about the timing. Perhaps he was also right about what part of me is permanent and which is not. These were the next thoughts bouncing around inside his life force sphere.

Lélek recognised it well enough now. It was his third cycle. But the environment was different. There were no moons or planets to gaze at, or magnificent galaxies and nebulae to admire. This place had seemingly no physical matter at all. There were no suns or blazing comets to illuminate the void. Yet it was not dark. Not ink-black dark. More like moon light dark but without the moon. Sparkling light without a physical source. Pulsing, cascading energy.

"Do you remember what the little rotund man said about the skills that had evolved into their sensory network? You are getting a little glimpse of that other realm of energies which are preparing for their next phase."

Lélek didn't even turn his head. He knew the voice. It was the voice of the one who had touched his mind with wisdom and knowledge before. The voice was silent now, letting him observe and absorb.

This must be the space between universes, Lélek mumbled to himself as all sense of physical life exploded out of his body. Isten watched his special charge explore the landscape of a new reality. To Lélek this reality felt warm, electrifying and exciting. In the diffuse light he could make out flashes of activity cascading in rhythmic regularity, originating from no particular location and heading nowhere in particular. There was sound; like a birthday party inside a beehive. Rivers of sparkling lights amazoned around each other, disappearing and reappearing. *There is so much 'intent' here,* the thought passed leisurely through Lélek's mind.

"There is indeed much intent in what you have just witnessed. You are not yet ready to understand. There will come the time, then you will be able to join them."

There seemed to be something extremely familiar in everything Lélek saw. It alluded to things that a man of science should know. He strained his mind trying to put a finger on it, not noticing right away that the phenomenon had completely dissolved. He was back in the normal universe he was familiar with, or so he thought.

Isten was content with his Lélek. *My seed of hope has germinated well and flourished … well beyond my expectations. It has strength and integrity, resilience and an extraordinary life force. It was worth the risk.*

For the briefest immeasurable moment of eternity Isten invited Lélek into his mind. There was no pain, only awe, admiration, wonderment, surprise, astonishment, fascination, amazement, but there was no pain. Overwhelmed by absolute incomprehension of the flood of imponderables, Lélek regained 'consciousness' inside his sphere after the very next immeasurable moment. He had not lost any part of his self. He simply lost what vestiges of fear still inhabited dark recesses of his melded mind.

Isten withdrew into his own reality to allow Lélek to continue his journey.

There were things Lélek had to think about, seriously, deeply, comprehensively. He turned his thoughts inward, invoking all the power of his accumulated beings to the task. First he wanted to understand what he had just experienced. *Is this what it feels like to be simultaneously inside a fission and a fusion chamber, with the energy of a billion suns illuminating everything. I could feel it all! How is that possible?*

In this new universe cosmic winds blew more strongly. Black holes here generated extraordinarily powerful winds that could push outwards to force the formation of stars and shape the future of galaxies. The winds now buffeting Lélek's bubble did not drive particulate matter: They carried the new additions to his complexity. A few who had escaped their confined physical existence, three in particular, made their way towards Lélek. Each in turn impacted with his sphere, the last impact destroying it altogether. He/they were now unencumbered by any need to be 'contained' in the safety of illusionary bubbles.

7th manifestation

a new world, a new life
3200 AD

"**W**ho are you people – where did you come from – what do you want?" Not realising they were his future melds, Lélek pressed for immediate answers. This coming together was not gentle like his previous encounters.

Idu, Mudutu and Nindanu all tried communicating with him simultaneously. It created an awful din inside his mind, to Lélek it was just static. Immersed in his thoughts he first noticed the buffeting which brought him back to his reality, only to be confronted by the static increasing inside his mind. It became so bad he could not concentrate on anything else except that. There was no specific moment he could discern at which the noise had morphed into three people talking at the same time. They were not actually doing that. It was Lélek who could not yet 'filter' out any one voice from the others. Mudutu soon changed that with a bit of tweaking.

The trajectory of the three was a pre-planned intercept originating from planet Restu orbiting its parent sun in a trinary system; the smallest of a cluster of planets in the system, played with by three of its suns which had nested orbits inside each other. It was a complex open star cluster exerting a strange influence on this Earth sized planet. Most things happened in threes on Restu. So it was not unusual that three entities should have chosen to transmute concurrently. Their shells were still perfectly functional, but they each felt it was more important to connect with Lélek than to see out the natural termination point of their respective shells. His coming was prophesied.

Three Restunians were chosen based on their professions, to meet with and meld with Lélek. Nindanu was already hard at work in her role as a teacher, picking up the loose threads of Lélek's thought patterns in an attempt to reduce the 'static' to a minimum and start converting it into communicable symbols. Mudutu, an awareness engineer, prepared the sub-routines ready to upload as soon as Lélek's thought energy pool was focused. Plenty of time before the planet's great knowledge smith, Idu, would be needed to integrate some of the data the other two were getting ready to upload.

Each of them knew at the outset that by melding with Lélek they would have to take a subordinate role. But they also realised that this particular agglutination yet to visit their system since its inception was considered to have the highest potential. That was estimated in billions of Earth years, though their species was not that old.

Nindanu took the lead role, feeling Lélek seemed to have an affinity for her gender.

"Lélek – we, us three, are your new melds. We have only very recently come from our planet, specifically to be with you."

He was well aware he was in transition again. But so much had happened in such rapid succession he had not had the time to reflect on his situation or to consider his previous transitions. It took Nindanu's authoritative voice to add a little perspective.

"I apologise. It's been a wild ride since coming through the black hole. The people I met before, came knocking at my door, not just barging in. It will be enlightening to know what other customs you have that are not so confronting".

"We are quite different to the species you had met before," added Mudutu, "and it was necessary to tweak your consciousness to avoid a dangerous overload, or worse, a feedback loop. Everything is safe now. We have given you a little knowledge to start with. So take time to consider your position. We will fade till you are ready".

Without any further preamble Lélek found himself disembodied, un-sphered, just a complex thought energy bundle occupying an infinitesimal volume of space in a new galaxy, betwixt realities. He may have died young and perhaps inexperienced in some ways in Earopian terms, but his mind was more than capable of deconstructing his situation and formulating a range of alternate courses of action. It wasn't as if he had much choice in the past. Still it was better to be prepared. First on his agenda was to find out about his three new appendages, then to ask a few critical questions.

As the first question began to formulate itself in his mind the trio surfaced, unbidden. Lélek saw the three of them, more or less as they must have been in their natural form, which diverged considerably from what he'd experienced in the past. Nevertheless, they were obviously sentient, intelligent and they were going to become part of him. The prospect gave him little twitches of excitement. He especially liked the most luminous of the three, Nindanu.

"Thank you Lélek. I also feel we are compatible".

Lélek kept forgetting that in his current energetic state, thought pictures were like the clearly spoken word. Beauty, one would have thought, was a highly subjective concept. There was no doubt Lélek found Nindanu attractive, even though her form, colour and texture were quite alien to his senses. The attraction surmounted the physical reality. Sensing she was more highly evolved than himself, added considerably to his amiable disposition towards her. Nindanu could read all these thoughts passing through Lélek's mind, and chose not to react at that time.

Lélek saw in front of him three different photon parties raging out of control. Almost the entire electromagnetic spectrum must have been invited. He allowed himself the pleasure of observing the intrinsic beauty of these beings. With Earth eyes he would have only been able to see the visible light; so he would only have seen three rainbows swirling in front of him, loosely contained in humanoid shapes. That would have done a serious injustice to the Restunians. In his current manifestation he had no such limitation.

They were twice as tall as himself shaped roughly like a human, but they did not seem to have boundaries. The dominant infrared effect swirled like orange/red smoke in a woven container, sometimes oozing out of the fabric like so much coloured haze and sometimes condensing into tight whirlpools. All the colours of light danced in that playground, running from the head through the legs, swirling back into a ball in the skull whenever one of them spoke. When Nindanu showed emotion, her whole being sparked with white photons diving in and out of her person. Lélek could not see any of their eyes. *I wish I could see into your eyes, Nindanu,* the thought flitted across his consciousness. And the trio manifested 'eyes.' Each of them showed an area around the middle of their face that could have been eyes. They were little whirlpools of indigo and dark blue with flashes of white. Although each of the three manifested with the same light show, they had individual nuances of tone and intensity, so it was not difficult for Lélek to tell them apart.

"We don't always look like this," Nindanu said to Lélek smiling," only when we are ready to meld. It is similar to what happens when we bond with a partner.

Otherwise our shells are really quite dull, mostly grey. We try to make up for that with decoration. You'll see."

Her voice brought Lélek's vagabonding mind back from its immersion in the light spectacle. He really only wanted to know two things.

"Tell me about yourselves before we melt into one another, and what's this business about having a shell?

"We have waited a long time for you Lélek. Welcome. I am Idu. Nindanu and Mudutu and I are related. But to get to the point - My reason for existence is to search out knowledge and make it accessible to our species. I'm not the only one doing this, there are many hundreds of us. We all specialise. My speciality is Post Transmutational Alien Melding. That's why I'm here. Once you are 'born' into our species you will remember your own history, as well as what we are going through now. You will be expected to share yourself with many others."

"Just how much coercion is involved in this 'sharing'? Do I have any choice in the matter? Forgive me for asking, but my recent past life experience has made me cautious."

"As an Awareness Engineer," advised Mudutu, "my contribution to existence encompasses exactly those kinds of feelings that arise in individuals. There is absolutely no force of any kind involved. Whatever you do, will be voluntary. As you become aware of the value and reason for your function you will willingly participate. However, my role also includes making others aware of how certain individuals may be feeling about their responsibilities. From time to time, people in my profession are required to ensure that matters related to the greater welfare are brought to the surface of people's thinking; regardless of whether it concerns dangers to the species, long or short term, or benefits to us."

"It all sounds highly Utopian, if you can understand from my mind what that means. Surely there are some characteristics of your species that are … not as … idealistic." Lélek tried not to make that sound too negative.

"There are some of our species who find it difficult to put others before themselves. Our method of dealing with that is rather Spartan. As is the way we deal with all 'defective' new entities," offered Nindanu. That last statement did nothing to soften the apprehension Lélek felt from the moment of meeting the three entities.

Whilst the conversation rolled from topic to topic, Lélek felt himself gradually becoming more energised. He did not exist as a physical entity in the realm of normal reality, even in this universe. When he tried to see himself with his mind's eye he saw a glow forming about his person. There was only one explanation for that. The meld was progressing quickly, more quickly than any of the others he had experienced. Nindanu had already said a few things about herself, but Lélek wanted to know more. In a small way he thought he would have liked to have her perhaps more as a partner, than as an absorbed personality.

"I understand what you mean Lélek," Nindanu said softly, "and I would not oppose such a possibility. But don't be too discouraged. I have a sister who is very much like myself." She detected an immediate digressing thought stream from Lélek, but decided to stick to her own train of thought. "I am a teacher. In our civilisation it takes a long time to become a teacher. It is considered to be the most critical function an individual can have. A teacher is placed above all others. I am here to help prepare you for that role. You will be subjected to great scrutiny. I am helping you right now. Even while we are speaking I am examining your thoughts. All your thoughts, from the time you were first given your name, your very first name."

"Do you mean the name my father Egek gave me?"

"Indeed, but for now concentrate on what I have to tell you. You will need to go soon. Yes, I can see you're impatient to know about your transition. When you are ready to sublimate, the three of us will guide you. Although Restunians have children whose shells have to be changed from time to time as they grow, you will go directly to an adult shell. These shells are simply a receptacle to hold our life energy within certain bounds to enable us to interact with each other, within physical reality, and to live out our shell's allocated time intervals. Without the shells we would quickly dissipate into the cosmos as heat."

Lélek kept silent. He had always felt there was more to be learnt by listening than talking, and asking questions of course. There were still details he wanted to know about life on Restu, about their beliefs, their interactions with other species from different planets. He was deep in thought about the idea of 'shells' having to be changed from time to time, when his attention was attracted by a sense of motion. He was being guided towards the planet Restu in the trinary system.

At first he could not entirely understand what he was observing, for he had not experienced anything like it in his own universe. Space-time fabric behaved in a different way here. He seemed to be suspended in the eternal moment, while the rest of reality moved at a much faster rate. So much faster in fact that he could see the mechanism of the trinary system in action.

Restu orbited its parent sun, much as the Moon orbited the Earth, whilst turning on its own tilted axis. The combination of these two orbited a much larger sun, and they in turn together orbited a third sun. It was like watching the cogs of a clock. As Lélek neared the system he could feel himself glowing more vibrantly, like the three who had now completely melded with him. Then for a time he lost awareness of suns and planets, turning his thoughts inwards. He considered all that had happened to him previously. All his deaths and births, meldings and transitions. It seemed to him there was a definite convergence of realities. The further his life energy travelled, the less distinct the boundaries became between his life in a body and his life between bodies. Only the experience within the mind of Isten stood out as a form of existence truly separate from anything he had previously experienced.

Once they had finished initialising Lélek's receptors and had given him ample opportunity to acclimate, the newly upgraded shell waited to receive him on the planet's surface. He would not have experienced that type of 'birthing' process before.

8th manifestation

meeting Ahatu
4300 AD

"Are you certain you want to do this, Nindanu?" asked Ahatu of her sister.

"I've been a teacher for two lifetimes. I've learnt a great many things and met many challenges. This is the greatest challenge of my existence. I feel this is what my existence is about. I could ask you the same question. You don't know this man at all. How could you possibly consider him to be a suitable life partner?" Nindanu asked without looking at Ahatu, absorbed in the spectacle of the setting of three suns over crystalline mountain peaks.

"As a Dream Technician I have had to learn many things too. I have studied our legends in minute detail. All I can say is that I feel drawn to this man. There is no solid reason for it, other than the yearning I have when I read about his life. It must be the same for you. But *you* will be absorbed into his being, and I'm not ready for that."

"Don't get me wrong, Ahatu, I'm not wanting oblivion. It's just that I think I've done all I can by teaching. It's time for *me* to learn. This man could be my teacher."

"When are you leaving?" Asked Ahatu.

"Soon. Are you ready for this man? What if he wants children?" Nindanu asked with a sideways glance at her sister.

"Well, you don't need to worry about that, do you sister dear! We'll work it out somehow, especially if the three of you going out there to meet him do your job."

"You can count on it." The two sisters walked back inside Ahatu's dwelling, the light having faded from the sky. "I have to go now and get ready. What are you going to do to prepare for him?"

"He will have to take me as he finds me. Tomorrow I have a special dream to give to a young man. He's become ambitious, too ambitious, and it has clouded his mind about his true nature. If I can't realign him, you know what will happen. There's still more research to do before I complete his dream. Don't you worry – I'll be ready for this man of wisdom and compassion – and I hope his mind is as handsome as the legends promise."

Two days after having administered the corrective dream Ahatu learnt her effort was successful. The young man's essence did not have to be sent into their nearest sun. She was in a particularly good mood when the birthing engineer delivered the adult shell and set it up against the wall in the birthing room. The man of legend could come any day now.

It must have been imminent as the engineer remained in the room with the shell, adjusting the sensors while Ahatu went to bed. It seemed she'd only just put her head on the pillow when the engineer woke her gently, "He's here."

Instantly fully awake, Ahatu rushed into the birthing room. The shell was no longer the dull grey of a lifeless inert crystalline sheath. It pulsed like a heartbeat, motionless and vibrant with concentrated life energy.

"Lélek!" He heard his name shouted from a distance.

"Lélek – Lélek!" Again from a little closer. He lost the thread of his reverie and began to concentrate on the sound of this name.

"Lélek – Listen to my voice – come to my voice," Ahatu called to him. He had to change direction to hear the voice more clearly. He started to move towards it.

'You are safe. We are with you. This is the precipitation process. You are about to move into your shell.' He heard another voice from inside himself reassuring him. *'I am Nindanu. I will stay with you until you meet my sister, Ahatu. She is waiting for you. Look at yourself. Look at your hands – see how you have changed. You are now an expression of light, the life of the light of our three suns.'*

Lélek looked at his hands and saw the same swirling mist of photon colours he had observed in the three Restunians who had met him. He'd gone through a metamorphosis so complete there was nothing he could recognise of himself from the past. But in his mind he was still Lélek. He felt different to the Lélek of Earth, and the Lélek of Erde. However, his uniqueness was not altered. His life was still the life of the seed of Isten.

Again his thoughts were interrupted by a sense of constriction, like someone was trying to force him to put on clothes too small for him. He tried to struggle to free himself.

Nindanu's voice again comforted him. *"What you are feeling is completely natural when putting on a new shell. It will not feel so uncomfortable after a little while. You'll forget that you're wearing it. Some of our people even get to the stage of thinking they are their shells. We have to help them remember that the shells are only temporary."*

"Lélek – try to open your eyes. I am Ahatu. I have been waiting for you."

This was a new voice ... a completely intoxicating voice. *I can't see you. Where are you? Keep talking – please.*

Though he thought the words aloud to himself, Ahatu could not hear him. He did not want to stop hearing that sublime voice. Lélek tried again to open his eyes. It was like trying to force a window open that had rusted in. At last, eyes fully open, he looked straight out at a vision of perfection! No other thought would enter into his consciousness. Ahatu stood in front of him, naked, unadorned completely open for him to perceive her in her entirety. She was inside her shell, resplendent in all the colours of her being as he looked into her eyes, and she looked into his.

"Ahatu?"

"Yes, Lélek, it is me."

In that moment their bond was formed for the rest of their lives. Lélek could not take his eyes off hers.

Ahatu did say a few other things but he could not remember what. He just kept looking into her. It was just not possible this was the first time they had ever met. *Why do I feel like we have already spent a lifetime together?* The deeper he penetrated into her being the closer he felt he was getting to eternity. He wanted to break out of the constraints which held him and started to struggle.

"Not yet – not yet," Ahatu whispered to him, coming very close, "it will take a little while to get used to your shell. Soon, very soon."

She moved away so he could see all of her. Ahatu slowly turned a full circle, knowing he would be surprised at what he saw; not because the Restunians were so strange, but because they were so similar to what he had known on Earth. For some reason Lélek had formed an idea these 'shells' Nindanu kept talking about would somehow be mechanical, metallic contraptions. He was not prepared to see the form of a perfectly proportioned woman, with all the soft curves one associates with a beautiful woman. He did not even notice she had no hair, and that her shell skin was made up of all the shades an amethyst crystal was capable of. Through her almost translucent skin he could just discern what he thought might be organs. Everything was bathed in the orange glow he saw when he looked into her eyes.

Slowly control of his voice returned. "Where is your shell?"

"You are seeing my shell. Before, you were seeing me. I wanted you to see me, before you saw my shell."

"I want to touch you."

"Soon. You have to give your mind a little time to understand how to motivate your shell. It is very rare for a person to sublimate directly into an adult shell. Sometimes it doesn't work. We have to be patient - I want to touch you too." Ahatu paused for a moment to savour the moment of their coming together. "We will have a long time together. It is time for you to sleep now, and to dream. I will give you some dreams which will help you when you wake up. I am a dream maker."

Lélek didn't quite hear the last few words for he was already drifting off to sleep. His shell, with him inside it, was held in an energy field. For the time being that energy was used to nourish his shell and to maintain his own energy at optimum adult level. He needed much more than a normal Restunian. Lélek had the life force of a few other entities besides the last three who had melded with him. In this, his current manifestation, he would be required to function to his fullest capacity so far. Or at least as much as was possible in that physical form.

Ahatu channelled some specific dreams into his mind. They were simple, happy dreams, introducing Lélek into the capabilities of his shell and how to manage it; in essence his sympathetic and parasympathetic nervous systems were being connected to his brain-mind. He dreamt about the time he was a little boy who had to learn to walk at a very early age to be able to keep up with his mother while they went foraging for food. Then he was running around playing a strange ball game when someone shouted out his name – Ptah. He had to stop playing and go to his teacher to learn to read and to write. Lélek dreamt about the past, but he was always shades of amethyst, always using his new shell.

By the time he had walked half way across Europe to the Bükk mountains he had full control of all the muscles of his shell. Ahatu gave him dreams of the two of them exploring his new world; what he would eat and drink, how he would travel and rest – where they were to live together and how they might make children. It seemed like a very long dream, and he didn't want it to end. It was so real and so pleasant. When he did finally wake, three days had elapsed, with only one thought in his mind – Ahatu. He desperately wanted to be with her. Although he was awake, he was afraid to open his eyes. *Perhaps it was all just a dream, and there is no Ahatu.*

"Ahatu," he spoke her name quietly, straining to hear her answering voice.

"I am here Lélek. You can open your eyes. It is all real. We will have some help shortly to get you out of the energy net."

"Did you say you were a dream maker?"

"Try to move your body while we are talking. Yes, I give dreams – mostly to children but sometimes to adults. We have natural dreams of course, but sometimes people need a little help. When we are sleeping our minds are very active and very receptive to learning and solving problems. Most of the dreams I give are to help children learn important lessons about how to live with each other. At other times I need to give reminder dreams to people who have forgotten those lessons. Occasionally repairing dreams are needed for injuries and illness – and sometimes correctional dreams need to be given to the primitives or even our own people."

"What I dreamt did not seem foreign to my mind. They were memories from my past, and some very pleasant ones about you."

"I only had to make sure your brain-mind would connect to your shell. The other dreams were just for fun."

By the time she finished talking, two tall technicians had arrived. Within minutes Lélek stood on the ground supported by the two men. He looked at himself and found it very strange. He still had a residual image of himself as an Earopian. "Do you have a mirror?" He walked slowly over to it, with a little help from Ahatu. In front of him stood two Restunians in their amethyst shells, with just a hint of moving energy inside each of them. They slowly, hesitantly turned to each other, embracing gently. Lélek could feel her soft coolness against his shell. He expected her to be warm. He could not actually feel where they were touching. It was as if the two of them had become united in the one shell.

It seemed they were in each other's embrace for a long time. The two men had left and they were alone together. He searched for words to tell her how he felt, but could not find a single one. Ahatu pulled back a little from him and put her hand on his chest. That felt warm, like the warmth of the sun on your face. Then she took his hand and put it on her chest, just above her breasts. Lélek felt his hand warming at her touch.

"Time to go for a walk," Ahatu said softly after a few minutes, and took his hand in hers, leading him around the dwelling. Eventually Lélek found his voice and wanted to say something – intimate – to Ahatu. But she put a finger to his lips.

"I know there are things you want to say to me, and I want to hear them. Wait a little while until you are feeling more yourself, more complete in yourself. Let me show you our home." *I think I can live a good life with this man.* Seeing and hearing him confirmed her intuitive feelings. *I have made the right choice. Look after him, dear sister.*

8th manifestation

exploring Restu
4300 AD

He has forgotten me. He has forgotten his potential. There is time. He needs Ahatu now – she can teach him – she will be able to let go.

...

For the first time since arriving Lélek concentrated on his surroundings instead of Ahatu, continuing to hold her hand.

The dwelling was an extraordinary sight. The room they were in seemed to be made from crystals. It was quite a large room and the walls smooth to the touch, glowing with a soft light. There were no windows, only several openings which obviously functioned as doors. One of them must have led to the outside as it was so much brighter through it. He recognised furniture – a large flat structure that must have been a bed; several things that must have been chairs around a table. Everything appeared to be crystalline in origin, with a strong translucence about them. But they were not sharp and cold. On the contrary, when he sat in a chair it was most comfortable and seemed almost to mould itself to his shell.

Inevitably the question came, "Why is everything so – crystalline?"

"That is the nature of our world. Our shells cellular structure is similar to biological cells, but they also have some unique properties. Our dwellings and our physical items are in fact composed of crystals, which we have learnt to work with in preference to mineral ores, metals or other materials that cannot be replenished. Do you remember seeing our suns from space? A great deal about our world depends on our three suns, and our evolutionary path was largely determined by them. Each of them emits energy of a different kind, which are all essential to our lives."

"Can we go outside?"

"Yes. We need to put on a protective cover. Step into that cavity, hold out your arms, spread your legs and touch the palm of your hand to the coloured spot on the wall."

Lélek let go of Ahatu's hand and with careful steps walked over to the cavity. In effect it was like a walk-in wardrobe. On activating the mechanism an opaque film formed itself over his entire body, including his face and head, but he could still breathe and see perfectly well. He stepped out, looked in the mirror and burst out laughing at the canary yellow figure standing in front of his eyes. Ahatu laughed with him, for she had also chosen the same colour. They just stood there laughing minute after minute. Lélek became exhausted and walked over to the chair to sit.

"Does everyone on this planet look like this?" He asked still grinning broadly.

"Only if you happen to choose this colour. Most people find a creative outlet in the way they colour their sheaths. In many respects it can reflect their personality. It is again because of the three suns and our atmosphere's inability to filter out some of the harmful radiation that we have to wear some protection. It is not lethal to go without, but can cause serious health problems by constant exposure. The sheaths also insulate against extremes of heat and cold."

"How do we change the design?"

"Go back into the cavity and pass your hand over the coloured spot twice."

As Lélek followed instructions a quarter size figure appeared on the wall, with a comprehensive colour chart beside it. All he had to do was touch a colour sample and use his finger as a brush to colour the figure according to his design ideas. As it turned out he was rather awkward about it. For some strange reason he tried to draw the outline of a hand on his chest, and then colour outside the outline in a kind of orange /red ochre. He rather liked the colour combination of the canary yellow and the ochre with the dark outline.

"Cute," She commented, "where did you get the idea?"

"I seem to remember seeing a similar design on a wall somewhere."

"Good. Your memory is starting to come back. I like your design. Can I use it too?"

"Sure. Is that a custom here, for partners to look the same?"

'Indeed, especially for partners. It is going to be an exciting life with Lélek – Sounds like he's accepted me.' Then aloud she continued, "Often partners will do similar designs."

It was the first real indication she and Lélek were indeed a mated pair. He did not realise it at the time, but the placing of the hands earlier was in fact a mating ceremony. Apart from the symbolic nature of it, the placing of the hands 'branded' each partner with the unique soul print of the other person. It was not something that could easily be changed. While Lélek watched Ahatu do her design, his mind went back a very long time. He was told not long ago that when he sublimated into the physical reality of Restu he would remember all of his past.

...

Ah! It is beginning, and so soon. First the memories, then the desire. Isten constantly monitored the seed's evolution.

...

As if solidifying from a mist, he saw a vision of his first self, as a young man, doing a very strange thing in front of a cave wall. He had placed his hand on the wall and was spitting a coloured substance at it. When he took his hand away, there was an image of his hand. Even as his mind dwelt on the vision, he began to feel again that first thrill of realisation – it wasn't just his hand that impinged on his consciousness – it was his personal, absolutely unique entity. He decided to learn how to do his hand print on the sheath and to use it as his personal design.

"It's not right," he said, "Ahatu, could you teach me how to do my own hand's print?"

"Yes, but only if I can have my hand next to yours."

That pleased, Lélek enormously, especially when she wanted exactly the same design on her sheath from that moment on. Whereas everybody else on the planet went to considerable lengths to adorn themselves in intricate patterns, Ahatu and Lélek became easily recognisable by the simplicity of theirs and the way it represented their devotion to each other.

Eventually they made their way through the opening to the outside world. "This is extraordinary! I don't think I've ever seen anything quite so beautiful, even on Earth, definitely not on Erde." Again at the most unexpected moment his past came to the surface. Though he had seen crystals with light refracting through them, their effect could not compare with the sparkle of this world. It was truly one of light. Their dwelling was one of a small cluster towards the top of a reasonably high hill. They were all smallish buildings, somewhat utilitarian in design, but with exceptional colours in their crystalline structures.

It seemed colour had become a seriously important vehicle of expression for the Restunians. Looking to the right, the road led down the hill to another cluster of dwellings, with large spheres parked all around them.

For a moment they caught his attention but they did not immediately go down there. Lélek turned to the left, "Let's walk up to the crest of the hill."

The view into the valley, rimmed with crystal mountains was overwhelming. He caught his breath, unable to tear his eyes away. "Is all of your planet like this?"

"Much of it is even more beautiful," explained Ahatu, "except where the Primitives live".

Lélek wanted to know immediately what she meant by 'Primitives', but his attention was distracted by movement down in the valley. As he tried to focus on what was going on he again had a vision from the past; from the time he and his two friends trekked across Europe to the Bükk mountains. Except for the numerous outcroppings of luminous crystal towers, it seemed remarkably similar. There were trees and grass, green with chlorophyll – animals grazing, and flying creatures in the air. The movement he noticed was a herd of animals all heading in the one direction.

Ahatu saw where his gaze was concentrated and volunteered the information, "They are some of our food producing animals. There are many creatures who help us to live. But because there are not many of us on this planet they are not exploited beyond what they are willing to provide."

Lélek made a mental note to ask about the population density as he watched a large flying creature ascend high above them. For the first time he noticed the three suns, each a different colour and different size in the sky. There was so much he wanted to know – and he wanted to know it then!

Still watching Lélek's reactions, Ahatu told him about their suns. "Our three suns are unique in this part of our galaxy. The way you see them now, with all three visible during the day, only happens once every three thousand years and it has deep significance for us. Each time it has occurred, a special event has taken place on our planet. Many of us feel you are our special event on this occasion."

That made Lélek spin around immediately to face Ahatu. All of a sudden he didn't feel as unconditionally happy. An enormous suspicion crept into his mind, and he simply had to ask the painful question.

"Is that why you were waiting for me?"

Without the least hesitation Ahatu answered immediately and without the slightest intonation of voice that may have suggested any discomfort caused by his abrupt question. Their relationship was very young, but she felt it was on a solid foundation – both on the personal level and on the historic level.

"There are two answers to that. The first is that I was *personally* waiting for you because of the kind of being I believed you to be. I will tell you more about that later. The second answer is that we, as a species on this planet in this universe, have a legend that tell us someone special was due to visit us at the next Three Suns."

Lélek eyes remained fixed on Ahatu's, searching, probing and finding no reason not to believe her. He took Ahatu's hand again. "I want to go down the road to the other dwelling cluster to look at those parked spheres."

The atmosphere between them had not changed. *I wonder what is so special about this 'visitor' she's talking about – and why should it be me?* Lélek wanted desperately to know. Patience was an attribute of his character that had been forming from the time he was a Neolithic cave man and it was well honed – so, first the spheres.

On the way down the hill, keeping his eyes on the spheres, his memory again brought him a vision. As some of the spheres moved away from their parked locations, he saw in his mind the planets of the Solar system making their way around Sol. He saw the photon sphere just before being engulfed by the black hole. They were all memories of his existence between corporeal lives. He considered that aspect of all his experiences – how his life and post life existences seemed to be converging the further down the space-time continuum he progressed.

They stopped next to the 'parking lot', watched some people get into a sphere and saw the sphere move away, then other spheres arrive empty. Obviously they were a transportation device of some sort. He could not see what made them move. The passengers did not seem to have to do anything. He walked to an empty one.

Ahatu explained. "Nobody owns the spheres. They are available for everyone to use. Empty ones are directed to places where their numbers become depleted. There are a variety of sizes for different uses. You simply tell it where you want to go and it takes you there. The thing you are probably most interested in is their power source. I can't tell you the technical details except that they use a certain type of energy from one of our suns, channelled by the crystals that are found all over our planet. They are themselves made out of another type of crystalline structure that grows naturally, which we have learned to fashion into these spheres."

"I'm getting very tired and hungry. Can we go back?"

"Perhaps it was a little too much too soon. Come on." Ahatu took him by the hand this time as they slowly walked up the hill in silence. Some people they met stopped and made a strange little movement with their hands towards Lélek. It was just a simple little turn of the wrist orienting their palms towards Lélek.

"That's a sign of recognition and potential respect. A respect," she reminded him, "that you still have to earn."

"You said 'recognition'. Do they know who I am?"

"Indeed they do." She smiled broadly at his bewilderment. "Everyone knows who you are, but not what you are."

"Already? I've only just arrived!"

Back inside the dwelling Ahatu showed Lélek how to prepare a simple meal and how to remove his protective sheath. Modesty was simply a matter of how much they allowed their shells to glow or how much intimate eye contact they allowed. Overcome by fatigue Lélek went to lie down, accompanied by Ahatu.

In spite of his fatigue, his shell started to glow rather brightly. When Ahatu explained it was a sign of arousal, he was a little embarrassed, but she showed him how to control that. Then she showed him how she felt, which made Lélek feel much better indeed. Being a very sensible person Ahatu convinced Lélek it really was time to rest, and that she would give him some pleasant dreams if he wanted. "We will have time to play later!"

It was another two days before he awoke to the sounds of tinkling noises coming from the other room. Ahatu was not in the bed. She was in the main room, playing music. Lélek felt very much refreshed and found it no problem at all to motivate his shell. So he went to see where that sound was coming from. As soon as Ahatu saw him she stopped playing.

"Welcome back. You've been asleep two days. Did you have nice dreams?"

"I'm not sure if I was dreaming, it was all so real."

"I am very pleased to hear that. Now it's time for you to start learning. After our learning period we could go out and visit some people if you feel up to it."

Knowing there were some specific burning questions in his mind, she started immediately on a short version of their history, concentrating in particular on their legends as it concerned Lélek.

Comprehending a predestined time for his arrival proved challenging. To him it felt like a completely arbitrary event, like most of the things that had happened to him during several manifestations. However according to Restunian legend it was a very specific occurrence to take place at a specific time. When Nindanu explored his mind before his sublimation, she had discovered something extremely exciting. Lélek had studied Earth history extensively when he lived on Erde. In particular, he was interested in the Akkadian civilisation, from the time when Lelke travelled with his friends to the Bükk people. She passed that information to her sister, Ahatu, before she herself was melded with Lélek.

"Try to remember some of your past. Think of my name. It's an ancient name passed down the generations to me. It was originally an Akkadian name."

"Really! How is that possible?"

"You're not the first person from Earth to come to our planet, dear," Ahatu replied as she put a gentle hand on his shoulder.

Distracting though that was, he cast his mind back to before his incarnation on Erde; to the time when it was his ambition to go to the place on Earth with the highest cultural achievements – the valley of the Tigris and Euphrates rivers. But he only managed to get as far as the Bükk mountains. Somewhere in the back of his mind the missed goal became the motivation for him to study that culture while he was on Erde.

Lélek began to remember places and names; the people's history and their cosmology. Enlightenment dawned on his face as he said to Ahatu, "Nindanu, Mudutu and Idu are all Akkadian names, as is Restu the name of this planet - as is your beautiful name."

Ahatu blushed, her amethyst colour turning a deep purple for a moment. "How much do you remember of their legends?"

"Not a great deal now – perhaps with time. "Does everyone have Akkadian names here?"

"Yes, without exception. It is a part of our heritage."

"How can it be a part of your heritage?" He was intrigued. Not only was this a very strange planet with three suns, seemingly in an entirely different universe yet with such strong links to Earth.

"A very long time ago, more than three and a half thousand Three Suns ago, we started having children that were different. Back in those days we were 'primitives'. These children told strange stories about a planet that had only one sun. Stories about a world where people had learnt to record their thoughts with symbols in clay. They remembered their own names and the names of their families and cities. As the centuries passed more of them were born to us. They remembered and told the stories of their legends. Then for a long time no more came. By then we had completely changed. Though there remained some who are even today primitives. They choose to know nothing about Earth and Akkadia."

"But how does all that concern me? I was never in Akkadia. I don't remember ever having even met anyone from there."

"Your fame started in your second life on Earth, when you insisted on discovering the world. You did not live for very long, but you had a great influence on many people. Two of those people were special, they were your friends."

"You mean – Tilit and Johee! Ah, indeed." Lélek recalled their names immediately. "How on Earth do you know about them – sorry slip of the memory – how on Restu?"

"Our legends tell us two men travelled from one end of the world to the other, to Akkad, and they took with them the story of a great man; a man of science, wisdom and compassion. A man who said his home was in the stars. A man who said he had been to the stars and would go back there again. We came to believe this man would come to us one day, like so many others had come before him in the past."

"You think that man is me?"

"Yes. We believe it is you."

Lélek found it difficult to comprehend such a thing. All his memories told him was that he'd had an interestingly varied life, which he thought was probably nothing unusual. Many things had happened to him, but they all seemed to be completely random. As for being a man of science, wisdom and compassion – well - *I just did what came naturally.*

"But I am not a great man. I may be a combination of many, but I don't believe I am particularly special in any way."

"Nevertheless you are here, and my sister has seen into your mind and knows who you are. She is now a part of you."

"This is very difficult for me. I have to think about this. Tell me honestly – why are you with me? Is it because you want to be with a great man?"

To that question Ahatu said nothing. Instead she took Lélek's hand and placed it on her chest. Then she put her hand on his chest and allowed him to see into her, as before. At that gesture Lélek allowed her to see into himself. He knew then he would never have to ask that question again.

After a long lingering moment Ahatu interrupted the intimacy. "It is time to go and meet some other people."

Lélek went to the cavity and practiced getting the handprints right. They went out, hand in hand, down the hill to the transport spheres. Ahatu instructed one of them to go the long way, through the valley, to their destination in the nearest town. Some of the road was straight, and some wound around, up and down following the contours of the smaller hills. Nowhere could Lélek see huge earthworks scarring the landscape. The roads themselves were more constructed to cater for the animals and foot traffic. The spheres had no wheels. They did not need to touch the ground.

From the vantage point back near their dwelling, the trees seemed to be normal trees like he remembered from Earth. Seen from close up the only resemblance was that they had leaves and the leaves were generally green. Otherwise they were enormous structures, tremendously wide trunks and so tall he could not see their tops if standing beside them. The rest of the vegetation was quite normal. It seems the energy channelled by the crystals buried deep underground plus the over abundant sunlight enabled these giants to dominate the landscape. Many grazing animals made use of their arbours not just for shade but as their permanent homes. Sometimes the people tending the animals had their crystalline structures near the trunks of these giants. From time to time Lélek could see clusters of dwellings in the valleys, or near the tops of hills, and often nestled against the sides of cliffs. Because they all looked like clusters of crystals it didn't appear there were many people living in that land anywhere.

Eventually he saw bright shafts of light in the distance. They were nearing their destination. The town itself was the busiest he had seen so far. Not that there were crowds, but there was plenty of movement with people going about their business, and spheres following their well organised paths. Some of the structures must have been dwellings, for they had similar proportions to their own. Others were at least three of four stories high, with spires of crystals jutting out at odd angles, giving out light of various colours. Some were built close together, and some strategically placed in what appeared to be parkland. This small city, with all its myriad crystalline structures was nestled against the side of a tall cliff, the top of which displayed an array of very thin and very tall crystalline towers. He guessed they must have been communication devices of some kind.

A small welcoming party met them at one of the more expansive structures. "Welcome Lélek," Ur said accompanied by the hand gesture of acknowledgement, "this is Umma and Larsa." He didn't say who they were, perhaps it was not customary in their culture.

"Thank you. This is truly a beautiful world." He reciprocated with the hand gesture.

The three already knew Ahatu. "We congratulate the two of you on your bonding," Umma said. "You have quite a unique design. Come for a walk with us in the park."

The planet was slowly revolving out of the light of the three suns and the rays came in at shallow angles lighting up the crystals and trees of the park into a most festive mood. It made Lélek feel very cheerful. Everyone they passed greeted him with the universal sign of respect.

"If I may ask," Lélek began, "how is it everyone greets me, seeming to recognise me. Ahatu has explained about your legends, but I still don't understand why it all seems so special."

Ur respond first. "This is a world of very few people by Earth standards. You already have some idea that we strictly control both the population numbers, and the quality of our genetic pool. That quality control is one of the reasons we extend a warm welcome to you. The other is because our legends have taught us of the possibility of an entity of great value coming to visit us for a short while."

"A short while?" Lélek cast a questioning look at Ahatu.

Umma hastened to clarify, "It is not meant as a restriction of the length of your stay, merely an expression of the transitory nature of all things that come to pass."

During the entire conversation Ahatu and Lélek walked hand in hand, a fact not gone unnoticed by the three dignitaries.

It was obvious these three leaders already knew a lot about him, partly from their legends, and partly from the information Nindanu had passed onto them. So when Lélek asked his worrying question about the importance they attached to him, Larsa responded without the least hesitation and in such a friendly way that it made him feel they had known each other for many years.

He put a hand on Lélek's shoulder as a friendly gesture before explaining. "We have no specific expectations of you. You can come and go as you please. If you like, you can join Ahatu in the work she does, or you can pass your time with us as you wish. The energy you carry with you will manifest itself with benefits to yourself, Ahatu, your children if you wish to have any and to our people. Simply pursue your life goals and be the person you have evolved into at this stage of your journey." Larsa's reassured him.

In spite of the weighty content of Larsa's words Lélek picked up on what could possibly be considered a minor side issue. "I hadn't thought about children." Ahatu gave his hand a squeeze which made him glance at her to see the smile and sparkling light in her eyes.

Ur interrupted the moment of intimacy with his own contribution to the discussion which made it clear to Lélek he was not on a holiday, but did in fact have certain responsibilities placed on him. "We have evolved in quite a different direction to the other sentient species you have come into contact with. Although we have space flight capability our strength lies in the way our communication skills have developed. This is partly due to the crystalline nature of our world, and more particularly because of the range of electromagnetic radiations we have been exposed to by our three suns. I am surprised you have not asked how we know so much about you."

The light of the three suns had almost completely faded, replaced by a glow coming from within the crystals in the park. They were so charged with energy the small group had no trouble in seeing one another. "Many questions have crossed my mind," Lélek said, "but I have been distracted by Ahatu," at the same time giving her hand a firm squeeze. She steered them towards a cluster of light crystals which appeared to function as a table and benches.

"I want to ask about your 'primitives' but first tell me about this evolved communication."

"Most importantly we are able to communicate with those who have outlived their shells. You met three of them before you joined us. Secondly, those of us who come back to our world don't forget their experiences off-world in that realm where you were met. However, there are limitations to our cycles of existence; limitations which do not seem to apply to yourself. We hope to learn more from you of the nature of realities that exist beyond our physical world."

Lélek got the strong feeling Ur had a prominent leadership role on this planetary community. He also suspected that if he had turned out to be 'undesirable' in any way, Ur would have the decisive word about his future. Lélek didn't feel this as a threat, more as a reassuring element of the structure of this society. He decided to think more about this communication capability.

"And the 'primitives'?" For some reason he felt that if Ahatu's people had any nasty tendencies, then those could be revealed by the way they treated the primitives.

"I can understand the nature of your interest in the other members of our world. Ahatu can take you to one of their colonies when you feel up to it. Suffice it to say for the time being, we share a common ancestry. When the energies of the cosmos manifested themselves in our children, some of our people accepted these extraordinary changes and some did not. Those who chose to remain unchanged have decided to live apart from us. When matters arise which affect the health of our planet, then we all come together to find and implement solutions. There are no restrictions on them or us about how and when we interact."

"Thank you." Lélek had enough information and sat immersed in thought, losing himself in the magical crystal twilight. The three leaders, content to see Lélek ponder, also enjoyed the splendours of the evening.

"With respect, Ur, Umma, Larsa, I will take Lélek home now." And so the conference ended most amicably.

"There is no need for us to meet again, Lélek, unless something of particular significance arises you may want to discuss," Ur said in parting.

Ahatu and Lélek walked over to a transport sphere in silence, at ease in each other's company. The sphere rose noiselessly, accelerating away from the park into the night blanketed countryside. Yet there seemed to be enough ambient light so Lélek could still discern major landmarks as they made their way home. Ahatu let him absorb himself in her world for a little while before drawing his attention to something she felt to be particularly significant.

"Perhaps you don't realise the great honour that has been bestowed on us, more precisely on you. The three people you met are the most highly respected individuals in our world. They are considered to be the guardians of our culture and our way of life. Each of them has outlived many adult shells. Their wisdom is beyond that of any others. They don't lock themselves away but rather spent a good deal of time travelling around our world. Very, very rarely do they consent to speak with anyone. Not only have they spent time with you, they have given you complete freedom of choice to live your life as you wish."

"Oh – I didn't realise. They were so easy to be with and talk to. They made me feel completely at home. They could have asked me to do anything, and I would have done it for them."

"The other significant thing they have done for us is to give us permission to have children," Ahatu blushed slightly, for child bearing and rearing was a special privilege, "and they placed no restriction on how many we could have." She blushed even deeper, turning a deep purple around her chest which even showed through her sheath. Ahatu blushed partly because she did not know how Lélek would receive that news. She had hoped he would want to have children. When Lélek didn't respond straight away she became a little anxious and tensed as she sat beside him in the sphere.

She need not have had any misgivings, for the next moment Lélek asked quietly and a little self-consciously, "Will you show me how?" He did not really see much of the outside world on the rest of the way home. It was dark, and he was too busy with Ahatu to bother about sightseeing. That night she did not need to give him any dreams.

The morning, like every morning he had seen so far was brilliantly lit by the light of the three suns. He wanted to go outside for a little while, but it was raining.

Ahatu said, "It'll rain for the next three days, it always does regularly at this time of the year. Most people simply stayed indoors. Work is not an overriding obligatory imperative of our society. Everyone has a life mission, which benefits themselves and the rest of the community. Mission co-ordinators ensured all things needing to be done are done in good time. The pressure of excessive population doesn't regulate people's lives. Crime does not exist. There are people who fall out of sync with the natural rhythms of need, acquisition and supply. But we don't consider them to be criminals."

"So why do you – make dreams, I think you said – in such an ideal society?"

"It's the way we treat people to bring them back into balance."

"Is there no violence here?"

"Yes, occasionally but rarely. These events are not publicised, nor are the consequences. It's not necessary. Everyone knows the consequences. Laws against violence don't exist, only the consequences. If sessions of dreaming with specialised dream makers do not alter the individual, then his energy is sent to the nearest sun, his shell ground to dust. The same process is administered to all their progeny. Genetic contamination is not tolerated. There are no circumstances that would moderate the severity of the consequences."

"This all seems rather extreme," Lélek commented, not at all judgementally. All these things Lélek learnt, as well as other more pleasurable things while it was raining.

The day the rain stopped Ahatu was called to a dream making. The message simply appeared on a section of the crystal wall of their home. To respond she had to inscribe certain characters in the same spot with her finger. The waiting sphere recognised her, was already programed with her mission parameters and needed no further instruction to convey them.

On the way she told Lélek what she was about to do. "Do you remember how my sister prepared you for sublimation, the way she was able to work with your thoughts to give you knowledge? I have to do a similar thing to a new entity. A little girl has just come into her shell and is having trouble sleeping. I may be able to help her."

It was not a long way, perhaps an hour before they arrived at a small cluster of dwellings. The structures were similar to those of their own village, but with much more vivid colours and patterns. These people were all image makers, using their own dwellings as experiments of expression. Both the mother and father greeted them, giving Lélek the special greeting of respect." Welcome, we are honoured to have you in our home."

I'm going to have to get used to this. It seems everyone on this planet knows me by sight. I wonder what I'll have to do to earn all that respect?

The mother turned to Ahatu, "Little Kaqquru is very restless when sleeping and it takes her a long time to get to sleep. She holds my hand and seems to be afraid of something." Kaqquru was playing in the corner of the room and got a fright when Ahatu and Lélek suddenly appeared at the door.

At least here is someone who does not know of me yet.

As soon as Kaqquru focused on Lélek, she went directly up to him. Lélek sat on the ground so he could be at eye level with her. Restunian fathers didn't generally do this. Kaqquru could not talk yet, but the sounds she made were obviously very friendly and directed very specifically at Lélek. Even to this day he doesn't know why he opened his arms. As soon as he did, little Kaqquru pressed hard up against his chest with her arms clasped firmly around him.

"How very strange," said the mother.

Ahatu answered Lélek's questioning look. "Restunian children tend to be extremely wary of all strangers. They feel vulnerable to outside influences until their entities and shells can provide safe insulation."

This little girl just opened herself up to him, and allowed him to look into her eyes without any reservations.

Ahatu and the parents stood there completely baffled. They had never heard of anything like this happening before. Ahatu went over to Lélek, put one hand on Kaqquru's back and the other on a comm panel on the wall; her data access to what she needed for the procedure. After a few of moments she changed her mind. Soon after, Kaqquru let go of Lélek and went back to playing, happily smiling to herself.

"Well it looks like your little one will sleep well tonight," Ahatu said, still baffled by what Lélek could have done. "This is my ..."

"Yes we know. It is Lélek. Thank you," and with that both the mother and father came close to Lélek to let him see them. "We wish for you the warmth of many suns."

So ended Lélek's first encounter with Ahatu's profession as a dream maker. Obviously it did not go as Ahatu had expected. She said as much to him adding with a smile, "If you're going to do my job for me, perhaps I should be *your* assistant."

He didn't quite know what to do or say and just shrugged his shoulders, smiling back.

"I'm not in the least upset. Don't misunderstand me. Besides, I have learnt today you might make a very good father for our children."

Well, what can a man say to that? He felt himself straighten a little in the seat of the sphere. Ahatu saw it and was glad. *This is a good man.*

8th manifestation

art of the dream maker
4302 AD

I couldn't agree more, Isten thought to himself. *I only hope the growth continues. He cannot enter the next level unprepared. Lélek must become fully aware of his true essence.*

...

Life began in earnest for Lélek from that day. They say good news travels slowly. On this world of crystal communications that was certainly not true. Within a few days the whole planet seemed to be aware of his special 'gift' with children. Never mind it was only Kaqquru who had given him one big hug. Apparently there were no more problems with sleeping for little Kaqquru.

There was a message from Ur, Umma and Larsa for Lélek when they arrived home. "Lélek, we are well pleased. Live your life among us as you desire." It made Ahatu puff out her chest just a little. She was proud of her choice. She'd had a reasonably busy life until Lélek came along and then she had to take a little time out to get him ready. Her little holiday was over. As soon as news got around of her new 'assistant' her services came into greater demand. Out of politeness, the invitations were always extended to her. Wherever they arrived it was soon obvious they were pleased with Lélek's attendance.

On one occasion they went to do a repair job. The man had fallen from the lower branch of one of those giant trees, hurting himself rather badly. His shell could not be repaired, so he lost an arm.

That in itself presented no big limitation to his life or his ability to continue his contribution to society. The problem was in his mind. Sorting out this kind of issue was exactly what Ahatu was good at. Firstly, she induced a three-day sleep for the man. Then she took out a small blue pointed crystal from her bag. Lélek saw her preparing it back at their dwelling, the crystal changing from a crimson colour to blue as she worked on it. As soon as the man was asleep she slipped the blue crystal into a small hole in the wall of the dwelling and kept one finger on it. Her other hand she put on the man's forehead. Staying in that position for several minutes with her eyes closed she seemed to 'download' the contents of the blue crystal. Lélek could only guess what was happening because the crystal gradually turned back to crimson.

The process seemed to tire her out so he did not question her until they arrived home. "What actually did you do back there?"

"This man's problem stems from a self-image issue. Remember that some people develop a sense of mistaken identity. They come to think of their shells as being themselves. That's what has happened to this man. His shell was damaged, but his essence remained intact. The part of him that used to energise the arm of his shell had withdrawn into the rest of his being. He'd lost nothing, but his mind hadn't realised that. To fix the problem, I gave back to him knowledge of his full and complete self. In our central control building we have a complete record of the essence of every person on the planet."

"Really?" Lélek interrupted, "me too?"

"I assume so, but to answer your question … I took a copy of this man's essence and put it back into his mind. He will now dream of himself as a complete being, who has only a slightly limited use of his shell."

"Has anyone ever not been able to be restored to the knowledge of their true selves?" Lélek asked the question with a little hesitation, because he didn't want to ask the next question: Or at least he did not really want to know the answer to it. This particular realm of thought had an undercurrent relevant to himself. As Lélek awoke to the extent of his past experiences there arose the natural question of who he really was. The issue, though not current in his conscious thinking, nevertheless needed some form of analysis and understanding in the future.

"Sometimes it takes more than one intervention," she replied partly side stepping the question she knew he would ask next.

"What happens to them if your procedure does not work?" He knew she felt a little uncomfortable with the answer she would have to give. What he did not know was the reason … which was because she felt his judgemental disapproval of the ways their civilization dealt with some problem people.

"If it looks like they're going to be harmful to others in the grip of their self-antipathy then their energy is sent to the nearest sun, and their shells are ground to dust." She tried to sound as matter-of-fact as she could.

"I can't help feeling that seems – harsh. Is there no other way?"

"Yes there is. You may experience that when we visit the primitives. Please don't form rash judgements. At least not until you've seen more of our culture and their culture."

"Is it possible to improve on your rehabilitation methods?"

"I can see you have a great kindness zand compassion inside you. These are perhaps questions Ur may be able to answer better than myself."

"Could you do something for me? Could you give me some dreams, using your crystal method, so when I dream them I'll be aware I am dreaming given dreams?"

That night Ahatu gave Lélek a dream about a part of her life, before she met him. She also implanted the desire to wake immediately after he had finished dreaming. When Lélek went to sleep at the usual time, she stayed awake. He dreamt his own dreams for most of the night. He dreamt about Kaqquru and what he saw when she let him look into her eyes. He also dreamt about the man with the damaged shell. In the dream he saw Ahatu again concentrating on her task. As he focused on her the scene changed gradually. He saw Ahatu as a younger person, sheathed in an aquamarine outfit dotted with magenta, white and cornflower blue round shapes of various sizes. It seemed to him to be a very extroverted way of presenting herself in public.

There was a reason for that. Ahatu was standing on a platform with other young people during some sort of ceremony. Ur, Umma and Larsa were there, Umma giving her a crimson coloured crystal. The audience made a tinkling sound by tapping white crystals together. The scene was replaced by a landscape that did not appear as welcoming as the environment he was now getting used to.

There was more barren, rocky ground. The crystalline structures showed many fault lines and a general milkiness, even the colours seemed less pristine. He saw Ahatu walking down a narrow road which wound its way through a cluster of dwellings. They were similar to their own home, but lacking the same clarity. Some people came out of one of these homes to greet Ahatu. Their attire was the same as he had seen in his own village; colourful and individual but a little dull, as if the shells were showing through.

Lélek followed the group into the house where Ahatu was expected to help someone lying on a bed. The ailment could not have been too serious because the person was chatting quite pleasantly with Ahatu. Lélek could see there was a difference in the glow that came from this individual. It seemed to lack a certain amount of lustre, a kind of vibrancy to his being. He realised that a depth of − character − for want of a better description, seemed to be missing. Lélek tried to focus more clearly on this person, but the next second he was awake.

Ahatu sat on the bed facing him and asked gently, "What did you dream? Could you tell when you were in the dreams I gave you?"

"Did you control all my dreams?"

"Not exactly. I thought you might like to re-live our time with Kaqquru. The rest was a gift from me."

"I saw you at some kind of ceremony, then you were at a place which seemed just a little depressing, helping a person who did not seem all that unwell."

"One of the most important stages of our lives is when we are bestowed with the privilege of our profession. You must have seen the crimson crystal. That is both a symbol and the most important tool I possess. I wanted to share that moment with you. It took a great deal of time and a lot of personal development to reach that stage."

"I saw the three leaders there."

"They only take part in those ceremonies with the people who have excelled above all others," Ahatu said slightly self-consciously. "The environment you saw me in afterwards was amongst our primitives.

Every graduate in every profession has to spend time at the beginning, and then regularly during their lifetime amongst the primitives. It is our contribution to what they do for us. The area they live in is their own choice. Once, before our paths diverged, all the planet looked mostly like that. As we evolved differently with the help of off-worlders we were able to make improvements in our environment. Did you notice anything different about them?"

"At first they seemed to be not as – clean. And when I saw the light of the man on the bed he seemed to lack the vibrant energy that you have."

"That is because they have chosen not to meld with other, foreign energies when and if they return to new shells. Many of them have only one lifetime. Only a few choose to return. We are different. Most of us have had many lives on Restu in this physical reality. We consider this experience to be as valuable as what comes after."

"I don't know about the free will aspect. In my experience I've never had the choice. Even coming to you seemed inevitable. Not that I regret it." With that statement came a little move towards her which she reciprocated very intimately.

After a little while the discussion resumed. Lélek found the bed time leisure activities most pleasant, including the intelligent conversation. On a more serious note Ahatu said everyone, that is everyone on the planet, was eagerly waiting to learn more about the post-shell existence. "We know for certain now there is an existence afterwards. We can even communicate to a small degree with those who had made the transmutation. However, there are still great unknowns we would like to understand. We're hoping you will be able to teach us."

"Perhaps I have had experiences that could be considered unusual. I don't really know. But I'm not very comfortable with large crowds of people."

"You can just tell me, or just a few of us. As part of the information we cherish, is the life experiences of all our people. We are able to 'record' that and share it as it is needed, if you are willing to agree to that."

"I ... like ... need ... my privacy, my private thoughts," Lélek hastened to add, fearing all of his self could suddenly become public property.

"As part of my profession of dream maker, I can selectively record experience captured in thought, as well as selectively give thoughts through dreams. It does need complete trust."

"You had that the moment I opened my eyes for the first time and saw you standing there." Ahatu moved a little closer to him, the cue to stop discussing dreams and practice developing intimacy. That was mandatory if they were ever to be ready to weave the fabric of new consciousness into physical reality.

8th manifestation

creating a life
4305 AD

Weeks flowed into months and months into years. The three suns slowly altered their relative positions. By minute increments the nights became just a little bit brighter, and the crystals glowed with just a little more inner life. Lélek accompanied Ahatu on all her expeditions. Sometimes he was able to help, like with little Kaqquru. Of all the people on the planet he was the only one with the combined energies of so many entities and with such rich experiences on many worlds and in the fabric of the cosmos.

Sometimes he would talk to people about his life as the original primitive Lélek on Earth, sometimes about his youth as Ptah in ancient Egypt. Occasionally he would tell stories about some of his life on Erde. A favourite became the episode of the time when he rescued Christin and returned her to her home on Earth. As he told the stories he would remember more through the telling. Sometimes he didn't need to tell stories at all. Letting the ailing see into himself and draw out the strength they needed seemed enough.

The symbol of the two palm prints became well known throughout the world. From time to time Ahatu and Lélek added a little extra colour to their sheaths, but their two palm prints were always there, side by side. Their activities fulfilled them, gave them a reason to live from day to day. Still there was something missing, which they both felt more strongly as time passed. Lélek had slowly graduated through the many levels of intimacy and had now become thoroughly proficient in the art. For it was an art form on several levels; in the degree of creativity of the partners, the expertise in building expectation, the possibilities it offered for weaving the fabric of a new life. It also involved making contact with individuals who had made the transition and were ready to return. The time had come.

Ahatu announced it one rainy three day, a little hesitantly, perhaps a little shyly, "If you would like, I could take some personal time from dream making to start a family."

She need not have been reticent about it, for Lélek had long had it in mind that the only thing he needed to make life complete would be a family. This would only be the second time he'd created life since his existence as a Stone Age man on Earth. Though he was successful then, the effort was minimal. Since then he'd invented many things, created wondrous machines on Erde, but never had he had the opportunity to put all of his intent, all of his life experience and all of his accumulated selfhood into such a wonderful task.

...

It gladdens me to see Lélek take such joy in a simple act of creation. He may yet be capable of greater things. Isten patiently followed the growth of his seed. *Soon it will be time to see if he is capable of flowering.*

...

That same day Lélek confirmed their intention with Umma. It was a co-ordinated effort. Replacements had to be organised for the work he and Ahatu were doing and the process of growing a small shell had to be started. Each shell was individually tailored to the genetics of the parents and the characteristics of the developing 'child'. The entire process would involve them for eleven months. Their responsibility was to create the fabric from their own essences that could accommodate the energy of the returning entity.

A specialist group of bio-engineers would provide the shell. Not least, one of Ahatu's friends, also a dream maker was asked to prepare the final part of the process; giving of the first dream to the newly sublimated life. Both Ahatu and Lélek wanted to contribute to the composition of that dream.

By the second evening of the rainy three-day, Lélek and Ahatu were prepared to begin. It started simply with freeform joint dreaming. They had to join hands, palm to palm, tied together so they would not separate during sleep and just go to sleep to dream. It was not necessary to discuss the content beforehand, nor to talk about it afterwards; it was a process of synchronisation. Their thoughts and desires had to converge in a completely free flowing way. As soon as the rain stopped, each day after the dreaming they had to lie in the suns on a clear crystal slab to recharge. Sometimes it took days, and sometimes weeks for people to completely synchronise. Each knew immediately when that happened, for then they would wake even if it was in the middle of the night. Just four days after the last dreaming they were ready.

"We don't need to discuss our dreaming, dear," Ahatu cautioned Lélek, "but we do have to initiate the next stage immediately."

"Is that going to be as involved?"

"No, but it will need all the energy we've accumulated if we are to successfully contact a waiting entity."

The process was as before, with the hands tied together but this time clasping a flat polished diamond to channel their combined thoughts. Night after night they dreamt the same dreams, each day recharging in the light off the three suns. Ahatu used her spare time teaching Lélek.

Sometimes she invited a Teacher, especially when Lélek had difficult questions to be answered; like whether they believed in a deity, or what their philosophy taught about the meaning of life. On those occasions Lélek made a lasting impact with his own particular perspective on things. Everything he said was recorded. Over time he had forgotten that. In the process of learning he became a teacher. Sometimes his Teacher would be angered by his declaration that life had no intrinsic meaning at all. Other times they would be in complete accord on the matter of a universe that had no God-hand regulating its mechanisms.

Every night the two future parents continued their search. Several weeks went by with busy days and tiring nights.

"Sinu!"

They woke simultaneously and spoke the name together. They had made contact. Sinu was to be their first child.

"Does the name have a meaning, Ahatu? It sounds very much like another Akkadian name."

"I'll have to take you to our knowledge repository."

That same day they were met by Larsa at the facility, something like a public library. "Hello Lélek, Ahatu. We have been following your progress with keen interest. Lélek, I have the information you wanted. 'Sinu' is an Akkadian term for the Earth's satellite.

"The Moon!" That made Lélek ponder upon something in his most distant memories. He told the story of his first encounter with the moon, then his other lunar encounter.

"I had a son once. His name was Gloppel. A bright boy but much too trusting. He learnt the art of creating a calendar from me using the phases of Earth's moon. This was at a time when I was first given my name, by Earth reckoning about 10,300 years ago."

"How advanced were your species then?" Asked Larsa, understanding the implications of such a duration.

"At the time I didn't know it, but later I learnt we had only just to begun to make tools out of stone. The calendar was a great innovation and much ahead of its time. After I died …"

"What does – died - mean?" Larsa again enquired.

"When my adult essence left my only shell. After I died - I was taken into our solar system and I saw our moon from very close. My father took me there and explained about the continuation of life energy after the end of the shell. He said we continued to exist as a bundle of thought energy, made up of all the thoughts and experiences we had accumulated during life. By the way, does Ahatu's name have a meaning?"

"Sister. It means sister. More of an honorary title, especially because there are so very few people who are allowed to have siblings. Ahatu's sister, Nindanu, was in the most highly respected profession of Teacher. As she was a teacher, you are now a Teacher. She has become a part of you, as you have become a part of her. You have already taught us many things. I have especially enjoyed your ideas about the intrinsic meaninglessness of life."

"Please excuse us," Ahatu said, "we are at the critical stage to begin creating the fabric to hold the consciousness for our child to be."

Lélek didn't realise the exhausting nature of the process. It required long sessions of ever increasing intensities of intimacy, with just as long sessions of recharging. No wonder Ahatu could not carry on with her normal duties. At every dream session, each of them had to take a single thread, a thin string of energy from themselves composed of specific characteristics, to be combined with every other string of energy, and weave it into a unique fabric, bundled inside Ahatu. This was a process that came instinctually to every Restunian. A critical aspect was the parents desire to create a life that would find physical existence fulfilling for the entity. When the fabric was complete, they had to *invite* Sinu into their lives.

Sometimes the waiting entity chose not to enter. It was never known why. The effect on the waiting parents was always devastating. Sometimes the entity would terminate the process soon after it had started. That also was a mystery. As the months passed and the bundle grew inside Ahatu, and she and Lélek became more and more fatigued, Lélek started wandering about the reason for the complexity of the whole process.

He asked Ahatu about that during the day. "How can your species possibly survive with such a difficult and time consuming process?" What he had forgotten was that the life span of each Restunian was many times that of Earthlings. He also failed to make a connection to the 'severity' with which the Restunians safeguarded their genetic health, and consequently their longevity. In fact, there did not exist a necessity for regular procreation to balance out large scale 'natural' attrition.

"Is this not a pleasure for you, my dear? We can't take a break now. The process has to be continuous."

"It is – yes it is," he responded, stepping up closer to Ahatu to feel her warmth. "What I meant was the practicality of it all." If the sessions of intimacy had not been as intensely satisfying, both in physical terms and spiritual terms, Lélek might have chosen to give up. In any case, he had developed such a deep affection, such an overwhelming sense of 'oneness' with Ahatu that it simply didn't enter his mind.

It was four months into the activity when Ahatu woke Lélek in the middle of the night. "I am ready. The fabric we wove for our son is ready to receive him. Just one more thing we have to do together – tonight."

Though feeling the effects of the effort he'd had to make so far Lélek cleared the fog of sleep from his mind. "Right now?"

"Yes, we need to start tonight. We have to synchronise our dreaming again to be able to invite Sinu into the tapestry inside me."

"This is extraordinary. Will you be alright? I mean, it's not going to be painful or anything?"

"No, silly. Now come close and hold my hand."

Lélek had a smooth transition to Ahatu's vibrations. In their dream they saw Sinu in all his vital scintillating self. They recognised him and he recognised them.

That morning Ahatu was not well. She felt completely drained. Lélek was surprised to hear her being so happy in spite of it. Apparently that was a healthy sign the entity had taken up residence, and was just making himself comfortable. The feeling would pass. There was no visible outward sign Ahatu's body was any different for its new condition.

"When my body changes ready for the birthing, which will come soon enough, you will not be allowed to be with me."

"Why, what's going to happen to you?" Lélek became suddenly alarmed.

"Nothing bad is going to happen, just that it's a very private thing. I'm letting you know in advance so you won't worry."

For now, their only task was to go immediately to the shell growing facility to register the initial parameters for the preparation of the young shell. Each subsequent month new data was needed to ensure the shell would match the energy profile. The process of sublimation was going to be traumatic enough for the child, without having a mismatch between him and his shell.

Life resumed some normality for a while. Of course the intimacy did not need to stop. It simply had another function, both to reinforce the bond between the parents and to give the child the experience of affection. He and Ahatu returned to some of their duties in the wider community, while each month sending the relevant data for the continuation of the shell's development. Lélek felt more and more as a Restunian. His experiences of past lives, and in-between-lives took on the semblance of memories of distant dreams, losing their focus as actual realities of the past. Without realising it, he no longer even thought about Christin. As those aspects of himself dimmed, the personalities of his last three melds started to come closer to the surface of his being.

It was Ahatu who noticed this first, in the little ways Lélek would watch her sometimes, just like her sister Nindanu used to. Lélek, on the other hand, actually started enjoying being in front of larger groups of people and telling them stories of his past, while sitting under one of those gigantic trees, surrounded by people of all ages. Her sister loved those giant trees, and the feeling of security they gave her. Lélek said to Ahatu one day that he wished they had one of those trees near their home. Exactly what Nindanu had wished for not long before her transmutation.

The day finally arrived. "Lélek dear, it's time for you to stay with my very good friend Kullaa. You've met her before — she lives in the next village, not far. Don't look so worried, I'm fine. Everything is normal."

"I've noticed you've been getting a little pale — I've not been able to see into you."

"It's what happens at this stage. All the energy is drawing into the core."

As Lélek prepared to leave that evening the new shell arrived. It was about the size of a three-year old child and a dull, lifeless colour. It arrived in a container, floating in a gel. They said it was a substance that aided the flow of energy. But the container was much larger than the little shell. Large enough for an adult. All they said was that Ahatu would explain it all tomorrow. By then two others had arrived, birthing technicians, and Lélek had to leave.

He had to take a transport sphere to Kullaa's home. There was nothing to distract him so his thoughts turned to all those unknowns about the birthing, which naturally began to torture him. By the time he arrived he was distraught at the thought of losing Ahatu. He simply didn't know what was happening, and no one was prepared to tell him. He was met at the door by their friend's child. A little boy, Kappu-Lélek. He smiled broadly and invited him inside. He was named after Lélek as a sign of the high esteem in which Lélek was held. The parents could see Lélek was distressed.

"There is nothing for you to be concerned about," Kullaa reassured him, "it's very rare for anything to happen to the mother during the birthing. It's always quick, not taking more than three or four hours. The birthing technicians really don't have much to do except keep an eye on the process and make sure the electrolytic gel is at the right temperature throughout the birthing."

"If you say so, but it worries me. It's nothing like I've experienced before."

"We know your deep affection for Ahatu. You will be able to help her very soon. Afterwards she will be drained of energy — you can help her re-charge. It's one of the responsibilities of a new father."

His friends seemed so relaxed and confident. It eased Lélek's trepidation a little. That night, for the very first time since coming to Restu, Lélek had to try and sleep on his own, and he found it was no longer possible, in spite of Kullaa's reassurances. It was like trying to keep the blood pumping through his body without a heart. The night turned out to be very long. Many things went through his mind. Mudutu, the Awareness Engineer inside him calmed him with her wisdom and Idu validated the information he had been given about the birthing process.

Lélek spent the night trying to think about all his adventures this side and the other side of life. By the morning he was relaxed though sleepy, ready and eager to go back to Ahatu and his new child.

He walked into their home as quietly as he could, making his way slowly to the birthing room. Ahatu was on the bed, with one Birthing Engineer beside her. The other one was tending to Sinu lying outside on the same slab of flat crystal Ahatu and himself used for re-charging. He didn't know where to go at first, Sinu was asleep so he went outside to Sinu. The child lay on his back, eyes closed, chest rising and falling slowly. Lélek didn't know what he should do: this was just another thing no one had explained to him. Quietly he stepped up to the crystal slab and stopped opposite his son's face.

It was remarkable, overwhelming! Here was his own son, already big enough to run around. He was beautiful! The most beautiful thing he had ever seen. At that moment Sinu opened his eyes and looked directly at him. Time suddenly stood still – his heart stopped beating – all his thoughts fled into the void. Lélek bent down, put his hand on his son's chest and opened himself up for his son to see. Without a single word, without any expression on his small face, Sinu gently raised his hand and put it on his father's chest and opened himself up for his father to see.

"Sinu," Lélek whispered almost inaudibly. It was the only thing he could say.

"Abu," his son whispered back, removed his hand and closed his eyes again.

"Sinu needs to charge his energy levels. He'll be out here most of the day," the attendant said. "You can stay with him for a while if you want." But Lélek didn't hear him. He remained there with his hand on Sinu, unable to move, so overcome by the experience, by the incredible connection he felt to this boy, *his* boy.

He'd experienced a great deal in his many manifestations, but never had he experienced a miracle. Never had he felt so utterly fulfilled. Before, he always seemed to be just that short arm's length from reality, even with Ahatu. Now he felt life actually had real meaning, even if he never found out what it was. He could not tear his eyes away from the face of his son.

Eventually, Ahatu's attendant came out to him. "Ahatu is awake. She's asking for you." The attendant had to help Lélek remove his hand. A great lethargy had descended on his arm and he wasn't able to move it himself. "That's Sinu drawing on your life force. It's an excellent sign. It means the boy has fully accepted you as his father."

Lélek more or less shuffled into the house, feeling drained. He looked at his beaming partner and could barely whisper as he bent close to her face, "He is beautiful, beautiful. The most beautiful …!

"Yes he is. Has he seen you?"

"Yes … he said Abu. What is Abu?"

"He called you father," and with that she pulled him to her. She was not at all sure how this strange man from the stars would react, and greatly relieved by the obvious outpouring of emotion from him.

The attendant went outside to leave them on their own. Lélek lay down beside Ahatu, and hand in hand they both fell asleep. While they slept Ahatu's dream maker friend arrived at the setting of the three suns. She brought the child inside and gave the little one his first dream. It was a simple dream. *Remember who you were … respect who you are … live the life you would dream of for yourself.*

…

Isten watched without emotion the moment of the coming together of father and son — satisfied, to a point. *Will he be able to relinquish his attachment? Is this as far as my seed is capable of evolving? There is so much potential in this being.*

…

When they first completed a dream for Sinu it seemed perfect. Yet upon reflection they realised the unnecessary complexity, driven mostly by desire and fear — their own desires and fears. It took Lélek and Ahatu many days and nights to trim out all the things crowding their son's first dream construct. They wanted so much for him, in the end realising Sinu needed the freedom to create his own life.

When mother and father eventually woke, they saw two technicians looking after Sinu, testing his legs, arms and all the connectivity between Sinu and his shell. The Birthing Engineers only stayed long enough to make sure the sublimation was successful and the mother was well.

"Ummu, Abu," the child called out. He wanted his mother and father. Ahatu got up, feeling a little more stable after the rest. Lélek had stabilised her energy levels overnight, so he was feeling a bit low himself, but couldn't wait to see his son again.

Sinu was perfect! Like a miniature replica of an adult. Lélek could have sworn Sinu had Ahatu's eyes and his own straight shoulders and back. But perhaps that was just bias. After all, they didn't grow the shell. Even the unique individual inhabiting the shell was only partly their work. Ahatu took Sinu's hand and led him to his father. Acting on the first impulse, Lélek bent down and picked him up to hug him.

"Ooh! You are heavy!" Turning to Ahatu he asked, "when will he be able to talk?" Sinu looked at his father and smiled. Putting a hand on either side of his head he scanned his father's face as if to make sure he would never forget any detail of it.

"You can start the teaching tomorrow. We'll have some help soon. If his mind is intact it'll only take a few months and he'll be able to express himself. Within a few weeks he will already start to understand most simple things." Lélek kept holding his son while they talked; Sinu happy to be in his father's arms.

"Before we fell asleep I was worried about how pale you looked when I first saw you. Are you well?"

"I am very well, my Lélek. The birthing takes a great deal of energy out of a person. It can almost completely drain them. That's one of the reasons for the attendants. But I'm better now after your help last night. Now we have to eat, and then go out into the suns."

Lélek reluctantly put his son down. He felt absolutely complete. *If no other thing ever happens to me again in my entire existence, I will be happy for eternity. To have to come such a long way to find this joy … why?* He let the question drift into the void, knowing well enough he would reclaim it.

…

Isten knew he could not interfere, could not coerce Lélek's thoughts to delve deeper into the realm of greater existence. Lélek needed to be exactly where he was, but he also needed to move into the future to fulfil his potential. *He needs to experience absolute love, absolute commitment,* Isten tried to convince itself.

…

After the meal all three went outside and lay side by side on the crystal, with Sinu between them. The suns were warm that day and the winds were gentle … and so the three of them shared the mystery of existence together in a state of contentment. Questions and answers, learning and teaching, and all other things could wait for another day. They did not seem so important just then. *Tomorrow — I'll ask Ahatu tomorrow how Sinu was born.*

Several short recharge sessions later the day came to a slow, peaceful end. Lélek led Ahatu and Sinu to the sheathing facility to remove their protective layer, where he designed a new symbol for themselves … Sinu's little palm print placed between his and Ahatu's. As the years passed, Sinu would have nothing else on his sheath, even when he formed his own bond with another.

Lélek cherished his role as Sinu's teacher. Aided by Nindanu's energy he knew exactly what would hold the young boy's attention, and what he had to teach his son. Sinu was always attentive. Even when Lélek was tired, he still wanted to go on with his lessons. It was a few weeks before Sinu was ready to meet his other teachers. Ahatu had become apprehensive about her son going out into the public, to a class of other youngsters. She alerted Lélek to Sinu's eyes changing colour. At first he didn't notice the transformation, or if he did he took no notice until his attention was drawn to it. They were going from the normal orange/red combination to shades of blue.

"Our eyes are always orange, with reds and yellows. It's only the primitives who've been known to rarely have blue eyes," Ahatu said.

Restunians had no pupils. They could look directly into the light of any of their suns for a short time without causing any damage. Their eyes had an eyelid, and also a third translucent membrane which was drawn across the eyes most of the time. That gave their eyes a pastel hue. It was only drawn back on special occasions; to get an energy boost from their strongest sun, during periods of intimacy or when there was a threat to their lives. Sinu had drawn back his membrane only a couple of times. That's when Ahatu noticed the start of the transformation.

"Should we discuss this with Umma," asked Lélek.

"I don't think it's going to cause him any harm or discomfort, but it does make him look quite different. Even you have normal eyes in spite of the complexity of your makeup. Yes, we'll go and discuss this with her. We also need to get Sinu to meet his new teachers and enrol him in some classes."

Umma agreed with Ahatu. "There is no reason for concern. I know how rare it is, but it's not a defect. Leave Sinu with me for the day. I'll arrange everything for him."

The two relieved parents walked to the park where Lélek first met the three leaders. Lately he'd had little opportunity to speak confidentially with Ahatu. Sinu was always with them, even at night in their bed. So he used this occasion to ask her about the birthing experience.

"Fathers are not a part of it is because of what it seems to do to the mothers. It's not really as bad as it looks, but it can be extremely frightening. If the father panics or tries to interfere in any way, that's where the real danger lies, both to the mother and the child. Both could be lost. As soon as the shell arrives complete with all the organs, floating in the gel, the mother has to get into the gel and place the shell face down on top of herself, enfolding it in her arms. They both have to be completely submerged in the gel. The moment she is ready to release the energy bundle of her child the attendant has to charge the gel. It goes completely opaque and almost turns to jelly. The mother's shell starts to glow with her own energy and the energy of her child as his begins to migrate through her shell into the gel. At that point they both seem to disappear into a swirling mass of highly charged material. You cannot see a distinction between the mother and the child."

"How long does this take? Can she breathe in all that stuff?"

"No, she can't. But it only takes a couple of minutes before the mother can lift her head out. As she does so and the energy essence of her child is in the gel, she can actually see it slowly diffusing into the new shell. That could take hours, and that's where the charge of the gel is critical. Her energy is also in the gel with her child's, and it has to diffuse back into her own shell and take control of it again. That is a short process because her energy knows her shell intimately. But that is not the case with the child. It has to find and connect to every nerve fibre, every muscle – find and recognise every organ and establish compatibility. If the parents had woven the fabric well, then it's only a matter of a short time before the child feels at home in its new environment. It will lift its head and take a breath when it is ready. By the end the mother could be as pale as a white crystal, for she has to support her child all the way. It is draining, but there is no pain. I could feel Sinu's joy as he became manifest. It is an extraordinary sensation that no man can ever know."

"Does it get easier with other births?"

"That I don't know, dear. Relatively few people are ever allowed to have more than one child." To change the subject she said, "That is a beautiful new design you created for our sheaths." There were some aspects of the birthing that were not exactly comfortable for the mother, and she did not feel like going into details about it.

Slowly, inevitably life resumed its normal rhythms. Sinu went to class each day on his own, in his own transport sphere. Ahatu and Lélek went where they were called, to administer to those who needed her help, or who wanted to interact with Lélek. It took Ahatu a while to regain full strength. Until then Lélek patiently attended to her without placing any demands on intimacy. He also took great joy in being with his son who was learning in leaps and bounds, leaving many of his friends behind. He seemed to know so much more already than the others. Ahatu said that was because of Lélek, and his deep life experience, some of which was woven into the tapestry they had created together.

8th manifestation

lost in the wilderness
4317AD

As Sinu grew from childhood into adolescence so did Lélek mature in himself having unreservedly taken on the mantle of personhood on Restu, absorbed in his son and Ahatu.

There came the time when Sinu had developed so much he was almost bursting at the seams of his old shell. By then, a new one was ready for him, almost as big as Lélek himself. The next one would be a full adult shell. Sinu at twelve years old, was same age as Lélek when he made an innovation in the way his father had used a calendar. Sinu had not only grown physically, but as a person within himself. So when Lélek and Ahatu told him about the colour of his eyes, a phenomenon known almost exclusively only among the primitives, he was ready to discuss it. He'd wanted to bring it up for some time but his parents seemed to be so busy. Besides, he wasn't sure how they would take what he had to say, particularly his mother. He felt his father would be no problem. Lélek was part alien anyway and was open to most things.

"We can see none of your friends at the classes seem to mind your eyes are so different from theirs. How do you feel about their changed colour?" asked his father.

"I can remember most of my experiences before coming to you," Sinu began. "The most vivid memories are from the time just before you were looking for me. I had been drifting for what seemed like a long time. At

209

first it was interesting to see the cosmos and our world from another perspective. But after the people around me left, some to sublimate again and others just disappear, I didn't know what I was supposed to do. It was the first time I had experienced transmutation. There was someone who met me. He was good to be with. He said he knew you, Abu. It was about the same time that I felt your energy searching. I didn't want to go back to live with the primitives. I wanted to go with that man, but he said it was not yet my time. It's not that I didn't want to be with you … I was just tired of all the effort of living before."

"What did this man tell you?" Lélek asked eagerly, for he suspected it was probably the same one who visited him each time he was between lives.

"I can't really remember the details, except I think he said something about waiting for you."

"Oh." Ahatu and Lélek glanced at each other, knowing of course there was a great deal more to life than their son had experienced.

"Before I transmutated I lived a long way from here - with the primitives. It was a longer than normal life span, and a difficult life. I was ready to leave it. That was the best thing for me, but my community didn't want to let me go. They said I was too important, not because I had blue eyes, but because of the things I did among our people."

The two parents just listened. They knew, and the leaders knew there was something special about this entity, this child of theirs yet not theirs. Nobody interfered with his development. Sinu had to experience his own enlightenment without being led or prompted to it. Sinu continued his remembering.

"Our people do not record history like you do. They don't keep an account of everyone's personalities, and they don't have dream makers like you, Ummu. They have what they refer to as the 'blue healers'. I was one of their blue healers. I used blue quartz mostly. Sometimes I used it to help people have healing dreams."

Hearing those words, Ahatu took Sinu in her arms and almost cried. She was so proud of him. He had to wiggle to get out of her embrace. He wanted to finish his story while the memories were coming back to him so vividly, for he could not always remember these things.

"Our lives were much harder than yours. I often had to help people to see their reality a different way, and help them to accept what they had; to see all the good things and not get depressed. The most frequent problem they had was forgetting who they really were, that they were not just their shells. Many of them started to forget about their true selves soon after their transmutation."

Now Sinu turned to his father and asked in a most earnest and youthful way, "Could you tell me the story of your life, your whole life. People say you have great experience and that you have lived on other planets … please Abu, I really want to know… Please."

"Yes, of course," Lélek responded without hesitation, "we can start as soon as you feel comfortable in your new shell." It was like hearing echoes of himself – how could he refuse.

During the few days they waited for the new shell to arrive, Lélek withdrew into himself to think about everything Sinu had said. He wanted to recount all the experiences of his life, all the lessons he had learnt. But most of all he wanted his son to understand the nature of reality. *No – that's not right – there were other realities - it was the natures of the different realities that is important.*

He took the transport sphere out into the open countryside, to sit under one of his favourite giant trees overlooking an especially green valley. The mountain ranges in the distance sparkled with the reflections of its many crystalline cliffs. It was the day after a rainy three-day period. The air sparkled like the crystals, everything was in sharp focus, brilliant in the light of the multiple suns.

He let his mind wander to ride the warm currents of air swirling through beneath his tree. Lélek tried to imagine what Ahatu had to endure during the birthing, and was sure she was not telling the full story. So much effort to bring a life into corporeal existence. Surely there must be a reason, a purpose for expending so much energy. He determined to explore that with Isten the next time they met. That jolted his thoughts towards something else that had been waiting in the shadows of his mind for a long time now.

The circumstances of being alive physically and then the conditions after physical life seemed to be so different by comparison. Yet at the same time there was so little separating the two states of existence. Casting his mind back to the time before his birth onto the planet Erde, he could remember the confusion he'd experienced. He had looked upon the planets and the sun of the galaxy that was to become his home. It was every bit as real to him as when he saw it from the space ship he used to escape from the planet. In that vessel he was physically alive, yet the cosmos was the same as before. There was indeed a serious blurring of the distinction between his physical life and his metaphysical life. He tried to simplify his understanding, thinking about the changes he had experienced and the strange things that happened to linear time. He thought about the relationship between change and eternity, and his mind just coiled and twisted like a string of energy trying to catch its tail. He could not get a firm grasp of it at all.

It was almost time to return home. Two of the suns had set and the third, the coldest and smallest sun had risen. It was getting cold. He'd stopped thinking about those big questions, disappointed he'd not come to any greater understanding than he had before. Putting his hand on the top of his transport sphere and just on the verge of stepping into it, a revelation gift wrapped in memory revealed itself - *I have travelled in my own spheres before!*

He suddenly remembered that little detail, and with that a rush of thoughts almost overwhelmed him, stopping him dead in tracks. It was absolutely clear to him now, whatever state one was in, one thing was absolutely certain – he must evolve! *There is so much more I have to do!*

…

If Lélek had heard he might not have been startled … *At last!* Isten said aloud to himself, rippling the fabric of the cosmos just enough to make Lélek feel the truth of his realisation.

…

All the way home his mind was clear. It was at peace. He could now tell his story to Sinu. As soon as Sinu felt up to it, he would take his son out into the wilderness where there would be no distractions, and talk together about the important things.

Sinu returned to his classes while Lélek was asked by Ur to address a small group of highly knowledgeable people.

Lélek began without any preamble, as was his custom at such gatherings. "It is a source of constant amazement to me that it should take so long to realise how much further there is left to go in my journey," he said. "I can now remember the very first time my father took me away from Earth to show me our moon."

Ur politely interjected before Lélek could immerse himself in philosophising about the deeper meaning of his unique experiences. "We are particularly interested in the events which brought you to us in such a round-about way. You existed in another universe: You experienced life as a species separate from your origins: You have spent time in transitional states and conversed with highly evolved entities. We wish to share in the details of all that accumulated experience, as captured in your being. We wish to see you in your current physical reality, from the perspective of knowing the details of your past. That is how you can teach us."

One advantage of those discussions was to force Lélek to delve deeper into his past memories to clarify many things which had become a bit hazy to him. He felt it would make the discussions with Sinu so much clearer, so much more comprehensive. Sometimes he forgot his son was only twelve years old. He was truly intelligent beyond his years, with a depth of life experience behind him from his previous manifestation, but he was still only a youth.

The time it took to give his presentations was enough to give Sinu plenty of opportunity to feel completely at home in his new shell. Lélek at last discussed his plan with Ahatu.

"I'm not at all comfortable with the two of you going off into the wilderness by yourselves. Neither of you knows the region very well. Certainly not you, even though in the last fourteen, fifteen years you've travelled widely with me."

Sinu joined the conversation. "We don't intend to go into dangerous environments. Just somewhere where it's quiet and we won't be disturbed. Anyway, it's only for a few days."

"Sinu is right, Ahatu. We're not going hunting like savages. It'll be just like an extended picnic."

"What exactly do you mean by 'hunting' and 'savages'?" Prompted Ahatu.

"Sorry, I know you don't do such things here. It's something from my past, which was indeed extremely dangerous. The 'savages' – perhaps that's the wrong word for them – the people who were at the very beginning of their civilized evolution."

"I don't like it. You don't know the true nature of our planet. Neither of you has ever been in a situation of having to use specific survival skills."

"But Ummu! I really want this. Abu and I have never had an adventure!" Sinu pleaded with his words and Lélek pleaded with his eyes. They both felt this great desire; Sinu for adventure and knowledge, Lélek driven by a memory from the past. The two 'men' managed to reassure Ahatu, though she did not consent without conditions.

"I will make sure you are properly prepared, *and* no arguments!"

They had to prepare extra rations, just in case of unforeseen delays – communications crystals, homing crystals connected to the sphere – first aid equipment – portable sheath pod – information crystal module containing detailed maps to a variety of scales – weather forecasting module and so on. Ahatu was inexhaustible in her foresight and wisdom. A few weeks later after everything was ready, there were just a couple of things left. "Sinu, take your father and register your intended route at the Main Information Centre for our region.

"We will only be away for three days – four at the most," Sinu told his mother, "do we have to?"

"Come on son, if it makes your mother happy." Lélek didn't see the need for all the fuss.

Sinu was very excited by the imminent adventure with his famous father. His teachers had already asked him to make a presentation afterwards to several younger classes about his adventure. Sinu felt very important. This was going to be his first big trip with his father, and it was not just any ordinary trip. He was going to learn about metaphysical realities, and about the cosmos. The universe of suns and planets and galaxies with black holes was much more interesting to Sinu, especially since their species did not engage in extensive space flights. The leaders were not interested in space exploration. They were much more interested in the nature of realities, and the nature of in-between realities. They wanted to learn the secret of the energies which gave living things their life essences, and all the mysteries of their creation and particularly their final destination. They felt Lélek's destiny was somehow connected with these things, and through Lélek, his son's.

"And while you're at it, teach your father how to control the pod." Among the most important preparations was Lélek's training on how to use the transportation sphere on manual control. To Sinu that was second nature, but Lélek also had to know it as he was the responsible adult on the journey. Restunians took such responsibility most seriously. So Sinu had the added pleasure of teaching his father something, as well as the official instructor of course. In some respects, the sphere behaved like a helicopter and needed good co-ordination of both hands and feet. Lélek found it much more difficult than piloting a space craft. At least there he had synthetic intelligence to help him. Pitch control came easily, he even found roll manageable each on their own. But putting the two together took him a lot of practice.

"Neither of you is going anywhere until I'm satisfied Lélek has proficient control of the sphere." Ahatu was adamant.

At last everything was organised and arranged and registered. The adventure seemed fool proof. Unfortunately, several characteristics came together in Lélek's makeup which could imbue risk into any adventure with him. First there was his own innate curiosity. Put that together with Ptah's adventurous spirit, Thales's thirst for knowledge and the scientist Fremd's desire for experimentation, little could have been done to forestall the likelihood of the two 'boys' going off the beaten track.

The first day

The first stage of their journey was uneventful. They followed established routes to go well beyond inhabited areas. The spheres could easily travel the equivalent of a thousand kilometres a day.

"Abu," Sinu piped up after hours of seeing the same kind of landscape, "couldn't we go that way, maybe just for an hour, cross country." The change of route was not registered on their plan.

"Why not, we've got all the maps. Maybe we'll find a good place to camp for the night." Although surrounded by mountain ranges the terrain was not difficult. Lélek felt quite in control zooming down canyons, up onto plateaus and out onto open plains. The two boys were having so much fun it didn't occur to them to actually check their maps. Inexperience is a cruel teacher.

"What about over there." Lélek spotted something vaguely familiar, though it was an overhanging accumulation of mixed rocks and crystals, not sandstone. It seemed like the perfect place to get out of the elements and stop for the night. It had been a perfect day. Both of them totally enjoyed each other's company, just being together, father and son, as friends, exploring the unknown. It didn't take long to set up camp beside the sphere. They watched the colours of the day's end in mutual wonderment. Exhausted, completely contented and well fed on Ahatu's prepared meal they fell asleep without the slightest thought as to where they were or what route had got them there. The anticipation and excitement of a new day did not let them sleep to their normal routine.

The second day

Both woke to the rising of the first sun, which had a slightly crimson, purplish hue so early in the morning. It brought back memories for Lélek of the times he had the early watch in front of a cave. They were hard, but happy days … uncomplicated days. Shadows turned from black to magenta, white crystals lanced the landscape with pink spears through the slight mist. Sitting side by side they awaited the rising of the second, yellow sun. It burst through the horizon as if it had been held captive for a thousand years.

They could not breathe, their souls having taken refuge in awe struck paralysis. How could anyone describe, let alone continue to exist another instant on seeing the transformation of the world when the rays of yellow light attacked the hordes of magenta shadows flanked by pink/lavender shafts piercing the highest peaks ahead of them. The spectacle lasted only minutes; minutes of splendour that could not be absorbed in an eternity. There was nothing either of them could say as the normal light of day reclaimed its domain. In a silent state of wonderment Lélek prepared breakfast, intending to go for their first short walk afterwards.

"When are you going to tell me about your life, Abu?" As with all boys who experience great wonders, their attention still remained focused on what they wanted.

"You see that cave over there? It might be worth exploring, do you think? I used to live in caves." That got Sinu's attention immediately.

"Yes, yes! It's not far – maybe half an hour's walk there and back." As often happened in that world, with virtually no chemical pollutants in the air, distances were deceiving. Everything seemed to be enlarged, making them seem closer than they really were.

Not intending to go far, they didn't bother to secure the sphere, leaving all their equipment around the campsite. The two of them were so excited by the prospect of discovering something interesting, continually talking about the most outlandish possibilities, that the half hour stretched into an hour before they eventually reached the entrance. The morning was very pleasant. They had had a big breakfast, plenty to drink, so felt very alert and very comfortable and very keen to explore the cave. Once again Lélek remembered the first ornamented cave he had found, with all the paintings – and – the hand print.

"Come, sit with me, son. I want to tell you about my first ever moment of enlightenment, many thousands of years ago."

"Are you really that old, Abu?"

"I am not old as your father, but I do seem to have some very old memories … like you have old memories you told us about."

Sinu listened with rapt attention. He had never heard of such primitive beings, having to go hunting to kill large animals for their food. Nor had he ever conceived of creating art on the walls of a cave to help capture animals.

"Now this is the really interesting part. When you have dreams they all happen inside your head, your thoughts, the images of what you see and everything you hear. Do you understand what I'm saying?"

"Of course, father – I'm not a child anymore."

"Well – imagine this … what if you took all your thoughts and experiences and put them inside a bubble, like our pod, and then travel into space?"

"When did you do that? Could I do it?

"Yes, of course you could. But it would have to be after you finished using your last shell." Lélek left the story there for Sinu to unravel the mystery.

All too soon the story ended and they continued with their initial intention to explore this cave. As one would expect, the young boy's imagination burst into life, thinking that around every corner there would be magnificent works of art and space travelling pods to use. His enthusiasm was so infectious Lélek almost felt himself transported back in time. But time was something that was getting away from them. Eventually growing weary, they stopped to rest.

"Can you remember which way we came?" Sinu asked his father.

Lélek looked around wondering which direction they had come from. They had no light with them. It wasn't needed. The energy charged crystals embedded in the walls gave off enough illumination to see well enough to walk about. "I can't recognise any features. We can't have come too far, but I think we'd better go back."

A wise decision, although a little late. They explored in every direction, not recognising anything about their environment. They were simply lost. Somehow Lélek remembered from his past life the rule of going up, always up if one was ever lost in a cave. What else could they do? So for a while they followed the route of least resistance. They went wherever the tunnels were larger and easier to get through. It was some time before Sinu noticed something.

"Can you feel it, Abu? The draught, coming from up there."

"There must be an exit somewhere close." They hurried with lifted spirits and did eventually find a hole, barely large enough to crawl through. Daylight!

"We made it!" Sinu spun around full circle trying to recognise the landmarks from the morning. "It's all different. We must have come to the other side of the hill."

Their vantage point was slightly elevated so at least they could scan into the distance. Nothing. Neither of them mentioned the fact they didn't even bring the sphere beacon with them. It was only meant to be a short walk. They went around to the other side of the outcrop. Still nothing familiar. The light had completely changed the appearance of everything. The countryside was totally different from the one they travelled through the previous afternoon. All the shadows and all the colours had changed. It was different again from what they marvelled at that morning. Now Lélek understood Ahatu's insistence on all that technology, beacons and maps and so on.

"Come on, let's just sit down and think things through," father said to son. "It must only be a couple of hours back to the pod."

"But in which direction, Abu?"

Lélek only half heard the question as he scanned the rocky hillside landscape. His Ptah memory came to the surface of his mind. He thought it would settle Sinu to hear another story.

"I remember being in country like this before. There lived in the wilderness a creature so ferocious with claws so large and sharp he could kill a man with a single stroke. And he was so cunning. We called him a Nubian Lion. I met this creature when on a journey as a young boy. That was one time when I died suddenly, and had to leave my shell prematurely."

Sinu became completely absorbed in the magical creatures that lived in a land that had a giant river flowing through it; a river so great one could barely see the other side.

While telling the story Lélek noticed one of those giant trees down in the valley in the changing light. "You see the tree down there Sinu, what say we go down there, there's often water nearby."

"Perhaps there might even be some people," Sinu became a little enthusiastic.

It did not seem so far when they first started towards it. Now thirsty and getting hungry the tree seemed to recede into the distance. Lélek was getting seriously concerned for their welfare. He felt their only hope was to either find people near to the tree, or at least a road or a path they could follow to a settlement. By the time they reached the tree the day was well advanced. The two suns would be setting soon. They had to split up and reconnoitre in the near vicinity of the tree. They were lucky to find the shelter of the tree.

"Did you find any water Abu?"

"Sorry son – nothing. There's no sign of people anywhere." They saw no paths, no animals, no glinting of crystalline homes huddled together in the distance. They were alone. As alone as Lélek was when he first travelled in his sphere with his father to Earth's moon, after his death by spears. They went back to the tree. At least it was shelter for the night. Finding a pair of large roots extending out from the trunk of the tree, creating a kind of narrow trough, the two of them settled for the night.

"Time for another story, come closer Sinu." This time Lélek told his son about his adventure in space after his first death by spears. "I started to tell you about travelling into space in a special bubble. Before a Nubian lion killed me, many, many years before that I had another kind of death. I was killed by my own people using a deadly sharp weapon." Sinu's eyes opened as wide as they could, enthralled by his father's many lives and deaths.

"Why would your own people kill you so violently? Did you do something really bad? Couldn't they give you the proper dreams?"

"That part of the story is rather complicated. What happened afterwards is much more interesting. My father met me after my death and showed me how to travel in one of those bubbles. We went into space together to visit our moon." Sinu was fascinated to hear about a planet that didn't have many lights of its own, like their three suns. Restu did not have a moon, and their astronomers had not discovered any planets in their vicinity which did. When Lélek explained how he could move from one place to another, just by thinking about it, Sinu clapped and shouted. It was exactly the way he moved before his sublimation. That was their first common experience and it further strengthened the bond between father and son.

"I'm so thirsty. It would be wonderful if we could do that now. We could just 'think' ourselves home!" A sentiment Lélek could not disagree with.

It was a difficult night to get through. Hunger and thirst kept waking both of them, as well as sounds they had never heard before. It could have been the wind through the arbour of the tree or it could have been wild creatures like the lion that killed Ptah. Sinu wished he could ask his mother to give him better dreams because the ones he was having were not nice at all.

The third day

Morning did eventually come, with no less a spectacular entrance than the previous day. But their ability to enjoy it greatly diminished. The tree had no fruit at this time of the year. They could find nothing else around that was edible.

Lélek looked up the valley and down the valley. He had no idea which way they should go. This was their third day out. There would be no rescue organised at least until the end of the fourth day. Could they manage to stay alive until then? Their biological constitution was far less resilient than Lélek remembered of his Earthly body. He was getting frantic.

How could I have been so negligent! It's not even my native planet, and I behaved like an absolute fool. Sinu had not said much over the last couple of days. Lélek felt perhaps his son was losing faith in him, losing respect for him. He was not losing respect for his son. This was his world – the second time over – perhaps more. He would let Sinu make the decision which way to go. Perhaps he had learnt some things in his classes over the years that would give him a clue.

"Sinu, the situation is very serious. I think you know this. I believe you know this planet better than me. I am going to rely on you now. Which way do you think we should go?"

Sinu made an immediate decision. No hesitation at all, almost as if he knew where he was going. "We'll go down the valley, that way." Lélek was afraid to ask him why, for shame in his own incompetence.

They headed down the valley. Restunian metabolism was not like that of Terrestrials. They could not last as long without sustenance. The charge from the suns was not enough to keep them going. They also needed the energy provided by their food groups. Susceptibility to dehydration was also a big issue. Now Lélek understood why Ahatu had packed so much food and water for them. At the time it seemed like enough provisions to last several weeks.

Along the trek down the valley, they had to stop more and more often to rest. Their energy reserves were running very low. Lélek found his mind starting to wander, and he'd meander away from the direction they were going in. Sinu had to bring him back several times. Behind them they could no longer see the tree, or the curve of the valley they had negotiated. How far had they come? It was impossible to tell.

"Son, I have to stop. Where is your mother? I wish she would bring us some water."

It was late afternoon when they eventually stopped to lie down in the shade of a boulder. Sinu could see his father's mind could no longer function. He had no choice but to stay with his father. He couldn't go far himself for help. Where could he go? "We'll get something to eat in the morning Abu." He eventually fell asleep lying beside his father, with his hand on his father's chest.

The fourth day

When Lélek and Sinu had not returned at the end of the third day, Ahatu immediately contacted Ur.

"How long have they been gone? - I see. Did they have plenty of provisions? - I see. And in spite of that you think they are in difficulties."

"Yes, I have no doubt of it. I can *feel* my Lélek. He needs help – they both need help."

The rescue party could find no sign of them along their registered route after two days extensive searching. Still she could feel they were alive. It would have felt quite different otherwise. Death to them was not a greatly distressing phenomenon. It was more the circumstances that caused pain. Especially if those circumstances were not known. Besides, there should have been some contact by now from the other reality if they had passed over.

The fifth day

Ahatu was correct in her feelings. Lélek and Sinu awoke another day later, not refreshed exactly but feeling much better. Some primitives from a settlement near to where they lay unconscious by the boulder found them on one of their routine excursions. Sinu was the first to recover after the ordeal. The minute he opened his eyes and their rescuers saw the colour their attitude changed. They of course helped anybody in distress, out of a sense of normal compassion. But they helped with an air of dispassionate unconcern. This young boy was different.

The eyes of a "Blue Healer" was a sign recognised by the entire primitives' society. There was a great man amongst them until relatively recently, who had come to the end of his time. His transmutation was still remembered each year. Their host did not know who these travellers were, but to have a young person with blue eyes with them was much too important not to alert the authorities. Within a couple of hours Sinu and Lélek were on their way to the capital city of that region. Lélek learnt later that the planet was divided roughly evenly into two segments; one where Ahatu's people lived and one where the Primitives lived. Their capital city was not far from the border between the two regions. Sinu and Lélek had managed to cross the border and were heading towards the city when they were overcome by exhaustion.

Nearing the centre of the city Lélek was surprised to see the density of population and the crowding of the buildings; some just a few storeys high, and some like skyscrapers. Obviously these people were not 'primitive' as he had originally imagined. The ones he and Ahatu had visited must have been fringe dwellers, perhaps not just geographically but on the fringes of their society as well.

Initially they were taken to a building where a lot of 'official' things seemed to be happening. Lélek had a feeling that it may have had something to do with security. It cast his mind back to Erde, and the overtones of control the people lived under. Sinu, quiet most of the time, didn't answer any of the questions he was asked during the trip.

"I remember some of these things," he said to Lélek quietly, "and I remember I didn't like how some people were being treated."

Argus, the person in charge, took them to a private, comfortable room in the building. "Would you like something to eat, drink?" He asked most amicably. This man was fully aware of the possibilities Sinu's presence represented so didn't want to make them feel 'unwelcome' or unnecessary alarmed. He spoke mostly to Lélek getting the full story from him about their unhappy adventure and the embarrassing situation they found themselves in. He was surprised to learn Sinu was Lélek's son.

While the interrogation was in progress the Spiritual Alliance was alerted to the presence of the youth with blue eyes. Their arrival at the security centre meant the end of the questioning. The two representatives, a male and a female wore sheaths that were overlaid by another material, in very stark black and white patterns.

"I can remember those uniforms. These people are friends, we can trust them," Sinu whispered to his father.

"Would you come with us, please," Gudrun, the female invited them to a larger than normal transport sphere waiting for them outside. Argus had no choice but to let them leave. He had no justifiable reason to detain them. "We are going home," Gudrun said. The sphere already had several occupants; one an elderly lady sitting back with her eyes closed. She didn't open them even when everyone got in.

'Going home' couldn't possibly have meant going home to Ahatu. It didn't make any sense to father and son, until about half an hour later. "Abu, I know this place, I recognise those buildings!" Sinu excitedly told his father he had been here and there. If they had been watching her they would have seen the elderly lady, still with eyes closed, smiling. That is what she wanted to hear. She knew the name of this boy. She knew who he was.

When the excitement in Sinu had settled and he was back in his seat, she opened her eyes and turned to the young boy. Sinu saw her movement out of the corner of his eye and also turned towards her. The old lady reached out her arm and placed her hand on his chest, at the same time opening her nictitating membranes. In an automatic response Sinu did likewise.

"Welcome home father," she said with great affection.

"Thank you daughter, but I cannot stay," responded Sinu.

The two uniformed individuals made some strange movements with their hands, several others came over to Sinu to touch him. Lélek could not believe what he had just heard. He was listening with Earth ears, not with the ears of someone who had travelled across realities several times. It was difficult to take in that he was sitting next to his son whose daughter was more than five times his age. But she was his daughter from the previous life. The others must have been 'distant' family members as well, except perhaps the two 'monks' for want of a better description.

That affectionate interchange broke the ice and the conversations flowed freely between everyone. The first thing Lélek asked, "Could someone please let Ahatu know we are safe."

"It's already been arranged. That's why you were first taken to Security Central. We will return you to our border in a few days," said Gudrun.

Lélek's next question … "Who was Sinu before his transmutation?"

The male monk, Trygve, confirmed everything Sinu had told his father back home. But Sinu had been very modest in revealing his importance. Not only did he carry out his healing work using a variety of techniques, he was also the head of the Spiritual Alliance organization of the Primitives. Lélek learnt that the title 'Primitives' was given to them by the others. It was not the name they called themselves. They referred to themselves as the "Puritanians" primarily because in the past they refused to be contaminated by energy essences other than their own species, originating only from their own side of the planet. The 'others' they called Polymorphs. Lélek was considered to be a Polymorph.

However, they showed him more than the usual respect, primarily because Sinu had chosen him to be his father. Secondly because his reputation had preceded him even into their region. He was a most unusual combination of unique energies, and who was as yet incomplete in his evolution.

"We could use your help, and your son's help to aid the Spiritual Alliance in re-directing our society away from the path of materialistic development," Gudrun said.

"We feel that certain technological advancements will bring catastrophe to our civilisation," added Trygve the monk. "Our scientists are determined to go out into the cosmos to find other species. Perhaps to even find a species that could improve our genetics."

Listening to the monk's story Lélek felt a heaviness descend on him. Memories of Earopian methodology vividly flooded back into his mind. *Could these Puritanians possibly be heading in the same direction?*

"I don't know why you think I could help. Please let me consider this." It was a worrying prospect and he felt he would have to give it deep consideration before responding. He wanted to talk to Ahatu and Sinu. He didn't feel sufficiently Restunian to be able to formulate any unbiased opinions, acerbated by his past unpleasant experience on Erde. During his conversation with Gudrun and Trygve, Lélek wasn't paying attention to Sinu's discussion with his past family. If he had, he would have realised that pressure was being put on him as well. The Puritanians wanted Sinu to return to them; to carry on with his previous work, and to lead the campaign against species exploration.

"Thank you all for your hospitality. My son and I would like to retire to rest for the remainder of the day." Lélek wanted to end the interaction for the day, particularly because of the direction it was taking.

The sixth day

Lélek and Sinu had created what amounted to an 'international' incident. It seems politics was bubbling not far beneath the surface of Restunian society. Their rescue, come 'detention' was considered so serious that the three leaders themselves accompanied Ahatu to retrieve her partner and son. The Puritanians wanted to hold onto Lélek because of his space faring experience, not only for the technological capability to get out there but also navigation, robotics and advanced artificial intelligence systems. Such a situation had the potential to set father against son; Sinu leading the revolt against space exploration and perhaps Lélek working to achieve it.

Argus, from Security Central, intruded on their recovery time. He was not at all happy to lose control of his prize. As convivially as before he greeted the two adventurers, "I trust you have rested well. It is a great pleasure to have you as our guests under such interesting circumstances."

"I can assure you we did not intrude intentionally," Lélek responded. He didn't like this individual. He was too 'smooth'.

"And you, young man – you must be proud of yourself for the way you looked after your father. You're a smart boy. If you would at all consider contributing to the great work we're doing I'm sure both of your contributions would be very much appreciated." Argus was careful not to be too specific, but clear enough to indicate the Puritanians were definitely interested in recruiting them into their society.

Lélek didn't make any commitments. "For now we would prefer to return home and recover."

Argus left with the usual formalities, not yet convinced it was a lost cause. Sinu was only twelve years old and a boy, despite his previous incarnation. The lack of current life experience precluded him from being able to make any kind of balanced judgement about what he could or should do in this situation. Lélek certainly did not want to be a party to the possibility of the kind of abductions and treatments the Earopians carried out. He didn't have the savvy and convoluted wiles of a politician to be able to say yes, while at the same time saying no.

Fortunately, the rescue delegation arrived early the following day.

The seventh day

Argus waylaid the Polymorphs, giving no opportunity for Ahatu to see Lélek and Sinu that day. Diplomatic protocols dictated the day's activities.

In the interests of peace and conviviality a reunion celebration was organised jointly by the Spiritual Alliance and Security Central. However, the issue of detaining the father and son team could not be agreed on, even at the informal discussions during the celebrations. The pressure did not ease up on the young boy. Sinu remembered a dream he once had. A voice in the dream said, *Be true to yourself.* The only way he could do that was by not turning away from the challenge he faced.

"Abu – I'm not sure what I should do." Sinu trusted his father and his opinions.

"Do you want to stay and continue the work you were doing before?" Lélek was half prepared to support his son's decision if that was what he truly wanted to do.

"I do want to help, but I don't want to leave my life with you and Ummu. I will find and nominate a successor for myself."

"A very mature decision, Sinu. I'm proud of you. I want to go home as well. But I can see some serious problems if these people continue with their research direction. And there is still a story I have to tell you, about what happened to me on Erde. But we'll leave that for another day. For now, I feel I must share my experiences with the Puritanians in that regard. It may give them some perspective."

When Sinu announced his decision it helped to ease the tension considerably, as did Lélek's decision to discuss the Earopian's strategy to rejuvenate their species, putting particular emphasis on the lack of success they had achieved and the methods that contributed to that failure.

The eighth day

It was not until the night of the eighth day that Ahatu and Lélek could express their feelings to each other about their reunion. Sinu was allowed to spend the night in the care of the two monks.

The days that followed were full of activity. Ur, Umma and Larsa used the opportunity to learn as much as they could about the Primitive's progress technologically and socially. Lélek gave his presentations about Earopian methods and Sinu eventually found a replacement Blue Healer; a young girl, about twenty-five years old and whose eyes seemed to be undergoing a transformation. Sinu saw in her a gentleness and a strength he felt would be needed if she was to be both a leader and a healer.

The Puritanians could not afford the risk of open hostility, so with a great show of magnanimity they accompanied the delegation to the border, with their 'treasures' safely in tow.

On the way home the convoy picked up Lélek's abandoned sphere. He was embarrassed to see how close it actually was to the cave where they got lost. If they had not gone to the tree, but in the opposite direction they would have found the sphere within an hour or so. Ahatu said no more about it and Sinu now had an extraordinary adventure to present to his class.

For Lélek it was a most difficult lesson to learn. He simply had to temper his enthusiasm with a little more wisdom and forethought. Certainly a lesson he would remember – well after his time on Restu. He also had to learn a great deal more about the "Polymorphs" before he was ever again prepared to put complete and unreserved trust in them. Ahatu was a different matter. They had a connection which transcended species and differences in universes. *If it is ever at all possible, I would like Ahatu to come with me when my time comes for the transmutation.* But this was not a subject he could easily discuss with her – not for a long while yet, perhaps never.

Given all the turmoil inside himself about this civilisation he found himself in, and the uncomfortable feelings the adventure had generated about the people on both halves of the planet, he was unsure how to proceed with the rest of his life.

9th manifestation

Lélek's transmutation
4415AD

Lélek devoted some of his life to study and some to helping Ahatu with her visits. He also spent more time with Sinu. As the boy grew into manhood, father and son discussed the more esoteric nature of Lélek's experiences. They became very close.

"Ever since you told me those stories many years ago, do you remember – when we had our big adventure – I've been inspired to study Thermometabolism."

"A rather rare science," Lélek commented, "even here on Restu."

"I want to understand the connections between energy within living systems and the systems of energy in the cosmic world. I've had this secret ambition to discover the fundamental principles behind the phenomenon I experienced after my first transmutation. And I especially want to know how you were able to meld with other energy entities."

"Indeed a worthy challenge for a man like yourself, my son. I am content to discover those things gradually as I continue along my path."

Lélek had not forgotten what he was told by the strange rotund creature – his evolution was not yet complete. The years had been kind to him and Ahatu. Neither had changed noticeably during Sinu's development. If anything, they had become more devoted to each other. Lélek discussed all his studies and all his thoughts with Ahatu. He even confided his misgivings about the apparent benign nature of the Polymorphs.

One evening, after an intimate reaffirmation of their bond to each other, he quietly told Ahatu, "You know things have changed since I met the Puritanians. I can't help thinking of myself as more of a Restunian than a Polymorph or a Puritanian. I feel uncomfortable with our system of keeping every bit of data on every individual. Not just the details of their daily lives, or their genomes, even the dream-giving technology."

"But you know the good work I do. You yourself have helped me innumerable times." Ahatu wasn't quite sure where this discussion was going.

"We even regularly record conversations; conversations which are just ordinary every day dialogues, as if people were discussing sinister subjects aimed at the ruling hierarchy. Why is it so important to do that?"

"You are in a strange mood tonight, dear. What's brought this on?"

Lélek stuck to his train of thought. "The very fact of having dreams constructed for people in order to modify their thinking, makes me feel extremely uneasy."

"Why haven't you said something before?"

"Don't misunderstand me – I appreciate the benefits of what you're doing and the good intentions with which you do it, but still …"

"Why worry so much. We have a good life amongst good people. Come close – let's get some sleep."

During his studies he had learnt how dreams were constructed and how they were 'given' to people. Although not as sophisticated as the technology needed for artificial intelligence, nevertheless in some respects the techniques were well ahead of anything else he had seen. Essentially, a collage of images would be put together and after digitisation, downloaded into the neocortex of the subject as electrical signals. The brain responded as if the signals were normal sensory input and integrated them into conscious dream thought and dream language.

An individual may ask for the procedure or give permission for the procedure. In some instances the decision is made by family members or other responsible adults. It had become obvious to Lélek that the process was tantamount to absolute censorship. As such it could easily be misused in all sorts of diabolical ways. So far he had not come across any examples of misuse, accidental or otherwise. Even Ahatu had never mentioned such possibilities. Lélek thought that one day he would have to bring up the subject with the leaders and gauge their reactions. Perhaps such interference could affect individuals after transmutation.

Another area of his studies was the methods of data collection and storage. Living a life as simple as his own, and seeing most people also living as simply, he could not understand why there was a necessity for such intensive data harvesting. What was done with all that information? Without divulging his reasons, Lélek decided to embark on a formal course of study with the intention of finding an occupation in the field of Information Intelligence. He discussed his desire with Ur, who was happy to fast track his advancement. Ur of course saw only the benefits to their science of cross pollinating Lélek's existing knowledge, with their own technology.

*

It was some time before Ahatu came to him for professional help. "You've now been in the Dream Maker's department for about two years. How is your expertise?"

237

"Quite good. I can find just about anything about anybody – with a few exceptions."

"I have a request for a male individual. Would you like to help gather some of his personal data?"

"Why?" He didn't mean it to sound so terse, but that's how it came across.

"Why do you think, silly," Ahatu chose not to react. "We've done this many times before. I need to attend a person who's lost his understanding about the dual nature of his existence; to re-align his thinking to help him remember his shell does not represent his entire being."

"Right. What do you need?" It was not difficult to gather the appropriate imagery and make it available to Ahatu.

During the process Lélek discovered many things about this individual. It worried him he could so easily do that ... understanding at the same time that he was in an important and privileged position to do so. But how easily the trust could be abused. This man had not transmuted before. They were the ones most susceptible to this kind of mental ailment. Lélek could also see the man's entire lineage going back many generations. He could see that from time to time some distant members of the family were 'vaporised' because of their alleged danger to themselves or society at large. The details of the transgressions or otherwise were not available at his security clearance level.

Admittedly it was a pleasure to be able to work with Ahatu from his new position, and it gave them long fruitful hours of conversation. Inevitably their discussions came around to the subject of transmutations, and how that was achieved.

Ahatu explained simply, using Lélek's conceptual base. "Everyone has to 'die' at some stage, even if they've had many renewals during their extended life span. There are only two ways that happens. Aided or unaided."

"What happens to them if there is no one to help?"

"Unaided transmutations often end in the energy of the entity being lost in the cosmos. It's rare for such an entity to find its way back for another sublimation. The general practice is an assisted voluntary transition."

Lélek learnt some of the theory from Ahatu, and rounded it off with personal research. The full impact of the process did not hit him until he went to such an event with Ahatu.

"Sinu, Lélek, we all are invited to a sublimation. Apu would like all of us to be with him when he goes.

"Do I know this —Apu?" Lélek asked.

"Why do I need to go," Sinu was mystified as he'd never heard the name before.

"Yes you do. It's an invitation to a special event in this person's life, a very personal event. There must be a very good reason for inviting all of us."

During the preparation Lélek helped put together the visual dream collage – some of it constructed from descriptions given by the person as there were few images available. All Lélek had to work with was a name. So he researched that individual only, without including his family. That was not important given the nature of the request. Lélek realised then one of the reasons for collecting so much data. This was going to be Apu's (short for Apuulluunideeszu), second transmutation, so he had a special request for his final dreaming. Apu choose to re-live his pre-sublimation experiences to remind himself of the nature of the upcoming reality. It was also a form of reassurance that existence did not all end with his passing. He thought he would feel less apprehensive during the journey, in case there was no one there to meet him. At the end of the dream Apu would be released.

Lélek, Ahatu and Sinu all went down to the transport sphere, Ahatu and Sinu chatting happily about various unconnected things, while Lélek became introspective. There were still unresolved issues in his mind about the 'tampering' that went on with another person's thoughts, even if it was at their request and their approval. Apu's home was about an hour away. The closer they got the more Lélek took notice of the countryside.

"Have we been this way before?" He interrupted Ahatu's chatter.

"Yes we have, but a long time ago. You might not remember the people."

When he finally saw the exceptionally colourful dwelling he was certain he had visited previously. Ahatu had said nothing about that.

"Ahatu, Lélek, Sinu, welcome to you all," Apu greeted them at the door, giving the sign of recognition and respect. His partner did likewise.

Still unable to place the face, nevertheless Lélek was taken by surprise. He'd wrongly assumed Apu would be unwell, so unwell he no longer wanted to live. Obviously that was not the case judging from the smiling faces that greeted them.

"Come in, please – make yourself at home." It was indeed a very warm welcome, given the nature of the event. Sinu followed behind his parents into the house, letting his eyes meandered around the room, alighting on the single most beautiful girl he had ever seen in his short, though eventful life. She paid him no attention at all, choosing rather to walk directly over to Lélek the moment she saw him.

"Do you remember?" She whispered.

That's when it hit him like a bolt of triple sun energy – It was little Kaqquru! He couldn't help himself, his arms opened automatically to embrace this not so little girl as she stepped into his embrace. Sinu didn't know what to think. He'd already lost his composure the minute he saw her, and now this. Ahatu and the two parents simply stood there soaking in the warmth of the special coming together of those two special people. No wonder Apu was all smiles when they arrived.

It was a long lingering embrace, at the end of which Lélek introduced his son to little Kaqquru.

"Sinu – this is Little Kaqquru – sorry Kaqquru." She would always be little Kaqquru to him. An instantaneous connection manifested between the two young people.

"Hello Sinu."

"Hello Little Kaqquru." Sinu couldn't help himself. He said it like a like a term of affection between two people who'd known each other for a long time.

"Come closer to me, Sinu." Kaqquru placed her hand on his chest and he put his hand gently on hers. They drew closer together opening their nictitating membranes, seeing into each other for the first time. The encounter seemed to signal Apu's readiness for the transition, judging from the expression of complete peace on his face.

Apu turned to Lélek while the two youngsters were still in their first embrace. "You are surprised, Lélek. Why so?"

"You seem to be in perfectly good health, even at your age." Several hundred years was not uncommon among the more resilient Restunians. "And from what I can see, you are a very happy man."

"Indeed I am, now my daughter has found her partner. Sinu is a good man. I've had a fulfilling life of creativity. As an image maker I've served this society well, bringing colour to many homes and institutions." Lélek's thoughts flashed back to the work he did on the cave walls to help his tribe and Ördog with the hunting.

"You've also pioneered the idea of recording outstanding events in our history with abstract images representing the nature of energies generated by those events, dear," his partner proudly reminded Apu.

"Yes, yes – many things. Now there is no more I can contribute – and I am very tired. My shell is wearing out, like the three others before it. It's time for me to re-invigorate my life force. There is only one way to do that," he looked meaningfully at Lélek.

The process was simplicity itself. After a pleasant meal together with his guests, Apu said his good byes. They all knew that sometime in the future there was always the possibility of meeting again. Apu lay on the main bed and calmed his mind to receive his final dream. Ahatu already had her blue crystal fully programmed and proceeded to download its contents into Apu's neocortex. Even before she completed the task Apu was asleep. This set of dreams was expected to last about two hours. Apu's partner had to monitor his EEG activity during the lucid dreaming stage. It was important Apu knew he was dreaming and why he was dreaming the content he was experiencing. A surge in Apu's EEG would mean he was on the verge of an out-of-the-body experience. It signalled his consciousness was separating from his physical shell. At that point little Kaqquru had to immediately de-activate Apu's shell to ensure the OBE would continue to its natural conclusion and Apu's life energy, totally intact in his thoughts, would transmute to the next level of reality.

Apu must have been in a hurry, because within half an hour he had crossed over. Little Kaqquru and her mother were both happy and relieved it had all gone so smoothly, and Apu had achieved his desire. They all retired back to the eating room to enjoy after meal treats. Lélek had some trouble with the seeming nonchalance with which the whole procedure was conducted. Always, in his past experience, 'death' was such a dramatic event, causing so much turmoil to the people left behind. This seemed so much more natural. The mystery and the darkness and pain and all the fear had been taken out of the event. He even started to feel cheerful himself after a little while.

Sinu and Kaqquru chatted in one corner of the room while the two women discussed something secretive, presumably their children's blossoming relationship. Lélek felt the need to collect his thoughts and stepped outside. The evening had progressed into night. It was dark enough to see the stars. He thought back to the first time he saw the Milky Way in his previous universe, and hoped Apu would find his future path also, perhaps with a little help from Isten. He then realised he'd not thought about Isten for many years.

I wonder if Isten had anything to do with the Restunians all having Akkadian names? A strange thought to have, so much out of context with the events of the last few hours. *Life goes on. Nothing changes and everything changes.* It was always at moments like these he seemed to have revelations thrust into his consciousness. *When my time comes, I don't know if I would want a 'foreign' final dreaming invading my consciousness – but I do like how they can just choose to go – and then it's done. I'll talk to Ahatu about it. I definitely don't want my passing to be unnaturally encumbered.* Lélek also resolved to find out more about the Akkadian connection with this planet.

This last avenue of research proved to be difficult. As good as the records were about individuals, the information about Restunian history, particularly cosmological theology was very sketchy. He remembered Ahatu telling him of a Restunian legend about a great man who would come to them from the stars, from a place called Akkadia. That was about all he could find in the official records. There existed no description of the man or of the era when he was supposed to have lived there. The event must have happened a very long time ago indeed. He had to rely on his memory of what he had learnt while he was studying Earth history back on Erde.

Lélek started to record everything he could dredge up from his past memories. Sometimes he needed to talk it out with Ahatu. Sinu was not around so much these days. What little time he had spare from his studies, he spent mostly with Kaqquru. Both he and Ahatu were most surprised to discover that in Sumerian cosmology 'Kaqquru' was the name given to Earth, the centre of all life in the known universe at the time. Apart from some other general knowledge he had acquired the thing that intrigued him the most was the Akkadian concept of the universe.

"I have not mentioned this before, about my preoccupation with spheres."

"Ah, so that's why you were so good with the pod on your adventure!" Ahatu couldn't resist.

He just smiled and continued, "I was intrigued to discover so many objects in the cosmos were round. Isten said all four universes were spherical and all were connected." When he put that together with the Akkadian idea that the universe was spheroid it made his mind stand to attention. "Just imagine what it was like for me … the first simplest thing I come into contact with here is a spherical transport vehicle … well … what was I to think?"

All these ponderings and discussions eventually became part of Restunian history recording the era when their legends came true, and a great man did in reality come to them from the stars. The longer Lélek lived on Restu and circumstances corralled him towards remembering and pondering his past, the more the distinction between realities began to blur in his mind.

There were times when Ahatu had trouble bringing him back to the present after a long presentation, where Lélek literally re-lived his past in the telling of it. He was now close to ninety-eight years old.

Some years ago Lélek had finally discussed his special desire with her … that he would like her to accompany him to the next reality at his transmutation. Ahatu didn't give him an answer for a very long time. Now she felt the time had come.

"Once, when we discussed your transmutation dear, you asked me a very personal question."

"Yes, I remember. Have you decided?"

"If we wait any longer to give you a new shell you will just disappear into interspatial reality. I don't think you want that." They often joked about that.

"You know I don't want a new shell. This is very painful for me. I don't want to leave you, but there is this thing driving me. I have to answer the call. I feel I'm ready to go."

"That's what I want to talk to you about. For some time now I've been in touch with Gudrun and Trygve – the two Puritanian monks."

"Yes, I remember them."

"Unfortunately, their fight to prevent the continued development of space exploration has failed."

"Why are you telling me this?"

Ahatu was not interested in the politics of the situation, but she was interested in whether a person had been sent into space. Apparently the growth of the technology had evolved at a phenomenal rate. Not only had a person travelled into space, it had become a regular occurrence. Lélek waited patiently to hear what interesting thing Ahatu had to say about that.

"I have a plan that might satisfy both my desire to continue life on Restu with Sinu and Kaqquru, and your need at the same time. I've made some special arrangements with the Puritanians."

"Oh?"

She went on to explain, "They are going to help with your transmutation."

"How could they possibly help?" It wasn't what he wanted.

"They will help me to go part of the way with you – But I will have to return."

He saw the sense in what she had to offer. He had to admit his own greater ambition precluded Ahatu from accompanying him. She was simply not sufficiently advanced to be able to cope with the environment he was planning on visiting.

"I've made all the arrangements in confidence with Gudrun and Trygve. Only our immediate family here knows what we intend to do."

"Good."

"Our three leaders might prevent us from going if they found out." Ahatu understood the situation better than Lélek thought she had.

"As much as I like them, I don't entirely trust them." Lélek was right to be suspicious so many years ago about the undercurrents of control in the Polymorph's society.

'We are going on a little holiday."

"Yes, that sounds good – when?" he was cautiously interested.

"Soon - an extended family excursion to visit the caves you and Sinu discovered."

"And ...?"

"You'll see. But you have to be certain of what you want for yourself."

The family of four set out towards the other side of the planet within the week. By the time they had arrived at the launch facility in Puritanian territory everything had been arranged. As well as the normal chambers on the craft, a special one was set up for Lélek's transition. There Ahatu could monitor his EEG and de-activate the shell at the right moment.

"You did this for me?" His hand was on her chest, nictitating membrane open. He could scarcely believe Ahatu had so much love for him – to want him so completely and yet be prepared to give him his freedom. "You did this for me! Ahatu – *Ahatu*." She was seeing him as he was seeing her – unreservedly.

"Don't say anything. This is for you, for Sinu, for all of us. This is how it must be."

Lélek was quite certain he would never again return to Restu. The temptation was considerable. It was the only place where he had enjoyed life. He was with Ahatu his perfect companion, and she had given him an extraordinary family. But he felt his time had come. He had lived long enough, longer here than anywhere else he had been before. Sinu was a wonderful son. Better than he could ever have hoped for. It was impossible to consider fathering a child on Erde, especially after he found out what they were really like.

There were certainly things about the Restunians he had difficulty coming to terms with - sure. Still, on balance, he was satisfied with his life. However, the pull of the great mystery could not be overcome.

At the last evening meal with the family, attended also by Gudrun, Trygve and Argus from Security Central, some of the practical details were sorted out.

"As soon as possible after your transition you must establish a communication link with Ahatu," instructed Argus. "We expect regular reports of your experiences, in detail."

"I will record everything and relay it down to Gudrun regularly," Ahatu confirmed.

After the meal Lélek was shown the technique he should use to communicate with Ahatu. Trygve explained. "Form an image of Ahatu in your mind, picture yourself putting your hand on her chest. When you feel she's reciprocated, simply think your words to her." There was no way to practice the procedure because he had to be 'dead' to actually do it.

The entire event was treated without any special ceremony. Although the Spiritual Alliance had a vested interest, they did not put undue pressure on Lélek. During his lifetime Lélek had earned the respect of many individuals and factions on the planet. The monks trusted he would supply as much information as he could about that next reality.

Early the following morning everyone said their farewells. Kaqquru seemed to be most affected by Lélek's leaving. There was some kind of special bond between the two which neither of them ever questioned. They were always especially contented in each other's company whenever the occasion arose.

Ahatu and Lélek made their way to the hatch of the spacecraft and continued on their way in without turning around.

An hour later they were in space, heading out beyond the orbit of their first sun. There was not much left to say. Ahatu knew his mind was made up. They spent a while enjoying the spectacle. Particularly Ahatu, for this was the first time she had ever experienced seeing their world floating in space. They did not speak. What was there left to say after a long and satisfying life?

Disengaging from a last embrace they both retired to the specially equipped chamber. Lélek lay on the bed. Ahatu didn't have to use her blue crystal this time. She just had to sit and listen to Lélek telling his story. The bed was comfortable and formed itself to his shape so perfectly that within minutes he could no longer feel the weight of his shell. Looking up at the ceiling, which was painted canary yellow and had the symbol of the three palm prints, made him smile – a little surprise arranged by Ahatu. He prepared by orienting his mind to dream of specific events from his life, culminating in the vision of seeing his son for the first time. He felt that would give Ahatu the clearest EEG peak signal for when he was ready. He reached out to take hold of her hand, which was already hovering near him.

With one hand on the deactivation button and the other in Lélek's embrace Ahatu listened to the beginning of his story. It had all the happy memories, from Lélek's previous lives and the lives of his melded entities. It was the first time she had heard so much detail. Eventually his words faded as he fell into a deep sleep. He'd let Ahatu's hand slip from his, but she placed her palm softly on his chest. She was intent on watching the monitor. There must have been many happy memories in his life for it was at least a couple of hours before she saw the EEG peak. She de-activating his shell.

Lélek had taken so long Ahatu had almost missed the moment. She had witnessed the process many times and there was nothing different happening before her. For a moment she almost wished she had joined him as she watched all the energy surge to an area in the centre of his forehead. It made Lélek's whole head glow, while the rest of the shell returned to a dull off-white, lifeless piece of inert material. The light continued to intensify in short bursts around the head until it almost pulsed to the rhythms of a heartbeat. Just as suddenly as it had flowed to his forehead, the intensity began to fade. Ahatu could not see where the energy was going, it was simply fading away. The transmutation was almost complete. An empty shell devoid of all life and all personality lay slowly caving in on itself. In a little while she could dispose of it, but for the moment Ahatu had to stay alert and concentrate.

The next little while would see the success or failure of her concept. She relaxed into the chair and let her mind drift. That seemed a better strategy than what she was told during the briefing. It seemed to her that if she was concentrating that could put up a barrier to thoughts coming from Lélek. In that she was right. The two realities were completely different, although intimately connected. The only hope of bridging the gap was to make the borders as soft and fuzzy as possible. Ahatu's mind became so relaxed she fell into a light sleep. No doubt the day's activities and the extended transmutation contributed to her languor.

It started more as a daydream. Thoughts of the day's activities slowly turning to images of their final meal, then to their approach to the space craft. The more her mind progressed through linear time towards the present moment, the more the images focused themselves until it seemed like a reality re-lived.

Ahatu saw herself sitting beside Lélek watching as her hand suddenly pushed the button. She saw again Lélek's essence gathering in the centre of his forehead, but this time, instead of seeing his energy fade, she saw an image of him reform itself.

He stood there beside her looking down at her in the chair. Simultaneously as she stood her observing self became part of the standing image and the interior of the vessel melted away to reveal the darkness of space. Lélek had already placed the palm of his hand on her chest and she automatically did likewise.

"Come with me, let me show you." At first Ahatu only saw his most wonderful, warm smile. She heard his words in her mind without seeing his lips move. Lélek was so concentrated on making contact with her he didn't notice a most important development – he was no longer a captive in his own thought sphere.

"Describe what you see," he asked while still absorbed in the spectacle before them.

Ahatu knew somewhere in her mind she was having an out-of-body experience. She had studied the phenomenon as part of her training as a dream maker, but this was her first personal experience of it. She turned slowly towards the spacecraft and saw herself sleeping in the chair, with Lélek's shell almost completely collapsed upon itself. With their hands still on each other they seemed to move further out into space, so far that the ship became just a speck in the cosmos. She looked around herself and saw their three suns orbiting in the darkness. Ahatu tried to use words to express herself, but they were not adequate to the task.

"We can go further." This was a shared experience of immeasurable pleasure for Lélek, the first time he was able to give of himself so completely. Lélek took her much further out. So far out she could see how their trinary system was only a small part of the arm of their galaxy. She saw what appeared to be a rotating disk of billions of lights, all part of several arms originating at the bright centre of their galaxy. She gazed at the immensity of the garden of their world, unable to describe the magnitude and the splendour. She looked beyond into the darkness and saw other nebulae phenomena she could not comprehend in any meaningful way.

She heard Lélek whisper, "I will show you more."

She turned to look at him but he was gone. She closed and opened her eyes several times to try and clear her vision. Ahatu was sitting in the chair and all she could see was the wall of the special chamber. She became aware of being extremely hungry. Her mind couldn't immediately recall the events of the last few hours, while concentrating on satisfying that hunger.

I must have dozed off for a minute …

Then images came flooding back; Lélek standing beside her (she glanced quickly at his shell – it was there and completely shrunk), saying something to her, then they were outside the craft.

What time is it? The clock showed eight hours had elapsed. Her mind began to clear. *Could it have been eight hours ago? I must have been out of my body. It was so real! He said he would show me more. How will I make contact?*

Before fully satisfying her hunger and even before disposing of the crumpled shell, Ahatu recorded her recollections, and sent them to the monks, who promptly confirmed receipt of the transmission.

Hunger had jumbled her thoughts and forced her to eat again. Back in the cockpit she checked her position in space. The ship was still travelling away from Restu. She decided to get some sleep right after cleaning up the transmutation chamber. *It feels so odd, his shell all shrunken. I was with him only a little while ago, strolling in the garden of the cosmos. So strange.*

Lélek was elated he was able to make contact with Ahatu. It was a decision of extreme difficulty for him to leave his family. *I just don't understand why the Great Design has to include such partings, to engender such a deep sense of loss. What possible purpose could it serve? I must ask Isten. Surely he knows all there is to know.*

...

Isten heard and considered. *He's right about the pain of separation. There is a reason, which you will discover soon enough, my little phenomenon. Knowing all there is to know – that may be up to you, my beautiful seed!*

9th manifestation

Lélek's legacy
2127 and 4415AD

"Context."

With that one word, Isten announced his presence. It was not surprising he made himself felt so soon after Lélek's passing over. An entity at a much advanced stage of evolution such as himself, should have felt he had an imminent rebellion on his hands. In previous existences the ties to physical reality had not been as strong for Lélek as in this last one. Isten felt heartened Lélek had finally started to ask questions in the more important realms of the unknown. There were many things he didn't know himself yet.

"It all depends on your perspective," Isten continued when he had Lélek's attention. "For example, reach out with your hands and tell me what you can feel."

In an instant, the old, wise, much experienced man of many realities had become a child again caught in the fascination of all things mysterious. "I can touch … nothing … where … is my sphere?"

"You are now as much a part of the energies of the cosmos as I am. There are few restrictions for you other than your own ignorance. Accept that you no longer exist as a physically solid object. Nor are you simply a bundle of thought energy. You have taken the first step towards becoming part of the fabric of the universe. Remember how Ahatu showed you how to weave the material with which to cocoon the entity of your son? This is something like that, but at much higher frequencies ... beyond anything imaginable by intellects formed of physical matter."

Lélek tried to concentrate on what Isten was saying. Little phrases set his mind wandering. *My ignorance ... fabric of the universe ... your son.* He meandered from the absolute unfathomable to the solidity of relationships. He started thinking about his second parents, Yon and Ide, his friends and his journey to the Bükk mountains. Christin flashed into his memories, his first real love, only to be lost because of an impossible situation. Isten recognised his needed to grasp something solid with his mind; some sense of his past – things that were real to his senses.

"Do you want to see Christin?"

It still always amazed Lélek that his thoughts were as transparent to Isten as crystal clear mountain water. Even before he could formulate the words of affirmation, the two of them were looking down at a small neat house in an idyllic setting on the outskirts of Wolfsberg, Austria ... Earth, in the year 2127AD. It took a little while for Lélek to realise that in a single instant they had travelled from one universe to another and from one time in history to a much earlier one. What now existed as reality for him no longer depended on a time framework. It was simply a function of its presence in his thoughts.

Christin was taking a young child for a walk across a field towards a wooded corner of the village. The child had lagged behind and Christin called out to him, "Come on Lelkem, keep up darling."

The child's name was obviously in remembrance of himself. It immediately sent his emotions into turmoil.

He is still too attached, thought Isten, fading from his consciousness. There was nothing to be gained by lingering in that singular manifestation. Isten had already taken him forward by the time Lélek regained some equilibrium.

He found himself staring at Ahatu's craft. Ahatu had tried everything after the first encounter to contact him. She tried the visualisation method as explained to Lélek, she tried going to sleep with dreams concentrated on him. Even tired herself out deliberately so she would fall into a daydream, hoping that would open the communication channel. Nothing worked. Weeks had passed and now her craft was well out of visible range of Restu. Communication with the monks had become sporadic and increasingly more difficult. Their three suns' magnetic fields were causing considerable difficulties. She didn't know whether to continue on the outward trajectory or return home. Ahatu determined to get a little rest, then with a clear mind make a decision.

Sleep didn't come easily. Eventually beta waves gave way to alpha waves as her mind started to relax. Worrying thoughts were replaced by vivid sensations. For a moment she felt like she was falling, then suddenly she heard her name called. It was Lélek's voice. *'Oh my suns, I'm hallucinating!'*

"Ahatu." There it was again.

She reached out her hand, and there he was, with his chest against it. He smiled and seemed to sit down beside her on the bed. They didn't go out into space this time.

"Why did you take so long? I thought you were not coming back. I was about to return home."

"It seemed like only a moment to me. So much has happened."

Ahatu remained lying down, and Lélek told his story, sitting beside her, with their hands on each other. He left nothing out. Not even the little boy called Lelkem. "I don't know if he's my son, yet I felt very close to the boy." Christin and Lelkem were both a part of him. There was no hint of jealousy in Ahatu. She felt even closer to him than ever before. The depth of his revealed feelings reminded her why she had chosen him in the first place. Most importantly he told her about Isten. "I've told you about Isten before. It said I was becoming part of the fabric of the universe, and I had to let go. I don't know what that meant. Perhaps it's some mundane process that just happens, randomly like everything else in existence, though I hope not.

Ahatu woke after a good long sleep. As soon as she was fully awake she recorded everything she could remember of her 'dream'. Whether it was dream or something else didn't matter. She was certain Lélek had been with her. But after what he had said about attachment she was not sure how many more times he would return. Ahatu finished the recording. After putting the craft into a slow decline back to Restu she settled into a more relaxed routine. She was prepared to wait.

Down on Restu the monks were getting restless. The last communication from Ahatu was weeks ago. Already she'd been out there longer than planned. If nothing had happened to her then her diminishing supplies would force a return soon. The information she sent back so far seemed 'ordinary' without any great revelations they could discern. Perhaps later, when everything was received, a picture would emerge. They fervently hoped the effort it took to get them into space was going to be worth it. They were starting to have their doubts. Still the monks put their best minds on the job to see what they could make of the things Ahatu had recorded.

While Ahatu waited and the monks deciphered, Lélek continued evolving towards his potential.

From Lélek's perspective Isten was not giving away very much. After his discussion with Ahatu, Lélek was again joined by Isten manifesting as a voice inside his head … no that's not accurate … he no longer thought of having a head … he just thought of himself as being there. Like a breeze wafting through a large stadium is there. You can't hold it or see it, but it fills the void with its presence. That's how he felt … like he was filling the void about him. The voice of Isten was simply a sound in that void, like the voice of his own thoughts. The sound invited him to expand his presence; to stay where he was, yet encompass in his presence the planets around him.

Lélek found it seemed to happen just by thinking of it, without any effort. He was no longer looking at the spheres in his part of the cosmos, he was containing them in his mind. Yet he could still visualise a form of himself as a corporeal entity. He concentrated hard on that for a moment. There were still things that physical manifestation had to do. However, his thoughts were interrupted by a harmony of sounds. They separated themselves into three distinct tunes. One of the melodies modulated to become words in his thoughts which did not originate from himself or Isten.

"We are Sound Masters. There are more of us, but not many. We sing the melody of the universe you are in. There are separate melodies for the other three universes. The symphony originates from the centre of all existence. Listen – learn – or return."

Although he understood the words, as single words, he could feel no sense of individuality from the originator of the words. They were extraordinary sounds of winds and storms and heat and cataclysms, of planets swirling in space and of suns and galaxies rushing towards each other. The sounds that followed were like a Siren Song – utterly irresistible – and etched deeply in his mind. They must have embodied the Great Mystery, all the questions and all the answers that could ever exist.

Why had it taken so long for me to hear this melody? "Can I become a part of the symphony?" He found himself asking. He couldn't hear the response. There were still attachments in him fighting for domination. He knew he must be of single mind, to use the full force of his energy for one purpose only. He must let go of his past. All of his past – his parents, Christin, his sons Lelkem and Sinu, and his Ahatu … the single most important part of his existence - Ahatu. He saw her again in his mind. She was resting in her craft, with her head on a table, breathing gently, rhythmically.

This visitation was going to be the hardest so far. He thought it would be his last. It was easier to expand into a void to hold a galaxy than to coalesce into a bundle of thoughts within a recognisable body and stand beside his Ahatu. He touched her mind with a soft thought. She opened her eyes and looked about the chamber. There was no one there.

"Lélek, is that you?"

He was barely able to bring enough of himself into the space for Ahatu to see a swirling light contained in an approximate outline of who he once was. There was not enough density in him to be able to put his hand on her chest, but she reached out and her hand disappeared into the cloud before her. Their thoughts touched. Ahatu looked into his mind and he told her about the songs of the cosmos. She heard everything he had heard when the Sound Masters came to him. She saw the galaxy contained within his aura.

As Lélek withdrew for the last time, he left a little of himself with her. She would take the sounds of existence back to her planet. When Ahatu had finished listening to the irresistible cosmic melodies, Lélek simply faded.

Altogether she had three visitations with Lélek, spaced many weeks apart. She had been in space for several months, much longer than anticipated, and she had travelled much further out than expected. So far away that all communication between herself and the monks had ceased. Towards the end of three months they had given her up as lost in space and were on the verge of discontinuing the surveillance when they received a message. It started with some descriptions again, ending in some strange sounds that were completely incomprehensible to them.

"I'm coming home. Lélek has departed on his journey."

The descriptions made some sort of sense, but the sounds left them bewildered. In their entire evolution, music had never become a part of their culture. The monks found the noises most unpleasant and thought at first they were produced by malfunctioning equipment. To have no music must have caused a peculiar blockage to their mentality, perhaps resulting from the restrictive influences of their systems of materialism and religion. Kaqquru, on the other hand cried when she heard the melodies. She was not sad or depressed. There was no other way she could express the joy and beauty she felt. Sinu was also greatly overcome with emotion. They did not understand it, yet heard Lélek's spirit talking to them out of those sounds.

Ahatu turned out to be an incredibly creative person with extraordinary powers of improvisation. She had used everything she could find in the spacecraft to reproduce the melody Lélek had given her. She was not satisfied with it, and determined to do it properly when she returned home. Though not happy with the quality of her reproduction, she did have time on the way back to contemplate what she had heard. With a combination of her own intuition and most probably with some help from the Lélek she once knew, she managed to work out a rudimentary message contained in the lilting sounds. Perhaps it was just her imagination, for she certainly did not understand much of it. Nevertheless, she made a note of her findings and on arrival passed it onto the two monks.

They, not being of a scientific disposition, or with any scientific training the message was gibberish to them. At best the message could be used by the Spiritual Alliance as a bargaining tool with the Puritanians.

Chaos is essential.

Imbalance is mandatory.

The universes are a change-space continuum.

Gudrun, the more astute of the two monks pointed out one interesting little thing they could argue over. "Interesting, don't you think, this idea of multiple universes."

Trygve was adamant, "You must have written it down wrong, Ahatu. Everyone knows there was only one universe."

"No, I've written it exactly as I understood it. I will not change it. If you recall, in one of my early reports I did in fact mention exactly four universes."

In spite of her adamant stance, Ahatu was welcomed with great excitement. She had been in space longer and had gone further than anyone else before. She was able to navigate her way back, and despite the mysterious content of her transmissions, she was successful in communicating in detail with a transmuted entity, one who was on their way out, not on their way in.

All three members of the family, Ahatu, Sinu and Kaqquru made an extensive study of everything Ahatu experienced. They became experts, sought after for their depth of understanding. An entirely new branch of philosophy arose from their contemplations. Kaqquru also proved to be extremely skilled in music. It was as if she had seen the soul of the man they called Lélek, and was able to create music to reflect every aspect of him. What she composed went even beyond that. The compositions gave listeners an insight into the nature of existence. The melodies were beyond the realms of interpretation; they were a spiritual experience. Sinu found he had a skill in creating instruments that could produce exactly the sounds Kaqquru needed.

Within a few years a whole new segment of society emerged dedicated to the purity that could be evoked by Kaqquru and Sinu. Ahatu had decided she needed a new shell. There was still much to be done to improve the quality of life in their small part of the cosmos, before she left in search of her Lélek. She spent a good deal of her time satisfying the needs of both sides of Restunian cultures in understanding the teachings of Lélek. Not just the messages from his departing journey, but also the way he lived his life and the stories he told of his past existences, both corporeal and the in-between states.

In spite of all her efforts very little changed on either side of the globe. The pursuit of materialism and technology by the Puritanians continued unchecked, as did the pursuit of power and control over the population by the Polymorphs.

These things were no longer the concern of the man once known as Lélek. He had not forgotten them; they just became a part of who he had evolved to be. Neither a small, nor a large part, just a part. It was no longer accurate to refer to him as Lélek, because that conjured up the spectre of an individual contained within certain boundaries. Limitations of his belief in his own capabilities, his longevity in linear time and the restrictions imposed by a corporeal shell: None of those now applied to him. He was no longer a 'him'. Though in his own thoughts he still recognised a sense of uniqueness, of having thoughts which were his only. He could still distinguish between what was himself and Isten or the Sound Masters, or existence expressed in physical form.

Lélek dispersed out of Ahatu's spacecraft cabin, severing all ties, perhaps not all attachment. He'd achieved greater freedom than could be imagined … at a considerable cost. Time became a toy, to bounce up and down or sideways; or perhaps simply a thing to forget. Space was no longer a medium to have to travel through. It was a state of mind. As fast as a thought could come and go, that was the speed with which he could manifest himself in one location or another, one time or another. It was all the same.

…

You have much more to learn, my darling, before your final journey. You are still thinking with a finite mind, you still think of yourself as on object of existence though you might think it strange and wonderful.

10th manifestation

the tetrahedral site
4415AD

Lélek felt a change of vibrations in his space before he heard the harmony of sounds. Isten also made his presence felt again. The harmony continued in the background. The sound vibrations somehow reorganised Lélek. They made order out of the chaos of his thoughts. Concepts that were right were given precedence over misconceptions, which were relegated to the background – but never destroyed, for they also carried with them some of the energy that was Lélek. Questions were prioritised, and knowledge suspended. For all knowledge was subjective and required an overhaul from time to time. Emotions were bridled, for it was imperative to bring such powerful driving forces under control. Memories, the substance of all his experiences, were stored with multilevel cross referencing to ensure the most efficient recall at the slightest provocation. After all, he was the sum total of his experiences, combined with his experience of others experiencing him, added to his experiences of experiencing himself.

The new Lélek was ready to continue his journey. He was aware he had been manipulated, sharpened – streamlined. He was also harbouring an exciting expectation that wherever he was heading, it was getting nearer. Not so much an end – more a focusing.

"Lélek!"

He felt compelled to move towards the sound of his name. He recognised that sound and knew it was Isten. The last time he had obeyed that command he had almost turned to stardust.

Isten opened his mind and Lélek entered. This time he could see and hear and communicate with Isten without Isten having to dilute itself to safeguard his mind. They must have travelled a long way very quickly. The melodies had changed and nothing Lélek saw was familiar.

"We are in the third universe," to answer your question.

Lélek saw nothing but clouds of interstellar dust and gas. The colours and patterns made him think of all the colours of crystal reflections at dawn on Restu, and the colours of the sheaths of the Restunians. Space darkness only highlighted the chaos of those colours, as a cacophony of sounds seemed to stir up the nebulae into discordant interaction.

"Is there sentient life here? It hardly seems possible in this exquisite chaos."

"There is the will. Thought energy exists but it does not know itself yet. Look into that purple yellow cloud. It is a stellar nursery. Soon a star will be born. If the will is strong enough planets could be born of the star or from the surrounding dust. But the will must be pure and strong."

"Whose will?"

"Those working with the Sound Masters. The Sound Masters can only create the waves of melody which activates the cosmic dust. It is gravity that must bring them together to dance in each other's embrace. Gradually thought will come to know itself out of that enfolding and be able to contribute to creation."

Lélek wanted to ask who it was that worked with the Sound Masters, as well as myriad other questions. Before the pattern of energies could form themselves into those words, the scene again changed dramatically. The discordant concert had morphed into absolute silence in a soup of complete blackness, absolute tangible nothingness invaded his mind. He thought something must have happened to his capacity to perceive existence. His mind made blinking actions to try and clear the obstruction. No change. He still felt Isten's presence, without which he would most certainly have panicked.

"When you grow accustomed to the stillness you will see all that can be seen."

Lélek turned his thoughts in every direction and had difficulty in acclimatizing to the sudden change from the nebulous universe. "Have we moved again?"

"Yes. This is the last of the four universes you need to experience. It is also your portal. I will not go with you from here, but I will wait for you – at your original home."

Gradually he began to discern circular patterns of different sizes. Some looked like circles turned sideways at various angles, some were distorted into asymmetrical ovaloids. Some seemed stationary while others appeared to rotate. As he watched he observed an even stranger phenomenon. He could not actually see them per se, or at least what he could not see were the faint stars hidden by their shapes. As always, Isten gave Lélek time to ponder and understand. But It could see these phenomena had escaped his understanding.

"They are a characteristic of every universe, except there are many more here, which can attract and swallow all substance and even light itself. It is the only force in the physical universe which can affect us in our reality. We must all be wary of not straying too close for they will surely swallow us. There is no escape from a black hole."

Lélek found the next sentence totally unexpected and totally terrifying. At his stage of his evolution he should not have felt terror, but there it was.

Just another indication the road still stretched into the distance ahead of him.

"You must go through a black hole." Isten said it quietly, without any undue emphasis on 'must'. Lélek was struck dumb, absolutely petrified. Not a fear of terror ... not a fear of unbearable pain ... the kind of fear that descends like a fog of insurmountable incomprehension. "Only when you feel you are ready." Isten prompted quietly, reassuringly.

Numbness slowly left his frozen thoughts and he blurted out, "How can I be ready – how can anybody be ready for this! It is worse than dying the physical death. I thought *that* was traumatic!" He was almost at the point of losing all composure when he felt a restraining force take control of his mind and steady it from completely careering out of control.

"I said I will wait for you. If you are to be with me, you have to do this. I too had to have the experience. You will survive."

"What do you mean 'be with you'?" Lélek was distracted from the terror momentarily.

"A part of you has grown from my seed. I am well pleased with its growth. I must reclaim that energy to maintain balance in the cosmos."

Isten's words gave him a lot to think about. It also gave him courage. With a sudden burst of intent he disengaged himself from Isten's presence and aimed himself directly at the closest black hole. "Where will this take me?" He asked as his energy already felt the pull towards the blackness.

"To the Tetrahedral Site."

That was not what he wanted to hear. Lélek was hoping for something a little more informative. Time was not on his side to work out the meaning of 'tetrahedral site'. Besides, he was distracted by another fabulous looking spectacle all his energy was speeding towards. This particular black hole had ornamented itself with an enormous sphere composed of photons moving along tangents to the sphere. All his life, in all his existences, Lélek had a preoccupation with spheres. This was the second most majestic manifestation he had ever seen. The first sphere from a distant other life could not compare. Such a sphere had to be observed and enjoyed. It had to be touched and experienced. Such a unique work of art is highly unstable. Consequently, when Lélek's energies, accumulated over eons, pierced the sphere, it exploded into a brilliant display of sparking photons. Some were trying to escape the pull, others succumbed to it, diving into the hole with Lélek.

The photon sphere provided enough distraction to prevent him from dwelling on the inevitable. Whereas before, when he had broken free of Restu and had expanded to encompass an entire galaxy, now he was getting squeezed. He could feel his essence being accelerated to speeds faster than thought itself, and crushed in on itself. No pain, just an omnipotent hug that threatened to annihilate even his memory of his own existence. He tried concentrating on his own essence.

I am Lélek - born of Earth - father of Sinu - husband of Ahatu – student of Isten … I am Lélek - born of Earth - father of …

He could not think beyond that phrase. He started again. *I am Le …. I am … I … I … I ….*

For an atto-second of infinity Lélek ceased to exist beyond the singularity of self. The "I" reverberated within itself almost to the boundary of annihilation. Lélek had entered the core of the black hole − from which he was ejected as if an impurity had infiltrated an omniscient sanctuary. The echoing "I" joined together with every other "I" into a long string of screaming, out of which emerged a consciousness, which recognised itself as having once been "Lélek".

*IIIIIIIIIamamamamLeLeLéleklekbornbornbornofofEarthert
hfatherofofofSinuhusband of o f Ah hatsustud entof I sten…*

With great effort his mind pulled together the fabric of his being. He examined the order that had been created by the Sound Masters out of the chaos of his thoughts and experiences, finding the record of his most recent experience … the journey into the black hole. Reassured he was himself again he turned his thoughts outwards and beheld a space teeming with manifestations of light. Most of the shapes he could not recognise. Some were just amoebic blobs of energy, others long and thin and flexible, with every variation of forms in-between. Yet others were almost recognisable.

His mind's eye focused on one of these, for no particular reason other than it seemed to be growing larger, as if it was approaching him. It moved without any visible means of locomotion, and as it neared, its form clarified. A halo of light was around it and inside the halo was a figure of turbulent energies, like the surface of the sun. The closer it came to Lélek the more he thought he could recognise the general 'feel' of the figure, the way it held its head, the angle of the shoulders, perhaps even the little stoop of the back.

Lélek caught his breath - *It can't be! Impossible* –

"Is … is that you Elliou?" The apparition had stopped beside him.

The figure remained silent. She took Lélek by the hand. He looked down and saw he had reformed his old self-image, including his hands – and Elliou led him well away from the swirling mass of entities. She pointed towards what looked like a nice comfortable rock to sit on.

I don't understand what is happening – I must be hallucinating – that black hole has restored chaos to my mind. That rock – I remember that rock!

So the two of them sat side by side and looked out into the Tetrahedral Space. They sat there for some time enjoying each other's company, marvelling at the spectacle around them.

"Did you find your favourite star?" Elliou asked his mind. Lélek immediately turned towards her and hugged her – he could not understand how he could do that, now that he was pure energy.

"Yes," he said after a while, with the voice of the small boy who was once her favourite. "It *is* you! How is this possible?"

"Always so full of questions. I thought I recognised you, looking all lost. I have had a complicated journey getting here. I don't know how long it's taken and I don't know how long I've been waiting. I didn't even know why I was waiting until I saw you."

"I have never forgotten you," whispered Lélek, with the emotional voice of a little child.

"Come back into your true self, my little one. There are things you must learn." Taking him by the hand again she led him into the middle of the frenetic activity.

"Watch."

Lélek couldn't work out what he was supposed to be looking at. It all seemed totally chaotic. Bundles of misshapen light moving about at random. A meaningless tumult of activity seemingly achieving nothing other than generating more pandemonium. Still he concentrated his mind because his teacher had asked him to. In his peripheral vision he thought he noticed new clusters emerging out of nowhere. So he focused on a particular area. Sure enough new formations arrived regularly, and from all directions, yet the place did not seem to get any more crowded or any more chaotic.

He let his mind meander around the arena of these manifestations. The further he extended his scrutiny the larger the space became but it did not feel 'open' or limitless. It had a sense of place about it. Not exactly like his original thought bubble, but sort of like it – though much, much bigger. Elliou let him explore without interrupting. The more he came to realise of his own accord the better. Lélek watched all that energy literally seething in and about itself. He tried focusing on a discrete bundle as it twisted itself through the throng.

It came into contact with another 'lost' wanderer. For a moment they stood motionless, then parted to continue on their meaningless way. Keeping an eye on this flotsam he saw it come into contact with another. Immediately the two melded, temporarily getting larger, then coalescing into a denser more vivid concentrated mass. He kept an eye on the same mass only to see it repeat the process many times. Each time becoming brighter and denser.

Broadening his field of scrutiny, Lélek saw that all the castaways were going through the same process, while at the same time new entities kept arriving out of nothingness.

"What is happening here?"

"I thought you'd never ask," Elliou teased affectionately. "This is where the engine of all existence turns. It is The Centre. It is from here that all that there is, is determined. Will it continue to exist? Will it remain the same? Will it change? The energy of life, all life, sentient and otherwise comes here to be reconnected, to be renewed. When they leave here they are powerful. They will re-energise each of the four universes as directed by the Music Masters and the Architects."

Who', he thought to himself.

"Ah – you think you have not met any of the Architects. You have, and you will recognise them when you see them again."

"But where are we?"

"We are at The Centre. There is a space formed as the four universes join together. Only four can join and still have each one touching every other one. There must be only one Centre. It is the Tetrahedral Site. The thought energy of all living existence must eventually come here, and from here go out again. As they fuse with one another they reach a limit. When at that limit, they must break through the intra-universal membrane and be ready to re-manifest. This process is the breath of life of the four universes. They must breath in and breathe out, they must contract and expand. Every now and again there is a dramatic expansion caused by an excessive accumulation of energy at The Centre."

True to form, during Elliou's monologue, Lélek was listening with only half a mind. The other half already considering possibilities. He burst into the middle of another explanation emanating from Elliou. "You said change is determined here. How is that change brought about?"

"I believe this is why I had to wait for you, to answer this one question. I don't know what role you are destined to play in the 'future', but you must understand the answer to your question before you can move on."

Elliou let him ponder the idea. He had to find in himself the desire to continue on his indeterminate path or to stay and meld and become the stuff of stardust. Lélek looked about himself, seeing again the continuous process of the evolution of energy. Suddenly he became very excited. *This is it! This is where it happens. I want to be a part of this!'*

"Will," said Elliou, hearing him going through his thought process. Lélek's mind immediately experienced a jolt of recall. He had last heard the word from Isten, in the universe of cosmic clouds and star dust, where the 'will' existed for life to manifest itself. He recalled the importance of the parent's desire to weave a fabric of consciousness that would give the new entity a fulfilling life. Then there was one of the first conversations he had with Isten, where he expressed the overwhelming desire to become a part of the new universe, starting with his incarnation on Erde.

Yes, he understood. The power was in the will; the total and focused iron will brought to bear with full force to achieve absolute potential. Lélek also understood that the radiation of the will must be spread across all of the incumbent citizens of The Centre to create a unification. *Do I need to be 'authorised' in some way to exercise my will?*

"The fact that you ask the question means you are free to act … as you desire," responded Elliou, "as you lived your life on Restu."

Lélek turned towards her. He wanted to touch her again, to feel her presence and her power. But as soon as she had answered his last question, her job was done. He saw her withdrawing into the mass of swirling energies, giving herself up to the chaos. *What do I want?* He realised that what he wanted was in his mind from the very earliest beginning. From the time he was forced to go hunting with Ördog. He had always hated having to kill just so he could eat, and live. *Why does life have to consume life in order to continue living?* He saw a fundamental flaw in that arrangement.

Long, long ago, standing in the freezing snow, waiting for the next kill, Lélek had not the remotest thought for the possibility of changing that reality.

Now he not only had the thought but also the means. He was going to change the nature of creation. He was going to remove the necessity of life having to consume life in order to survive. The ramifications were incomprehensible. Survival would no longer need to be violent. Aspirations, 'desires', the evolution of soul could focus on greater goals. Life itself would be considered to have greater value. Perhaps life was sacred once. Maybe it will be again.

Lélek didn't know how he would achieve that change, but he knew he had to implant that 'desire' into all who inhabited The Centre at that very instant. From the rock at the middle of The Centre he focused his intent and with single mind, projected it.

chamaeleontidae manifestations

the Rose galaxy

Something monumental should have happened. Perhaps everything should have ceased to exist and the next instant manifested into reality again - looking different for his intervention. No. None of that happened. Instead he found himself somewhat more diffused than his previous manifestation and occupying an indeterminate area of the cosmos, which was no longer the tetrahedral site. The luminosity and the chaos were gone. Lélek felt different. There was noise in his mind, which he had not experienced before … the voices of all who were at the Centre … they were all a part of him …. the centillions of individuals.

He found himself in his original universe, in front of him the Milky Way. The greater Lélek was in danger of losing his self-awareness. Already he was having difficulty isolating his thoughts from the myriad voices inside him.

"Lélek!" The clear sound of a commanding presence found his attention. "Focus on my voice. Listen only to what I say. Use your will to gather your essence and channel it in my direction."

As at every other time previously, Isten made its appearance at the critical moment. It had been waiting for Lélek. "Think how you looked when you were with Ahatu. Imagine your energy encased in a shell."

Distant ripples of sound formed themselves into the softness of a voice from the outer reaches of space.

I a m L e l e k - b o r n o f E a r t h - f a t h e r o f S i n u - h u s b a n d o f A h a t u — s t u d e n t o f I s t e n - I am Lélek.

The voice arrived out of the cosmos carried by the form of a man who had called himself Lélek. The Restunian shell was missing from the writhing bundle of energy that was his essence, and the essences of the centillions, swirling upon itself like the surface of the sun. This new, focused Lélek was again able to listen to his own thoughts without the noise which had threatened to engulf him.

"What happened? I can remember everything except what happened after the photon sphere. Elliou was with me, teaching me. I focused my will and suddenly I was lost, until I heard your voice."

"You are now like us. We each had to be a catalyst in the process of evolution before we could be released from The Centre. You have made your contribution. Experience will be your teacher now. Yet there are still some things you must do before we can be together."

Just like every other time It was gone and he was left by himself to sort things out. Still the question lingered; *What did It mean − to be together? What things must I still do? It said I had made a contribution. But I've done nothing − nothing yet, except fulfil my desire.*

An Act of Creation

Questions and more questions filtered into his consciousness even as his attention was drawn back to the Milky Way. Gazing at the familiar sight he thought again of his friends Tilit and Johee and how he amused them with his panorama of round pots arranged in orbital patterns. Those were happy, exciting creative days. A tiny little thought started wiggling its innocent round-about way to become a very prominent thought.

Could I maybe … yes, YES … but not here … this galaxy is too old. Another, younger one! A great excitement took hold of him. Not since he had completed the planets around his hut had he felt the same creative drive come over him.

Not even his contribution to the birth of his son Sinu could compare. *We wove a fabric out of ourselves to enable Sinu to manifest.*

It all seemed to be coming together. He allowed his mind to encompass the far reaches of the cosmos around him. Always drawn to order and beauty, he found what he was looking for; a flower in a universe of galaxies, The Rose. Two galaxies had come together, a larger and smaller, with the smaller one distorting the larger resulting in the shape of the head of a short stemmed rose. There were many young solar systems in that galaxy. *This is a good place to start!*

Lélek could barely contain himself from the exhilaration of what he was about to do. He focused himself and moved towards The Rose for a closer inspection. Casting his mind into the various spiral arms he wasn't clear about what he was looking for. He let inspiration guide him. Lélek could 'feel' the plasma energy of every sun and flitted from one to the other, rejecting each in turn, until suddenly he saw it.

There! That's the one!

Alive, full of power, a solar system with many planetary children. A jewel, the fourth of the sun, sparkled in its infancy. It had cooled sufficiently to form a crust, and for oceans of water with clouds drifting above the blue and green. Photosynthetic life had claimed a foothold.

This planet was a lot like Earth, but unlike Earth it had two moons. A larger and a smaller one, playing together in frivolous orbits around the planet, denying life a stable environment on it.

This will not do. I want just one moon – That one!

And the will became the reality. He watched as an asteroid, almost as large as the smaller moon decided to go and play with them, but it and the little moon clashed. Neither survived the fight. The planet gained precious minerals and exotic molecules from the confrontation, that would be needed by life in the future - life that now had a creator and did not have to rely on random mutations in order to actualise.

Lélek looked upon this planet considering with awe what he had just done, and what he was about to do. Isten had left his seed on Earth. Life around it had grown and matured into consciousness and self-awareness. It had achieved its maximum potential very early in its evolution. By the time that sentient species had attained the ability to explore the cosmos, it had mutated into weeds, killing themselves and their home. Lélek did not want that. He loved beauty and peace and harmony. He wanted to see life that did not consume life - either for food or entertainment or out of envy or anger, jealousy or revenge or for survival.

He focused his energy until he was able to stand on the surface of the planet. *This is going to be my garden.* He spent an eon walking in his garden, and when he became tired he lay down to rest at the base of a mountain. Lélek slept for a very long time and while he slept new mountains and new seas were born of his dreams. Even the moon became lonely over the eons without it's playmate. The power of the sun diminished and Ice Age after Ice Age travelled the surface scouring the land cleaner with each passing.

Lélek awoke after his long sleep and looked out upon the land. He remembered all his geological dreams and nightmares. He remembered dreams of playing with the simplest forms of photosynthetic life, nurturing them towards their new potential. He remembered paddling in all the oceans' waters, cleansing them even as they refreshed him. They promised him that no life would arise from their waters that was contrary to his desire.

His first work of creation had begun, his and the centillions of souls that were a part of him.

Egek, my father.

What else must I do? The creative exhilaration that had taken control of Lélek since his departure from the Tetrahedral Site seemed to have abated. Though he slept, he had not rested. A very large portion of himself became the life of the new planet. Lélek felt drained. With fatigue came a certain lassitude, and with that an ennui he could not shake. He tried going for walks in his new garden. Though he admired the many wonders that had evolved during his long sleep, he felt somehow – unsatisfied.

Extraordinary as it was to breathe life into a planet, to infuse it with his aspirations for perfection, it did not give him the same sense of fulfilment as seeing his son, Sinu, for the first time. Then there was Kaqquru.

Kaqquru. Beautiful, fragile little Kaqquru.

He recalled the first time he saw the little girl, playing quietly in a corner of her parent's house. She was not his daughter. He did not help to weave the fabric of her consciousness, yet he felt such a close affinity with her. Even her name, when he checked Restunian history, meant 'The Earth'. Perhaps that's why he felt so close to her. Lélek had not thought about the Earth since he returned to the Milky Way. For a while longer he remained on his planet garden, Ahatubibbu – he named it in memory of his wife, Ahatu's planet – walking the breadth and length of it, committing to memory all that he saw.

As the majesty of this world flowed into the fibre of his being, his mind turned more and more towards Earth; a sapphire in the heavens. Lélek had come a long way, but the Earth was still his home. It was the origin of his mind.

Perhaps if I visited home for a little while – He hoped it might help to lift the depression that had begun to settle around him. A renewal of the spirit might give him a little perspective, provide his existence with stronger purpose. Even though the thought of seeing his past appealed, it also frightened. He wanted to see his old friends, his parents and Christin – especially Christin's little boy. Humanity, as a species, held no appeal. It had already been on the wrong path when it crawled out of the sea. Humanity was alien. As alien as the Earopians. Evolution after all, was a process of trial and error. It had failed mankind. To contemplate Humanity's devolution only served to make Lélek feel worse.

Better to think happy memories. Linear time had ceased to have meaning for Lélek a long time ago. It had ceased to be elastic or even circular. To him it was like splashing around in a puddle. To facilitate his point of entry into linear Earth time, Lélek had to decide when he wanted to be, as well as where he wanted to be. As he could remember all of his history, he felt it to be more interesting to move the window either a little further back, or a little forward.

My father, Egek. I want to be with my father at the edge of the lake.

And so it was.

A young boy stood beside his father, hand in hand by the side of a lake. They were watching the fish drifting lazily near the edge. Together they saw the Moon die in the water. Those were happy days. There was no future then. Just one day, then another and another – each isolated from the others: Each day holding the threat of dying and the promise of living. Yet they were happy days. The little boy knew exactly what he had to do each day – simply survive. Lélek moved his shadow slightly, and his father glanced behind him for a moment. Lélek would have to be careful not to be discovered.

Ördog, the new tribal chief, ruled for a brief period. With his treachery discovered, a replacement was found.

Lélek felt proud to see his son, Gloppel, as the new leader. People like Ördog were destined to be the future of mankind. All ripples reach distant shores.

Being a ghost did not give Lélek the 'feel' of his past reality. *I want to be more than just an observer. I want to interact with the past as it moves into the future without me.*

And so it was.

Tilit and Johee

Tilit and Johee decided to honour Lélek's passing by continuing their adventure in search of knowledge. So a year or so after Lélek's death they set off towards the East, from where news of a great civilization had filtered into the mountains of Europe. Several months after their departure, just as the light of day began to fade and they searched for a safe place to camp, they came across a wanderer.

"Tilit," Johee warned, "there's someone coming."

Johee strained his eyes in the failing light. "He's – I think he's – let's invite him to share a meal," he said at last. The man came towards them out of the light of the setting sun. He was tall and thin and walked as upright as a spring sapling. From under an ample hood he greeted them with a nod and words they could understand.

"May I join you, friends?"

Johee scrutinised him, something stirring deep in his memory. The face of this man shone almost as if he was a source of light itself. Johee immediately invited the wanderer to spend the evening with them and share a meal.

"You are welcome, stranger. Share with us."

Lélek felt again the warmth of the company of his friends. He could not help comparing all the wonders he had lived during his existence, with the simple, uncomplicated joy of those few hours. They spoke of many things and more than once Johee interrupted Lélek, "Have you not met our friend Lélek by any chance in your wanderings?" Johee more than Tilit felt something different and familiar about this man.

"Describe this man to me." Lélek could not help satisfying his curiosity of what they truly thought of him, for surely they would not conceal that from a stranger. Their words filled him with such a gladness, he confessed to having met their friend.

After sharing a meal, the stranger invited them to sit with him away from the camp fire. "I will tell you about the man I met. Come sit under the stars with me and I will talk about the heavens."

Tilit especially was more than happy to do so. He launched into telling the stranger about their friend. "Our friend knew all about the stars," and very confidentially he said, "he had visited the moon." As soon as Johee heard the words coming from Tilit he fully expected the stranger to laugh and ridicule them. Not so. This strange man continued the conversation by entertaining their minds with stories of his adventures among the stars. The two friends listened, entranced, like they used to listen to Lélek.

"This man has told me many tales about his adventures. Perhaps he was your friend."

The hours drifted by all too quickly. Fatigue claimed the two friends and they retired to their makeshift shelter. Hardly had they put their heads down when Johee jumped up and ran over to where he thought the stranger had settled. He was gone. Completely gone, except for a small round pot on the boulder he was sitting on, with a handprint inside it. Johee could not even see his footprints in the morning. For many days they discussed this stranger, fearing to think the impossible. Lélek's heart was full with the affection he felt from his two friends. They gave unconditionally without even knowing who he was. For the rest of their journey Lélek kept them safe until they reached the city of Ur in Mesopotamia.

Lelkem, my son?

There was only one other person he wanted to see – no – needed to see – Christin. She was the first woman to whom he had opened up. Perhaps because it was safe, knowing at the time they would never be able to make a life together. Then there was her little boy, Lelkem. *Is he my son?*

That was a question that had never left him since Isten first allowed him to see Christin and Lelkem together. An uncertainty began to torture his mind. *Should I reveal myself to Christin? Would she even recognise me? What would it do to the boy? No doubt she has a partner. I can't interfere … I must see them!*

And so it was.

Questions and fears chased each other around in his mind, until he found himself outside their home. He had chosen an Earth reference time only five years after the last time he had seen them.

A man stood in the field and waited. He looked like a gamekeeper searching for lost deer.

Tall and spindly with thin arms adorned with long fingers at the ends of his palm, and a ready smile which he bestowed on a young boy who came running up to him. The boy chatted away excitedly about it being a school holiday and going on a picnic with his mother.

Soon enough his mother caught up and cast a suspicious glance at the stranger. This man had never been there before on their numerous previous excursions. Lélek caught his breath. It was Christin and Lelkem! The boy had grown so much he didn't recognise him at first.

"Hello. New around here?" Christin asked, wary.

The gamekeeper turned towards her and she looked into his eyes. Neither of them could speak, paralyzed by doubt, apprehension – until Lelkem interrupted, "Do you want to come with us on the picnic?"

"Yes … Yes, why don't you join us." Christin invited, confused.

Her previous suspicion of seeing a stranger in the middle of the field had turned to another suspicion. She could not voice that suspicion, even to herself. Christin wanted to run away, yet she could not. A dozen men could not have dragged her away at that moment. *I want to be with this gamekeeper!* She admitted to herself, even more confused.

"I have something as well. We can share," he answered cheerfully to Lelkem. It was difficult to tear his eyes away from Christin. His emotions were coiling like serpents ready to strike at him.

I must leave it up to her.

Without hesitation Lelkem took his hand leading him towards the picnic spot. The boy chatted away and the gamekeeper stole glances at the boy's mother. Every now and then their eyes met. Each look burnt itself into his memory. No thought of Ahatu came to the surface. She was from another time, another universe.

"This is our favourite place," she said when they had arrived, adding, "It's the best place from which to see the stars at night."

That made her blush. She didn't mean to say that. *Why did I say that, to a complete stranger?*

The gamekeeper looked up into the sky and remarked what a beautiful, perfect day it was. He had lived many lives, seen extraordinary things, visited many universes – yet this was the most beautiful day.

She knows who I am! "Have we met before somewhere?" Now it was his turn to chastise himself. *I didn't mean to ask that.*

The boy, oblivious of the drama being played out in front of him, happily unpacked the picnic basket. The gamekeeper gave him his little box of food to share out as well, taking the opportunity to examine the features of the boy closely. Lelkem was tallish, perhaps even a bit lanky – large expressive eyes. Hair like his mother's, and a way of holding his head just like her.

"It's a pity your father couldn't share the picnic with you." *Ah! I shouldn't have brought up his father.* The gamekeeper felt he was losing control, giving his emotions sovereignty over him.

"I don't know my dad," The two sets of adult eyes flashed at each other, "I have a dad, but I've never met him."

"Oh …" Was all the gamekeeper could say as he and Christin continued gazing at each other.

Exquisite agony. There was no other way to describe the moment when Lélek saw the light of recognition ignited for a moment in Christin's eyes. Lelkem was sitting in the middle of the rug, with Christin and the gamekeeper on either side of him.

The boy suddenly jumped up, and with sandwich in his hand ran over to a small hill with a large rock on it.

"That's our star gazing rock," said Christin, trembling ever so slightly.

"I used to like to sit on a rock just like that and watch the night sky," he said, pretending to adjust his seating position, moving a little closer to Christin. *What am I doing!* Christin noticed the manoeuvre, but didn't move away.

Her mind kept racing around in circles: *This is a stranger … why am I having a picnic with a stranger … yet … I … know … this man!* That last little revelation to herself completely unbalanced her composure, what little there was left of it by then. The next thing she heard him say raised goose bumps over her entire body.

"Have you ever wished to travel to the stars?"

Fear had given way to the courage of those who are about to die. There was no galaxy, no black hole, no photon sphere that could compare to the moment when she reached out her hand and put it slowly, hesitantly near him on the rug. The impossible could never be possible. Her hand was so close he could feel her warmth.

"I have been to many places, a long way away," she said ambiguously. In response he moved his hand closer to hers, just touching its side. If he had dived into the hottest sun of Restu he could not have felt a greater heat surge through his body. An unwanted rescue arrived as Lelkem came running back to get another sandwich. It gave Christin and Lélek a chance to look at each other. It was not possible across the gulf of forbidden hope before.

"Let's go to the river!" Lelkem shouted happily. It was turning out to be the best picnic he'd ever had. He liked this man. He liked him very much. While sitting on the rock he stole glances at his mother and the gamekeeper sitting close together, smiling at each other. Yes ... he liked this man a lot.

Before he'd realised it, the gamekeeper had picked up the basket in one hand and Christin's hand in the other. Christin did not take her hand out of Lélek's. It was at home. She walked with him following Lelkem to the river. It was the best picnic she had ever had, and the most painful.

She didn't have the courage to ask him the question. He did not want to hear the question he knew she wanted to ask. They arrived at the river at a clearing, and a sandy beach. Lelkem ran down to the water as they watched, still hand in hand. Without letting go, they sat on the grassy embankment, then turned their eyes away from the boy for a moment. They exchanged a look of knowing and both visibly relaxed. Just sitting there, hand in hand, watching Lelkem play by the water was enough - No. It was not enough. It would never be enough. They both wanted so, so much more.

Again Lelkem disturbed them. He saw their hands in intimate embrace, and with the happiness of it in his mind, asked, "Can you come and play with me?"

Lélek slid his hand slowly out of her clasp so he could feel every nano second of the embrace. She loosened her grip ever so slightly, so he would have to withdraw his hand slowly. He was half way to the edge of the water when Christin heard her son asking,

"What's your name?"

She also heard him say, "Lélek."

"That's almost like my name," the boy chirped happily.

It seemed that for an entire hour Christin could not take a breath. At least not until her two men returned, wet and happy. She no longer saw a gamekeeper. Like a family, they spread the rug again and sat to finish the rest of the food. All three spent a lot of time looking at each other, with few words of meaningless nothings passing between them. Gradually the shadows grew longer and there was only time for one more little play for Lelkem. Christin and Lélek sat side by side again, much closer this time, again with their love communicated through their joined hands. He desperately wanted to ask, but did not have the courage. She did not want to hear the question she knew he wanted to ask.

"Your son looks a lot like you," Lélek went searching, emboldened by their time together that day.

Turning to look directly and deeply at him she said, "He also looks a lot like his father."

If the universe could have stood still, this was the moment for it to do so. But it did not. Still he was not sure. *Do I really want to know?*

The inevitable had arrived. Lélek knew he had the power to prolong the day and re-live the picnic over and over again. But that could not happen. He helped to pack up all the things, said good bye to Lelkem and Christin. He heard himself say the words, those painful words, knowing they would be the last. He stood there, by the edge of the river overcome by the long shadows of the dying day, watching them walk across the field.

He did not hear Lelkem ask his mother, "Did you know that man, mummy?"

"Yes darling. He is your father."

They had moved too far away and he did not hear her answer either. Lelkem turned immediately and started running back to the river. His mother turned to watch him. But Lélek was gone. Christin did not want to see him gone. She wanted to remember him standing by the river.

The Dark Angel on Erde

Heaven and hell were concepts Lélek had become familiar with from his studies of Earth cultures. They had become ideas that lost their meaning as he progressed along his evolutionary path. The differences between the corporeal state and post death state were minor. Both presented great opportunities and limitations to a sentient being. The most powerful of those originating from their own belief systems. Obviously heaven and hell did not exist – not as locations nor as states of punishment or reward – each existed as unfulfilled desires. Heaven being the anticipation of fulfilment, and hell the denial of it. For hours that day, on Earth with Christin and Lelkem, Lélek existed in a state of ecstatic agony; an experience known to many, probably by multitudes of alien civilizations as well. But not to the depths of his encounter. It felt absolute.

All hope was extinguished the moment he saw her and spoke to her. If only he could have resisted, hope would still be alive; and if hope was still alive then so would have been his attachment. The price of his freedom was the very agony and ecstasy he endured for those few short hours. It was the fire which tempered his soul.

Drifting out through the solar system, aimless and disembodied, Lélek started to question – everything. Perhaps there is greater value in experiencing the full spectrum of possibilities through attachments.

Why should I have to end up without hope?

'You cannot understand what you have not experienced.'

Was that his own thoughts trying to find justification? Was it the tumult of the tide of experiences of the hoard of souls embedded in him, voicing their collective disenchantment?

'Your growth now depends on absolutes. Partial measures are a luxury denied to you.'

So where do I fit in? Lélek asked without realising the conversation was mostly with himself and partly with Isten.

'When the Sound Masters set your house in order, you became one of them. It made it possible for you to give Ahatu your songs with some of the secrets of the universe. Your graduation from The Centre gave you the power to influence creation. As you lay down by the mountain side on your special planet you became one of the Architects of the Cosmos. Yet your potential forced you on. However, there was still a great attachment in your soul, and the souls of all within you, which had to be purged.' 'You knew the path and you took it. In so doing, you freed yourself. Christin's life

can now also move forward. She is complete. She needed to be with you just once more for that to be possible. Lelkem had a father for a day. That day will sustain him for the rest of his life.'

Then why do I feel so — desolate?

'Acceptance.'

That was the last word he heard himself say to himself – no – that was the last word Isten said … Lélek found the distinction harder to discern. By now he had drifted a long way from Earth. Not so far he could not recognise the planetary system with the red dwarf sun and its fourth planet which had no moon. He was looking at Erde, a world without fond memories for him, except for Christin.

Christin! Scritchen! Why didn't I think of it before! He'd had such a depth of affection for his stone age mate, and she for him. Their society did not encourage emotions to be publicly, or even privately exhibited. It would have been a sign of weakness, a hindrance to survival. Christin reminded him so much of Scritchen. The realisation of the connection between the two lifted another huge burden of uncertainty.

The desire to revisit Erde was extinguished long ago when he had to flee for his life. Curiosity seduced him to look a little closer.

And so it was.

Lélek had drifted through space and through time to the future. That dark angel, Change, had been busy on Erde. Population density had increased so much over the millennia that little of the planet's surface could be seen; partly because of the structures covering it and partly because of the pollution of the atmosphere. He felt strangely removed from this world. He looked upon the people and saw that the human gene had triumphed over that of the Opians. Perhaps even the human mentality had taken control - probably. The world no longer looked healthy. It didn't have the aura of a living being that could sustain the life of its inhabitants. Whichever species would have ended up dominant, Lélek felt it would have made little difference. The flaw in them was obvious. It was time for a new soul-set in the minds of sentient beings.

Ahatu's shadow

That was all the thought he was prepared to dedicate to the lost world of Erde. But there was another world that had a special being living on it, and the thought of that being awoke in Lélek another desire. He approached it with no less trepidation than Earth. Again he was not at all clear about his intention. *I want to see Ahatu.* That was certain.

And so it was.

He wanted to see Sinu and little Kaqquru, who was now a member of his family. Would he be able to resist revealing himself to Ahatu?

Engrossed in his own thoughts he did not become immediately conscious of the rising volume of sounds around him. Not since The Centre had he been aware of so many individuals. Some had just transmutated, others were ready to sublimate. Many wanted his attention. Lélek had not realised he could be so visible – so accessible. One voice in particular rose above the others. Lélek could see into her mind and a surge of warmth washed over him as they made closer contact. It was a woman, times nine. She had lived a number of lives on Earth, melding many times in between. She was here because evolution on Earth could no longer fulfil her hunger for growth. Christelle had been set on the path by the spirit of one of her ancestors, whose name she still remembered.

Christin!

He read this in her mind.

"How did you know?" Reading his thought. "Who are you!" Christelle demanded.

When he carefully released his identity both to her and the rest of the throng Christelle cried out, "Lélek! Is this possible? Your name has been handed down through generation after generation to me. The family legend said I should search for you."

His name was echoed by all the others around him. They were all Restunians. Some "Primitives" and some "Polymorphs". Though little time had passed on their planet in this other universe, the local legend of a great man who had come to them from Earth, had spread far, aided by the activities of Ahatu and her family. Christelle's voice had softened considerably as the eminence of this entity pervaded her energy.

"Am I ….?"

"Yes, you are where you should be. They are good people. You can help each other."

Lélek stayed with her mind until one of the Primitives came to meld with her and help her sublimate. He realised this was a considerable departure from the past he had known, aware at the same time that his short presence on Restu may well have had something to do with this development. Perhaps the Puritanians realised there were important advantages to be had for their future evolution by not shutting out non-Restunian energy. Opening his mind to the multitude of others, he found he was able to connect with each one, individually and personally. He listened to himself using words of reassurance, just like Isten had done for him. Few words, most of them raising more questions than giving answers, just as before.

This brief, unexpected encounter had softened his desire to see Ahatu. The curiosity was certainly still there, but not with the same intensity of desire.

Perhaps if I don't see her I may still be content.

'Obviously she hadn't forgotten you and had lived a productive life contributing to the evolution of her species,' he heard a familiar reassurance.

Ahatu was still living in the same house that had been their home. Although he wanted to spend some time with her, the compulsion to reveal himself had diminished. Lélek felt again all the emotions he had for her, but they did not dominate him. They could not force him to act against himself. With the freedom to manifest in any form, devoid of the driving force of attachment, he found a way to be with her and with his family.

It was the period of one sun on Restu. Only one sun during the day, and two dim suns during the night. He'd forgotten how beautiful the planet of crystals and green fields with giant trees was. He was stunned again by the magnificence of the amethyst glow of the bodies of the inhabitants, even in the light of a single sun. Lélek had not been alive there during the last one-sun period and hadn't seen the reflections of the rays of the two night suns as the light played mischievous games in the myriad facets of crystals. The wilderness of that planet under those conditions was indeed a most suitable environment in which to get lost. He smiled to himself remembering his ill-fated adventure with Sinu.

For many weeks he accompanied Ahatu on all her travels, never once giving himself away. Lélek synchronised himself with her shadow so he could be always present with her. She gave him that sense of fulfilment which was missing even after the acts of creation on his garden planet.

Seeing his son with Kaqquru filled him with such a deep joy. They gave his existence deeper meaning. Lélek had not realised before that the one thing missing from the magnificent evolution of his being, was the 'meaning'. He had achieved unbelievable miracles in his many manifestations, but the capacity to become immersed wholly in the beauty of the being of another, surpassed everything.

'I too have had that element of 'meaning' missing in my existence.' There it was again. That voice from within himself, as if it was an equal.

Sinu and Kaqquru had just entered the house, which they now occupied with Ahatu, with a momentous announcement. It completely distracted Lélek from his own thoughts.

"Ahatu! We've received permission to weave the fabric of consciousness for a child of our own!"

Ahatu rushed to hug them. Lélek was so surprised by the sudden movement he almost lost phase with her shadow. In fact, he had, just slightly, but no one noticed in the excitement of the moment. *Ahatu's going to become a grandmother, and I will be a grandfather.* His seed was continuing the act of creation. Lélek thought about that and its ramifications for what he had started on another planet, in another universe. *I am going to stay until the little one arrives. I have time − I am time.* The new Lélek was learning quickly that no matter what happened, all experiences were a source of contemplation and the foundation for revelations.

For the following months he went everywhere with Ahatu, always with careful attention to his connection with her. He noticed that her mood was changing a little. When he first arrived, she tended to be more on the serious side − somewhat introspective.

That could be explained by the nature of work she was doing. Dream making had become subordinate to Ahatu's more complex function of teaching a philosophy of life based on Lélek's own teachings, his songs of the universe and his comprehensive life.

Lately her mood had lightened up. Perhaps because of Sinu's news − probably. *Maybe she can feel me.* It was more a hope than a definite feeling. He'd been extra careful not to give any hint of his presence. But there had always been such a profoundly strong connection between them that it was just possible she could feel his presence.

On one particular evening Ahatu went outside just to enjoy the night atmosphere. She was extraordinarily beautiful. The shades of her amethyst overtones bathed in the light of the two suns refracted from crystalline forms nearby. He was so absorbed in the vision that when she moved her position, his shadow didn't make an immediate corresponding movement.

Ahatu glanced at her two shadows. *'They didn't move!'* The next moment they did move.

She was confused. *'What just happened? This cannot be.* Losing interest in the allure of the evening, she went into the house to lie down for the rest of the night, disturbed by impossible thoughts. Lélek was grateful she fell asleep quickly, but he couldn't see into her dreams. Ahatu started re-playing that moment in her mind. The moment when her shadow had stood still. Then her mind drifted; to the shadows at the end of the day on which she had rescued Lélek and her son; to happy images of Sinu and Kaqquru so happy with their impending parenthood.

As with all dreams, without restrictions or boundaries, she saw again the darkness of the cosmos Lélek had shown her; that frightening immensity of the universe at the doorstep of their little planet.

Where is my darling Lélek now? What is he doing? It was inevitable her thoughts would lead her to dream about him. Especially now that a new life was going to come into the family. She had not done that for a very long time. Every day of her life had been saturated with her partner since he had transmuted. There was no need for her to be dreaming about him. *Why now? ... I know my shadows did not move!*

Lélek knew his time to depart was getting close. One evening a few days later, when Ahatu was particularly tired and sleepy, sitting on the edge of the bed in half light, Lélek did something unexpected. Almost half asleep, Ahatu still on the edge of the bed, watched as her shadow slowly, deliberately shrunk away from the wall. It slid down to the floor and moved towards her. All perfectly normal – when the person's body is moving into a horizontal position. But she was still sitting. She had not moved. Her day-dreaming mind watched the phenomenon with fascination. *This cannot be happening.*

"I must be dreaming already. No – no, not yet. My eyes are open." She experimented by moving one arm. The shadow didn't make a corresponding move. "Oh my suns!"

That was the last thing she remembered the following morning about the shadow. She did not remember Lélek moving from the floor to sit beside her and gently lower her onto the bed. She did not remember Lélek placing one hand on her chest and the other on her forehead. But she did remember her dreams.

Ahatu remembered hearing the sounds of the Siren Song, as she heard that first time. The song continued to expand into improvised melodies; She heard the songs of The Centre and of the Universe of cosmic dust clouds. Lélek even gave her the song of the picnic by the river. He saw her smiling in her sleep. It gave him a profound peace. Before the relentless attack of the morning light could infiltrate the room, he gave her the images of his garden, his world, Ahatubibbu, which he called Ahatu's planet. She saw him walking in his garden and relaxing by the sea. Her very last image was seeing him lie down at the base of a mountain and go to sleep.

Ahatu awoke from her deep, deep slumber relaxed and bewildered. *Where did those dreams come from? What does it all mean?* She realised instantly as soon as she saw her morning shadow on the wall. "Lélek was here!" As she remembered apprehension crept over her. *What will happen to the shadow if I move my arm? If I don't try, I'll regret it for the rest of my life.* If she did, and the shadow moved then she would be disappointed for the rest of her life.

Looking down at her hand she watched it make a slight movement, as if it had a mind of its own. Fearing to raise her eyes to the shadow, nevertheless she forced herself. It was an hallucination. *It must be an hallucination!* The shadow of the hand moved. No! She had stopped moving her hand. She moved her hand again and began to raise her arm. Oh, the supreme joy! The shadow did not move. The arm dropped to her side, impaled to the spot. In total turmoil her chaotic thoughts couldn't focus on reality.

"Mother - mother - - - Mother!" Came Kaqquru's shouting voice. "What's the matter with you!"

That broke the spell.

"Have you a name for your girl child?" Ahatu asked as soon as her eyes focused enough to see Kaqquru in her room.

"Yes, Akamu. What happened to you just then?"

"I've had a dream. There is a planet, Lélek's garden planet, called Ahatubibbu." She did not need to explain.

Kaqquru looked into Ahatu's eyes, and she into hers. They sat together for a little while. Kaqquru had never seen her mother as happy in the entire time she had known her. "If she will agree, may I call our daughter Bibbu?" She asked.

Kaqquru was sitting opposite her mother and saw the light of joy in her eyes. Kaqquru did not see her own shadow on the wall. Ahatu watched as that shadow duplicated itself, moved to the side and raising one arm, put its hand on the shadow of her daughter's chest. Tear's started streaming from her eyes. No one on Restu had ever been known to cry. It was anatomically not possible. Yet tears of pure energy streamed out of her.

"I am very happy," she whispered to Kaqquru. When she had composed herself she knew Lélek had gone. "I hope one day your daughter's daughter might visit a garden planet in a galaxy that looks like a rose."

Ahatubibbu, in the Rose Galaxy

Lélek stood on a hill overlooking a large lake, with snow-capped mountains in the background. Everywhere he looked it was clean and healthy, full of the energy of life. A great deal of time must have flowed under the bridges of change, for he saw the greenery of the planet in motion. When he was last there, giving of himself and of his desire to this world, he had no expectations other than the promise given to him by the waters of the seas.

This time he joined forces with the breezes circling the planet. He could not be seen, yet he could be felt – and he could touch his creation. He let himself be carried at random, over water and over land. Sometimes he would slow and almost stop. This was indeed a garden world, for everywhere he could see forests of great trees and rows of bushes and fields of waving grasses. They were all stationary except for the action of wind and rain. But there was other life that moved. It was green also, every part of every individual. They were not wearing green clothes; they were green beings. Large and small and in-between. He could hear their voices, like the rustling of leaves; dry leaves of summer and wet leaves in a storm, the voices of children like the whisperings of tiny leaves in soft breezes.

Civilisation.

Have I been gone so long? Looking about for signs of social decay, all he saw was the healthy decay of energy returning to the earth to be reborn, to feed the sentience that depended on it. There was a society, many societies covering the planet. All spoke with the same voice. Whether it was some plants that had become mobile, or an entirely new species, it did not really matter. The long journey had started towards a complex culture and technology.

He travelled around the planet many times on the back of the wind and saw the seas had kept their promise. He could not see a single instance of killing as a part of the fabric of life. *"This is indeed a wonderful world."* It showed the promise of a worthwhile future. "I will stay a while to see it grow."

He thanked the winds for carrying him, then re-manifested as an image of himself. Recognising his previous resting place nearby he thought it was a good time to have a little rest. The base of the mountain was by the sea, so Lélek wandered down to its the shore.

"You have kept your promise. I am well pleased."

The end of the day was calm and the many rock pools inviting with their mysteries and warm, still waters. Standing beside one such pool he saw an image which did not match the image he had of himself. He snapped his head around to see who was behind him. There was no one there. Looking more closely at the reflection he thought he could recognise some characteristics which could well have been his own.

We are together.

At the least expected moments that voice kept coming back to him. He'd heard something like that before, many times. Too much to think about now. *"I am tired. Five billion years is a long time. I will think about my voices tomorrow."*

Finding his way back to the base of the mountain Lélek lay down in its shadow to sleep and dream a while.

There was a small, slender green boy, sitting on a hill watching the clouds move across the sky when Lélek manifested by the shore. The boy saw the image, which was greater than any other living thing he had ever seen. It was like the fiery surface of the sun in a shape he could recognise as it walked slowly towards the sea. Then he saw it turn and go into the shadows at the base of the mountain and he saw it lie down on the earth. The boy saw the fire of the sun swallowed by the mountain, and disappear into the ground it lay on.

When he first laid down to rest, photosynthetic life had just become sentient and mobile. When he woke, they had learnt to travel into the void.

That little boy, when he had grown into a man, told the story of the birth of the God of the Mountain who had come from the Sun, to give life to his home. He visited that mountain many times, to sleep where the God of the Mountain had laid down to sleep.

epilogue

*I can remember the birth of the Earth and the single seed I
planted. Now I have created a world and life upon this world.
What more must I do?*

When he woke, it was Isten who rose from the
ground. But it longer thought of itself as Isten. The seed,
his seed, which it had planted so long ago on a planet
called Earth, had matured and was now a part of its
greater self again.

*Who is this man on the hill, who is able to see me? He tells
good stories and comes to sleep in my bed. I will ask him his name.*
The man gave his name gladly and asked in return,
"What is your name, Groundsman?"
"A very small part of who I once was, used to be
called Isten," he replied. He had finally placed one foot
on the first level of divinity, realising in that achievement
he had attained his absolute potential. He looked
thoughtfully at the inquisitive green man.
"Would you like to come on a journey with me?"

--------------------- * ----------------------

Zsoall, born in Hungary, was brought to Australia by his parents after the 1956 uprising.

He currently lives a creative life with his wife and animal family in the Northern Rivers, New South Wales, Australia.

His life has changed direction a number of times. After gaining his qualifications as a Sculptor he worked as a Secondary Teacher before becoming an Administrative Officer. Neither offered much in the way of creative involvement. That began when he embarked on a career as a computer programmer. Whilst in that profession his continuing compulsion to create made it inevitable that his life would change again. Completely giving up programming he immersed himself in creativity as a Sculptor and Painter. Much of his time is now dedicated to creating glass paintings and sculptures and to writing Science Fiction.

Another change is looming on the horizon as the art of recording future visions in written form takes a firmer hold of his creative energies.

www.ingramcontent.com/pod-product-compliance
Lightning Source LLC
Chambersburg PA
CBHW050141120726
47903CB00002B/442